T0037472

"Thrilling story! The story took off in the first line __ cuffed until the last. A must-read for every romantic suspense reader. Goddard's novels keep getting better and better."

DiAnn Mills, author of *Concrete Evidence*

"Elizabeth Goddard's *Cold Light of Day* is an exhilarating, page-turning race to the finish! Highly recommended."

Carrie Stuart Parks, bestselling author of *Relative Silence*

"In *Cold Light of Day*, Elizabeth Goddard has created a novel that immerses the reader in small-town Alaska. From the first page, it's a race to stay alive and solve a number of ever-spiraling mysteries. From who the hero really is to why one body after another is found, the reader will be sucked into a story that presses forward from page to page at a rapid pace. I highly recommend this novel."

Cara Putman, award-winning author of *Flight Risk* and *Lethal Intent*

"Gripping and hard-hitting. Grab a cup of cocoa to keep you warm, because the cold and danger on these pages are as real as it gets."

James R. Hannibal, award-winning author of *Elysium Tide*

"A simmering romantic suspense with an explosive ending. Once more Goddard proves she is a master storyteller and deserving of her place as one of the best Christian romantic suspense authors of our time. *Cold Light of Day* is a book you will not want to miss."

Mary Alford, author of *Among the Innocent*

COLD
LIGHT
OF DAY

Books by Elizabeth Goddard

UNCOMMON JUSTICE SERIES

Never Let Go
Always Look Twice
Don't Keep Silent

ROCKY MOUNTAIN COURAGE SERIES

Present Danger
Deadly Target
Critical Alliance

MISSING IN ALASKA

Cold Light of Day

MISSING IN ALASKA • 1

COLD LIGHT OF DAY

ELIZABETH GODDARD

Revell

a division of Baker Publishing Group
Grand Rapids, Michigan

© 2023 by Elizabeth Goddard

Published by Revell
a division of Baker Publishing Group
PO Box 6287, Grand Rapids, MI 49516-6287
www.revellbooks.com

Printed in the United States of America

All rights reserved. No part of this publication may be reproduced, stored in a retrieval system, or transmitted in any form or by any means—for example, electronic, photocopy, recording—without the prior written permission of the publisher. The only exception is brief quotations in printed reviews.

Library of Congress Cataloging-in-Publication Data
Names: Goddard, Elizabeth, author.
Title: Cold light of day / Elizabeth Goddard.
Description: Grand Rapids, MI : Revell, a division of Baker Publishing Group, [2023] | Series: Missing in Alaska ; 1
Identifiers: LCCN 2022018326 | ISBN 9780800742041 (paperback) | ISBN 9780800742720 (casebound) | ISBN 9781493439775 (ebook)
Subjects: LCGFT: Mystery fiction. | Novels.
Classification: LCC PS3607.O324 C49 2023 | DDC 813/.6—dc23
LC record available at https://lccn.loc.gov/2022018326

Most Scripture quotations are from The Holy Bible, English Standard Version® (ESV®), copyright © 2001 by Crossway, a publishing ministry of Good News Publishers. Used by permission. All rights reserved. ESV Text Edition: 2016

Some Scripture quotations are from THE HOLY BIBLE, NEW INTERNATIONAL VERSION®, NIV® Copyright © 1973, 1978, 1984, 2011 by Biblica, Inc.® Used by permission. All rights reserved worldwide.

This book is a work of fiction. Names, characters, places, and incidents are the product of the author's imagination or are used fictitiously. Any resemblance to actual events, locales, or persons, living or dead, is coincidental.

Baker Publishing Group publications use paper produced from sustainable forestry practices and post-consumer waste whenever possible.

23   24   25   26   27   28   29   7   6   5   4   3   2   1

To Dad:
long ago you took us on adventures in the mountains,
and that's where my heart remains.

The mountains are calling, and I must go.

—John Muir

To act justly and to love mercy and to walk humbly with your God.

Micah 6:8 NIV

PROLOGUE

never should have come.

What was he even doing here? What had he been thinking?
I'm an idiot!

He wasn't so stupid that he couldn't admit he was lost. Dusk
was almost on him, and if he didn't find his way back to civilization soon, he could very well die.

Kenny thought back to his uncle's open invitation to find
refuge at his place in the mountains. The man often bragged
about "wild" Alaska. Eagles. Bears. Bigfoot. Spawning salmon.
Whatever. Kenny wasn't much of a fisherman, but he could
learn to fish. What better place than Alaska? Or he could hike
on a glacier. Take up dog mushing.

"You can escape what holds you back, son. Here in Alaska—
the world is at your feet," his uncle had said.

And like the proverbial fool on an errand, Kenny had finally
decided to take his uncle up on that offer and purchased a one-
way ticket to surprise him. With its record-breaking snowfall,
his hometown of Sault Ste. Marie in Michigan's Upper Penin-
sula couldn't be that different than Southeast Alaska. Could it?

And since Kenny had spent half his life on a snowmobile, he could make his way around the snow-covered Tongass National Forest, a temperate rain forest, the same way.

He'd worked up a sweat hiking, and the cold wind whipped around him, cutting between the layers of his fleece-lined winter jacket. With the lush evergreens covered in fresh snow, early May seemed like winter. The frosted forest closed in around him as he hiked on the snowshoes he'd brought from Michigan.

He'd taken the snowmobile up the road and thought he could continue up the trail, but the vehicle had gotten stuck.

Stuck!

Of all the stupid things to happen. He couldn't believe it. That was on him. He shivered and glanced at his cell phone. No signal, but he hadn't expected one.

Still . . . he should have made it to his uncle's by now. Had he missed an important marker? The man had sketched him a map, for crying out loud. Kenny pulled the drawing out of his pocket and clumsily held it in his gloved hands. All he'd had to do was follow the trail. And *that* was the problem. The path had kind of disappeared with the heavy snowfall today. Another blast of wind whipped over him along with huge flakes, reminding him that his life was in jeopardy if he didn't find his way back—and soon.

A sliver of fear slid through him, cutting deep.

If he backtracked down the mountain, he might run into the main road again. And if he died out here?

Mom is going to kill me.

Now, too late, he could easily see the big mistake he'd made. He'd allowed emotions to drive his decision to come to Alaska, but this wasn't the first time he'd been impulsive.

A gunshot cracked the air.

He stopped in his tracks. That sounded close. Heart pounding, he stood perfectly still. A hunter out looking for dinner?

He started hiking again and picked up his pace, hoping he'd run into someone who could help.

Then, through the trees, he spotted a man in a black ski mask. Nothing unusual about the cold-weather garb . . . except . . . he stood over a woman in a bright-pink parka.

She lay on her back. The man pointed a pistol at her head and shot her point blank. Instantly, her blood turned the white snow crimson.

And Kenny's blood turned to ice.

Move, move, move.

Panic exploded in Kenny's chest, the glacial air knifing through his lungs.

I have to get out of here.

Kenny headed away from the killer.

Except . . . oh no! His tracks would give him away if the killer spotted him.

I can do this. I can survive. He willed himself to believe. He picked up the pace, going deeper into the forest. A glance over his shoulder sent dread blasting through him.

The killer was tracking him.

Legs shaking, Kenny powered through the fear before it paralyzed him. Keeping to the thickest trees for protection, he snow-jogged. Outlasting the killer, giving him reason to give up the hunt, was the only way to lose him.

Except Kenny had already been out here for too long. His lungs ached. Muscles burned.

Pressing his back against a spruce to rest, he sucked in cold air.

Kenny pulled out his Buck 50th anniversary–edition Ranger knife in case he had to face off with the man who had a long gun as well as a loaded pistol. What did the hunter want with him? Dumb question. Kenny had witnessed him commit murder. But he hadn't seen the man's face. He'd just have to do what a lot of people came to Alaska to do—vanish.

Pushing from the tree, he tried to keep up the pace as he jogged through the snow toward higher elevation. Another possible mistake, but he wanted to lose this guy.

He hadn't gone far before he couldn't catch his breath, which meant he couldn't keep going.

Even if his life depended on it.

The temperature was dropping fast. He stumbled forward and out of the tree line . . . just a little farther . . . and spotted the lights shining from the town below.

He should be sitting next to the fire at his uncle's cabin and eating moose stew instead of running for his life.

A shout brought him around. Standing twenty-five yards away, he spotted the killer. The man aimed his rifle right at Kenny and looked through the scope.

Before Kenny could react, the ground rumbled and shook, and the snow shifted under his feet. He glanced up at the peak above.

A new terror gripped him as realization dawned.

The hunter would kill him to make sure he didn't climb out from the avalanche racing toward him. Alaska would make him disappear forever.

No one would miss him—no one who cared even knew he was here.

 # ONE

Autumn Long had no plans to give up without a fight, even though it might be killing her a little every day.

As the bush plane sank lower, her view of the glacier spilling into the valley behind a forest exploding with reds, oranges, and browns fell away. Lofty mountains on each side of the fjord filled her vision.

"Hold on, Chief. We're almost there." Pilot Carrie James flew her bush plane straight up the Lynn Canal—one of the longest, deepest fjords in the world. The snowcapped Kakuhan Mountains rose lofty on the right, the Chilkat Range near Haines to the left. And across from Haines to the west—Glacier Bay National Park.

Autumn ignored the mounting dread she felt and focused her thoughts. She had better get her act together and earn back the trust of the city council and the people she swore to protect in the small town of Shadow Gap, one of many communities dotting the Inside Passage of the Alaska Panhandle.

She'd stayed overnight in Anchorage for a meeting that left her drained to her bones. She'd taken an Alaska Airlines flight

13

to and from Juneau, and now Carrie was delivering her up to the northernmost part of the Panhandle. Wearing her brown bomber jacket and a headset, sitting in the cockpit of her Helio Courier—the ultimate bush plane—Carrie was a bush pilot poster child.

The plane flew lower, following the Chilkoot Inlet until Carrie banked east, flying over the Lewis Inlet that branched off. "That's why I'd better say this before I lose the chance."

Autumn wasn't sure she wanted to hear it.

Carrie angled her head toward Autumn and arched a brow. "I know you didn't ask for my opinion." Carrie looked forward again. "But you didn't do anything wrong. Out here we take care of our own. The land is harsh. Brutal in ways the lower forty-eight can't imagine. We have to watch out for each other, and that's all you've ever done for the people of Shadow Gap."

"Yeah, well . . . thanks, Carrie." *Tell that to Wally.* He'd had it out for her from the first day she took her position as police chief.

Carrie waved a hand in mock incredulity. "Shadow Gap isn't even classified as a town, much less an organized borough, so who needs a city council anyway?"

Or a police department, some might say.

Autumn cracked a smile. "Glad to know at least some people still want me around."

Despite the many limitations of a small-town budget, they'd at least equipped their chief and three officers with loaded Ford Police Interceptor SUVs. After all, her officers were trained to carefully collect and preserve evidence as well as to tend a wounded moose in the road. They had to know how to do it all in small-town Alaska. Because, yeah, she thought of Shadow Gap's community of 1,252 people as a town. Shadow Gap was just outside of the Haines and Skagway Boroughs. Alaska didn't have counties, so there were no sheriffs.

Best of all—or worst of all, depending on which side of the

law you were on—Shadow Gap had lost their Alaska State Trooper. Not enough crime to support one or budget to afford one if there was enough crime.

Autumn had nothing to complain about, except the results of her trip to Anchorage left a—

"What's that?" Carrie drew Autumn's attention to the water. "Someone's out there, floating in Lewis Inlet. I saw hands waving, signaling."

"Have you got—"

"Here." Carrie handed off binoculars.

"Fly in close, Carrie. I want to get a better look. We have to help if we can." Autumn peered through the binoculars and struggled to find what she was looking for, instead only capturing the deep, dark waters. Then . . . "I see the hands. But, oh no, whoever is out there is going under."

"But look! Someone's swimming out to them. So maybe there's a chance."

"They won't last long. Those waters are cold." Autumn adjusted the binoculars, searching, searching . . . there. "I see what looks like the rescue swimmer." Was that . . . Grier? "How close can you land?"

"Close enough. Once on the water, I can angle in closer."

"If he can get to the woman, we'll take them both the rest of the way to get help."

Because there was no way the woman wasn't going to suffer from hypothermia in these temps, unless she had on the appropriate attire. Same for Grier.

Come on, Grier . . . save the girl.

Shadow Gap needed a hero. A ray of hope shot through her, and though maybe she shouldn't have the thought, it popped into her head all the same. She didn't mind that a town hero would take the attention away from the police chief's long list of transgressions.

Though, if she were choosing heroes, she would have chosen

a longtime resident over an outsider—or as the locals liked to call them, cheechakos, and meant in a negative way. She wouldn't go so far as to use that term for this particular man. Grier had shown up in Shadow Gap a few months ago to fish in the Shadow Gap Salmon Derby. A tourist who decided to stay. Wasn't the first time and wouldn't be the last.

Autumn dropped the binoculars as Carrie skillfully landed the plane on the water. The pontoons smoothly connected, and Carrie guided the plane, heading toward where they'd last seen the woman in need of a rescue.

Her struggle could well be over.

Please don't drown . . . don't die.

But Autumn didn't see her anywhere. A fist squeezed her heart.

TWO

Grier Brenner only had one job to do. One rule to follow. But he couldn't seem to keep his head down. He hadn't meant to get involved, but he couldn't watch someone drown, even though he strongly doubted he could make it to her in the frigid waters. He had to swim out to the middle of the Lewis Inlet in record time. He wasn't so arrogant to think he could, but he couldn't stand by and do nothing.

Slicing through the cold water, he lifted his head for a breath and heard her terror-stricken cry for help. He could tell from her voice that she was getting tired and losing the battle. He prayed his efforts wouldn't be for nothing.

To give them both the best chance of success, he'd taken a few precious moments to slip into his GORE-TEX dry suit and call emergency services before he jumped in the water. If he lost use of his limbs, then he would be of no use, and they both would die. He had no idea how long she'd already been in the water, and the Lewis Inlet averaged about fifty degrees even in August. That meant she could lose dexterity in under fifteen minutes if she wasn't also wearing protective gear.

He had no way of knowing anything, really.

All he did was act.

Acting without thinking first had gotten him into trouble before.

He swam, arm over arm, cutting through the chilled water, his thoughts wrapping around the life-and-death situation—his life and hers. How had she ended up in the middle of the inlet, no boat in sight?

Questions for her to answer—if she survived.

"Stay in the shadows, Grier."

The voice whispered to him from the recent past, and he shook it off to focus on saving the woman. As he pushed his head up and out of the water, he caught sight of her arms—still waving.

Grier considered himself to be an experienced diver, but that didn't mean he was a long-distance swimmer. Maybe he should work on that too, because right now the muscles in his arms and legs were complaining, but at least they weren't going numb.

"I'm coming!"

He had no idea if she'd heard him, and it was more likely she was watching him, willing him to swim faster toward her, so he should save his breath. The fact that she hadn't tried swimming toward him told him she might have already lost her ability to control her limbs enough to swim. She was going to sink into the cold depths.

One more glance toward her and he saw . . . nothing.

His already-pounding heart jackhammered.

She'd been waving for help right over the SS *Tate* that sank over a century ago—he'd gone down to look at it a few weeks after arriving in Shadow Gap.

God, help me make it!

Even if he made it to her, he'd have to swim her back. Grier dove down deep into the murky, cold waters, pushing himself forward with every kick until . . . there . . . he caught a glimpse of her sinking body.

Arms. Then hands.

The visibility improved as he got closer.

Come on! Only a few more yards separated them, but she was sinking faster than he could swim. Grinding his teeth, he gave one last thrust to propel his body deeper. He was so close to saving her.

God, if you're listening, help me!

At this depth, the visibility grew to less than five feet, and she disappeared again in the murkiness. Desperation flooded his soul as he searched, reached, and grasped in the cloudy green waters.

His lungs started burning.

No. He couldn't stop now.

White flesh flashed in his line of sight, and he again spotted her hands and arms, her tangled hair lifting up and floating in the current, obscuring her face. Grier reached forward and gripped her hand, tugging her body upward behind him as he pushed to the surface.

Come on . . . just a little farther.

He was trained, had practiced holding his breath, but his heart pounded too fast, burning through the oxygen he held in his lungs. Gripping her cold, limp hand, he pulled her up . . . up . . . up.

He breached the surface and sucked in air as he pulled her up with him. That was half the battle. The next half—swim them back and pump the water from her chest.

Given his line of work, he'd faced certain death before, and as he stared back at the shore, he knew he was facing death again—head-on. He stared it down and started for shore.

A fire truck and an ambulance were crossing the bridge, which was still a couple miles out from the beach. In Alaska, people learned to live on their own or die on their own, because help wasn't always around.

A deep vibrating thrum in the water and in his ears drew his attention. A floatplane?

The red-and-white prop had already landed on the water and maneuvered toward them. A woman held open the door and shouted, but he couldn't make out her words. But he didn't need her words to understand the plane would save them. He swam toward the welcome sight, the plane much closer than the shore by far—and probably the reason he would live another day. The drowning victim too. Still in his arms as he swam to the plane, she twisted into a fit of coughing up water. Good . . . this was good.

"It's gonna be okay." With his free arm, he grabbed the pontoon. Because she couldn't use her limbs, she remained limp, dead weight, which made her seem heavier than she truly was.

The woman could still die of hypothermia, but she wouldn't die a drowning victim. He noticed she was wearing only slacks and a fleece jacket.

She hadn't meant to go for a swim.

The two women in the plane reached forward and tugged her from him. She might be pale and have blue lips, but for the moment she was still alive.

The hand reaching out to him pulled his attention from the drowning victim. He looked up into a beautiful face framed by crazy brown curls, with a set of light-blue eyes he could never get out of his head because spilling out into the blue iris of her right eye was a deep, golden amber. Partial heterochromia—he'd had to find out about her eyes the first time he'd seen her. And now, he couldn't take his gaze from her as he held on to the pontoon.

Her expression was stern, filled with concern, but the corners of her lips hiked up—just for him? "Hello, Grier. Looks like you're the hero today."

I'm no hero. "Hello, Chief. Or can we still call you that?"

 # THREE

His question took her aback. Grier was direct, she'd give him that to go with his irritating, roguish grin, but she didn't answer as she assisted the guy onto the small plane. He probably didn't need her help, but then again, he must be exhausted after that strenuous swim.

With the woman he'd rescued secured in the second-row seat, a blanket draped over her, Grier took the seat next to her. His presence made the compact cabin feel even smaller.

Autumn buckled into her seat next to Carrie and twisted around to take in the shivering woman who looked barely conscious.

"Call for the ambulance to meet us at the dock." They'd done all they could do.

"Already on it." Carrie got on her radio. "As soon as everyone is secured, I'll head that way. There's another blanket in the back-row seat with my emergency preparedness kit for you, Grier."

"Appreciate it." Grier twisted around and found the kit, then yanked the silver-lined blanket out. Instead of putting it on himself, he placed it over the woman to go with the one she already had.

The plane started forward, taking longer to lift from the water than it did from land. Once in the air, Carrie flew them around a ridge—Eagle Bluff—in the deep fjord up the Lewis Inlet, then landed on the water again. Shadow Gap was located at the mouth of the glacier-fed Goldrock River where it flowed into the inlet. Carrie maneuvered the plane up to the dock right as the ambulance steered into the parking area. Two EMTs—Dooley and Harlan—jumped out and grabbed a gurney they rolled to the end of the dock to meet them.

Autumn, Carrie, and Grier got out of the plane and out of Dooley and Harlan's way so they could carefully move the woman onto the gurney. Watching them roll the gurney back to the ambulance, Autumn decided she would go see her later. She wanted to question her, but she could wait until the woman's life was no longer in danger. As it was, she hadn't gotten her name and hadn't found any identification on her.

Grier lifted Autumn's duffel out of the plane and set it on the dock. He stood next to Carrie, watching Dooley and Harlan load the gurney into the ambulance, and Autumn was guilty of watching Grier instead. Was it her imagination, or did the neoprene suit make his arms look bigger, his shoulders broader? Definitely a swimmer's physique. He was in top shape even in his midthirties, a good five years older than she was.

Carrie glanced at Autumn, catching her staring, and arched a brow. Time to shift gears.

"So what happened?" Autumn asked. "Who's the woman? You two out for a swim or what?"

He threw up his hands in either surrender or defense. "Whoa. I don't know any more than you do. I'd just come from down the road and caught a glimpse of someone in the water. I had my dry suit in the back with my scuba gear. I figured that to give her the best chance of survival, I'd need the dry suit. It only took a couple short minutes to put it on."

"Thanks for your quick actions, Grier. Like I said, you were a hero today." Autumn took in his still-wet hair that, when dry, was almost blond, as well as his strong jaw and deep-green eyes that reminded her of the lush Tongass Forest. On the inside, she berated herself. She knew entirely too much about his appearance and almost nothing about his background.

Carrie shifted toward the plane. "Listen, I'd love to stay and chat, but I have work to do before the sun sets, and I'm already late." Smiling, she waved and climbed back into her Helio.

"Thanks for the lift." Autumn returned the smile. "Be careful out there." Then she looked at Grier, who acted like he expected more questions from her.

"If I think of anything else I need to ask, I know where to find you." She picked up her duffel.

Then he gave her his rakish grin.

Ignore, ignore, ignore.

Oh. Wait.

"I'm going to need a ride, if you don't mind," he said.

Right.

"I never mind helping a hero." Her duffel in tow, she headed to the Interceptor she'd left parked at the landing dock.

"Please don't call me that." He hiked next to her, his suit booties making a squishy noise.

Okay, then. She wasn't sure what that was about, but he projected the kind of confidence Autumn wished she had herself, especially after the vote of no confidence she received yesterday.

Once she and Grier had gotten into the Interceptor and buckled up, she started the vehicle and steered quickly through town and the few miles out to where he'd left his truck near the water, during which time she queried him more about his swim out to save the woman.

But she learned nothing new. He'd spotted the woman only a few moments before she and Carrie had from the air. They'd all converged onto the water at nearly the same moment, and that's the only reason the woman was still alive. And maybe Grier too.

A tragedy avoided.

Once they were across the bridge south of town, Autumn

steered down the rocky terrain to park next to his red Dodge Ram 4×4.

"Thanks for the ride." He opened the door and hopped out as if glad for the escape, then marched over to his truck and unlocked the back.

She glanced up at the dull, gray sky. The rain had stopped, but probably not for long. She got out of the SUV too because she wasn't done talking to him yet. He started unzipping his dry suit, his dark-green eyes lifting to meet hers, and for a moment she expected him to hesitate, but nope, he continued to disentangle himself from the complicated water gear. And Autumn should step away.

But she lingered long enough to see he had on a shirt underneath—and still, it felt inappropriate to watch him "undress" as it were. Hating the warmth that rushed to her face, she turned away and walked to where water lapped against the pebbles, the smooth inlet reflecting the mountains on the other side. The beauty of Southeast Alaska never grew old and always took her breath away when she managed to stop long enough to appreciate God's stunning creation.

It was in the sixties today, so not too cold. She drew in a deep breath of fresh air and tried to imagine swimming in the inlet's fifty-degree water. Why had the woman been that far out? Maybe she'd intended to commit suicide and then changed her mind? Or had she taken a boat or kayak out and it sank? In that case, why wasn't she wearing the proper clothing, like a life vest? She could have at least set off an emergency beacon.

Like far too many in Alaska, she might have been lost to the world forever.

Missing, never to be found.

They still hadn't found Monica Nobel, who'd gone missing back in May.

Time to head back to town. Instead of going to see Dad first, she'd better go to the hospital to check on the woman. Get her name and ask questions. But first, Autumn lingered because she wanted to answer Grier's earlier question. He hadn't pressed her on it, but just how much did he know?

He finally approached. Hands in his jeans pockets, he stood next to her but said nothing. The man had a sturdy presence about him, one to which she found herself inexplicably drawn.

Not that she owed him an explanation, but she said, "Yes, I'm still chief."

After a few heartbeats, he responded. "Glad to hear it."

"Are you?" The words slipped out, and she wasn't sure why she cared what he thought.

Her question seemed to surprise him too, and she felt his gaze on her but continued to look out across the pristine water at the lush forests of spruce, hemlock, and pine carpeting the landscape, topped with snowcapped mountains. An eagle flew out over the water.

"Why wouldn't I be? You didn't do anything wrong."

Carrie had said the same thing. Autumn always tried to do what was right, of course, but her confidence was shaken, and she felt as if she had to prove herself over and over. But maybe not to Carrie and, yeah . . . not even Grier Brenner. She didn't know why, but she was glad she had a fan in this stranger who seemed a long way from home. She still tried to make out his accent, but he didn't have one, which was odd in itself. Maybe he'd lived all over the place, and Alaska was just another brief stopping point.

She glanced sideways at Grier.

Lines furrowed his brow as he leveled his intense gaze. "How does that work, exactly, that you're still chief?"

Her heart beat a little too fast. A little too loud. Wasn't he a bold one? He kept surprising her today, and she was getting way off track. "Alaska state law doesn't require chief administrative officers to hold a state certification."

But it remained to be seen if the city council would allow

her to keep her job since she had at least one enemy in a high place, who in turn had friends in high places. And now, she definitely needed to redirect the conversation.

"What do you think happened? I'd just like to know how she ended up so far out."

He shrugged almost as if he didn't care, but concern lodged in his eyes. "Right, because there's no boat. I wondered the same thing. She wasn't wearing the right clothes either, so it doesn't seem like she was planning to go for a swim. Whatever the reason, it doesn't feel right to me."

It didn't *feel* right? Interesting comment.

He remained an enigma, and she only felt comfortable when she knew the people who made up the town she swore to protect. People often came to Alaska to start fresh or disappear, and she should give him the space for either. But like her police chief father before her, she listened to her instincts, and her instincts told her Grier was trouble. Oh, she had no doubt he was a hero through and through, especially after his actions today, but he was also trouble with a capital *T*. She hadn't decided if her instincts were warning her about him in a more personal way, though.

Either way—personal or otherwise—the last thing she needed was more trouble after yesterday's hearing. She could still lose her job and disappoint her grandparents, who ran the iconic Lively Moose. Her father. And even her Alaska State Trooper brother, Nolan. But mostly herself.

Grier said nothing more, then left her side. She listened to the crunch of his footsteps. He started his truck and it rumbled, then the tires crunched as he turned the truck around. Enough looking out over the water. Her question wouldn't get answered by staring longer, so she headed back to her vehicle. Grier's truck sat idling as he hung his elbow out the window.

"I hope you find out what happened . . . *Chief.*" He shot her that grin, then drove off.

FOUR

f he'd heard it once, he'd heard it a thousand times—no good deed goes unpunished.

Grier cranked up the heat to chase away the chill. He might never get used to the cold waters of the Inside Passage no matter how much he adapted to this environment. The rain had picked up again—nothing new there—and turned the road back to town slick. He floored the accelerator without concern that Chief Autumn Long would pull him over for a traffic violation. She'd called him a hero, after all. Never mind that she hadn't left yet. He would be out of sight before she pulled out.

Grier sped along the two-lane road, traveling in the opposite direction from his earlier excursion. The road didn't actually go anywhere except to connect to a trail and a few cabins in the woods or where the Chilkoot Inlet branched off into the Lewis Inlet, which is where he'd been diving with Tex, his friend from Haines. Tex had taken his boat home, and Grier had driven. He preferred to meet away from prying eyes rather than at the very public small-town marina.

And that's why he'd been the only one around to see the drowning woman, but saving her had drawn unwanted attention, all the same. Grier slowed as he entered the main drag in

Shadow Gap. The small town was nestled in the Tongass Forest along a stunning waterway surrounded by mountains.

He steered slowly through town, passing the IGA grocery store, Brothers Outfitters, the Rabid Raccoon Pub, and then his destination—the Lively Moose, the iconic restaurant owned and run by Pearl and Ike Lively since the beginning of time, or maybe at least the beginning of Shadow Gap—so he'd heard.

He parked and sat in his truck. Caught his breath.

"You were the hero today."

He pounded the console.

She had no idea what she was saying. He wasn't a hero. Shouldn't be acting like one. People would talk, drawing unwanted attention. They'd get the wrong idea. Any ideas about him at all were not part of the plan.

He should have gone completely off-grid. And now he should just go home, but instead he planned to head into the Lively Moose—a place he frequented far too often, hanging out with his new friends.

What am I doing?

He pressed his palms to his eyes. He'd tried to keep to himself, but he'd never been a hermit and couldn't start now, even in his dire circumstances. Besides, the warm, friendly people of Shadow Gap had a way about them and had drawn him out with their small-town-Alaska charm.

Enough fighting his next step—it was a losing battle. Second breakfast was calling to Grier, so he got out of his truck. Hiking up the boardwalk, he longed for a bright sunscape to replace the gray, rainy days and lift his spirits, take away the chill in his bones. He spotted the chief's Interceptor crawling up Main Street and, smiling to himself, kept his head down. Chief Autumn Long, with her striking multicolored eyes and dark, curly hair, possessed the fiery spirit of a survivor. Yeah . . . he recognized a kindred spirit when he saw one.

They were both in survival mode, though completely different kinds of survival. But over the few months he'd been in Shadow Gap, their paths kept crossing for some reason or another—both big and small.

Today was a big one.

Shoving his thoughts of the chief aside, he focused instead on breakfast. After he got a good meal in him, he'd head back to his cabin and feed Cap—short for Captain America—the husky with one blue and one brown eye he'd inherited when he rented the cabin. Besides, Grier might be able to get some salmon scraps from Ike that he could feed to Cap. Now, there was a perfectly good reason to hang out with his Shadow Gap friends at the Lively Moose—scraps for Cap.

Oh, Grier was good at justifying his every move, all right—even down to the smallest detail. He spotted Otis's old, rusted-over pickup truck with the giant wooden cross attached to the back sitting in front of the restaurant. The display was impossible to miss and brought Grier comfort he hadn't known he needed. The truck was painted with "Jesus Saves" and various Christian phrases and symbols over the top of the rust. Something else to make Grier smile.

He paused to stare at the enormous log cabin that could be mistaken for a lodge but was a hopping diner that served breakfast, lunch, dinner, and everything in between. The owners lived in the second-story apartment, so in a way, it *was* a lodge of sorts.

Grier opened the door and walked in, let his eyes adjust, then quickly scanned the large dining hall—a counter at the front, booths along the windows, and tables through the center for the larger dinner crowds. Rustic chandeliers hung from the lofted ceiling lined with rafters, and the typical mounted wildlife trophy display—moose, elk, bear, and more—hung on the walls.

He was grateful the place wasn't too crowded this time of day and breathed easier as he headed toward the booths at the back.

"Grier!" one of his buddies called out to him from the booth by the window—where he usually sat—and Grier joined him.

"How are you doing, Sandford?"

"I'm breathing. God is good." Luis Sandford looked to be in his late seventies, though Grier wasn't sure. The man, an army vet who'd served during the Vietnam conflict, was fit as a horse. He'd come home intact and sometime during his life ended up in Shadow Gap for reasons Grier didn't know. But Sandford had been here long enough to become a town fixture.

Otis joined them, sliding in next to Grier, who scooted over. These men had become Grier's fast friends when he'd wanted none, but they were characters with colorful histories and he related to them. He hadn't expected the camaraderie, or he would have guarded against it. But it served to confirm how desperately he wanted his life back.

"You look anything but relaxed. I told you that you should have gone fishing with me." Sandford chuckled, revealing a few missing teeth, and his laugh filled Grier with light, pulling him out of the shadows where he definitely needed to stay hidden.

Hanging his head, he joined the man and laughed. "Maybe next time."

Nina brought Grier a plate of fry bread and reindeer sausage, and he looked up at the waitress, trying to hide his surprise.

"You come in here five days out of the week, and this is what you order. I took a chance." She winked and smiled, giving him the feeling that her smile was for him alone.

He didn't have the heart to tell her he'd been thinking peach cobbler. "Thanks, Nina. You're the best."

He might have caught a slight blush in her cheeks. He hoped he hadn't given her the wrong idea with his compliment. Grier turned his attention to the food and contemplated the best place to start on the reindeer sausage.

Nina left, and his booth companions chuckled.

"You've got a secret admirer," Otis said.

"Only it ain't no secret." Sandford had to add his two cents.

Both men laughed again, enjoying their joke at Grier's expense. It was all in fun and he didn't mind, but he ignored the teasing and bit into the warm fry bread and savored the moment. He definitely needed to lay off the rich food if he wanted to stay in shape.

"I heard you saved someone from drowning today," Sandford said. "So probably best you didn't go fishing with me."

Otis nodded. "I knew the first time we met that God brought you here for a purpose greater than your own."

To save a drowning woman?

What was he supposed to say to that? Peering out the window, Grier caught sight of the smallest police station he'd ever seen right across the street. At that same moment—of course—the chief exited and climbed into her vehicle. She had donned her chief-of-police attire in short order and moved with determination and confidence. He couldn't help the admiration. She was . . . something. She drove off, and he watched the vehicle until it disappeared.

"Uh . . . huh. I see how it is." Otis cracked a knowing smile.

Grier hoped not. "There's nothing to see."

"If you say so."

"You two enjoy your day." Sandford slid out of the booth and stood. "I've got places to go and people to see."

Sandford was fit but still hobbled as he left, offering Nina a congenial nod when he passed her. Grier had hoped to catch Ike so he could get those salmon scraps for Cap, but he only spotted Pearl chatting it up with customers at the counter, and he wouldn't interrupt.

Otis sat in the other side of the booth to face Grier.

After finishing off the sausage, Grier looked up at Otis, who'd been watching him too long. "You got something to say, go ahead and speak your mind."

"You can't hide the truth forever, son, but I'll tell you my

31

piece about the chief. You'd better be sure before you get in too deep."

"I'm not . . . you've got me wrong." He had no plans to get in too deep with the chief.

Maybe Otis saw more than Grier was ready to admit. He shouldn't get involved for a hundred reasons he could never tell Otis or anyone, not the least of which was that he'd come here to disappear. To get lost and be forgotten.

Problem was, he had a feeling he was already lost—at least to himself—before he even arrived. Now that he was here, he felt almost . . . well . . . found. As if those thoughts made any sense.

Otis glanced around and sipped his coffee, and Grier was glad the man wasn't pressing him, though, actually, Grier kind of wanted to press Otis. What did he mean about being sure before he got in too deep with her? What was there to be concerned about as far as Otis knew?

Grier finished off his breakfast and tried to put those questions to rest. But something else Otis had said floated to the surface.

"God brought you here for a purpose."

If Otis knew the whole story, he would say something different.

Grier usually appreciated Otis's cryptic speech, but not today. Agitation crawled over him, and he wasn't sure why. He sensed a subtle shift in the atmosphere. The Interceptor returned, and the chief hopped out of the vehicle, looked up and down the street as if to cross, then stared at the Lively Moose, her eyes catching him staring at her through the glass.

The way she looked at him . . .

"I think that's your cue that it's time to work." Otis set his coffee on the edge of the table to signal he needed more.

Grier's pulse jumped. "I don't work for the chief."

"Sure you don't."

Otis was only teasing, but Grier knew something was up. He

left enough money on the table for his breakfast and Sandford's and Otis's, plus a sizable tip for Nina, then slid out of the booth.

Cutting his gaze to Otis, he nodded. "See you later."

"Watch your back."

Always.

Exiting the restaurant, he didn't catch sight of the chief. Relief washed over him as he made a beeline for his truck. Time to get out of town for a few days. He started up the engine. The chief's face suddenly appeared outside his window, startling him. She knocked on it, her strange eyes pinning him in place.

He lowered the window, dreading what she might have to say. "Can I help you?"

"I thought you'd want to know that the woman you saved—Sarah—is doing well. She said her boat sank."

He shrugged. Made sense. "And?" *I can't get involved more than I already am.*

That was for the best.

The chief glanced up and down the street like she thought someone might overhear if she wasn't careful. "I'd like to confirm that and see what exactly happened."

Huh. Interesting. Well, he'd thought something hadn't seemed right.

"What else did she say? Is she filing an insurance claim? You could start by finding that out." *I need to keep my mouth shut.*

"I asked, and she said she would call them."

But the chief clearly didn't believe her. "I'm not sure what that has to do with me." He could put on his best nonchalant expression and pretend he didn't care. But if he was being honest, he wanted to know what happened too. After all, he'd risked his life for this woman.

"I'd like you to dive with me to find her boat, if there *is* one."

If there was one? Otis's words rushed back to him. *"God brought you here for a purpose."*

Sorry, God, but I can't get involved. "How did you know—"

33

Oh, right. He'd been wearing a dive suit, and he'd told her that he had scuba gear in the back of his truck.

She arched a brow, her lips curling up slightly. "That's some serious equipment you've got."

Then it hit him. "You dive?"

She nodded, her blue-and-amber eyes mesmerizing him. He hadn't known, and knowing now shouldn't make a difference, but it did. It absolutely *did* make a difference. He liked the chief even more. *Like* wasn't a strong enough word.

"So, what do you say?"

He pulled his gaze from hers—because she held some kind of power over him—and stared down the street, watching the traffic and passersby and trying to clear his mind.

Then he angled his head and looked at her. "You have to be dry-suit certified, plus that dive is about a hundred and fifty feet at the deepest part and—" At the look on her face, he stopped. "But you probably already knew that." And no one else around here was equipped for such a dive. She could reach out to other local communities—Haines or Skagway or even the state—for search-and-recovery divers, but after her recent experience with the state, he supposed . . . not yet.

I don't know if this is a good idea.

She met his challenging look and waited for his answer. "Well?"

He shouldn't, he really shouldn't, but he found himself asking, "What time?"

Because Grier had never been good at following the rules, even when those rules were the ones he'd personally set in stone.

34

 # FIVE

C atching her breath, Autumn shut the door to her office and leaned against it. Had she really just asked Grier to dive with her tomorrow? Of course, he was the man of the hour, and she would go with the flow.

But her pounding heart had nothing to do with the fact she needed his skills at the moment and everything to do with the way his eyes seemed to look right into her soul and search the hidden places, and she feared that one day he was going to find what he was searching for. She'd pegged him as trouble when she first met him, and she'd been right.

Unfortunately, she might be just a little addicted to his particular brand of trouble.

Oh brother. I've lost my mind.

Or at least she lost it when she was in proximity to Grier.

Autumn shoved from the door, moved around her desk, and plopped into the chair. She couldn't afford this distraction in her life right now—or to lose her mind.

Hanging on the wall across from her was Dad's plaque from when he was chief, which she'd left there because the Scripture said it all. Birdy and Ike gave it to him when he first started in Shadow Gap.

"'To act justly and to love mercy and to walk humbly with your God.' Micah 6:8."

Just the words she needed to adjust her attitude. She had a job to do. Time to get back to the reality that was her world—sans Grier Brenner, at least for the moment.

Autumn's day hadn't gone anything like she'd expected, but, well, she should have expected her arrival back in town wouldn't include fanfare. Instead, she and Carrie had been able to assist Grier in rescuing Sarah. Maybe there was nothing to look into regarding the young woman, but she would follow her instincts. In the meantime, she would bury her head in her work and try to put the disaster of her recent decertification behind her. She was still the Shadow Gap police chief until she wasn't.

She stared at the pile of paperwork on her desk.

Go figure. Nothing about the daily grind magically changed in my absence.

That included politics. Per usual, city affairs got in the way of every aspect of her life, it seemed. Police work was no exception, especially since a member of the city council, Wally, had a second cousin on the Alaska Police Standards Council to whom he complained—as in, he provided a long list of Autumn's alleged misdeeds.

That has to be the reason my certification was revoked.

At the thought, she clenched her jaw.

Everything had been misconstrued and spun in a way to make her look corrupt or like she was playing favorites, and honestly—even if that were true—she didn't believe it warranted her losing her certification.

Nobody's perfect.

And if someone were to go on a witch hunt looking to list her every little mistake, then that list could be made. The allegations—or to her way of thinking, slurs—had been stacked against her.

For one, she'd taken her intoxicated father home instead of arresting him for public intoxication and disturbing the peace. And she'd let him ride in the front seat with her—which, technically, was a violation. Though that was all within her discretion, if someone wanted to push it—and they did—she'd made the town liable by transporting someone who wasn't under arrest.

Her pulse quickened.

If she let the accusations get to her, she would start fuming, because the stress level was high enough without having to deal with the previous police chief . . .

My father.

Another thing on the list was that she'd bid out the contract for the towing service the police used for accidents, DUI arrests, and abandoned cars to give someone else a chance instead of always using Wally's brother, who hadn't won the bid. She had nothing to do with it. Terence Unger's business won the bid fair and square.

And lastly, or probably firstly, Wally had wanted his nephew, Officer Craig Atkins, to be the chief.

Oh yeah, Wally has it in for me.

Big time.

And ever since she was named in her father's place, Wally had been needling her. Nitpicking at every small thing. And frankly, she didn't have time for the games. She had this stack of paperwork, reports to read through, three officers to manage, and a town to keep safe. The Shadow Gap crime rate remained at 5 percent below the national average for US towns, and most of those crimes were tame in nature.

Maybe that's why the nearly drowned woman intrigued her. *What happened?*

She sighed, stood from the desk, and looked out the window at the back parking lot and the trees beyond. She thought back to her visit with Sarah, who'd regained full consciousness and was being pumped with warm saline via an IV in her arm.

Autumn had peeked through the door after getting a run-down of the situation from the doctor, HIPAA laws notwithstanding. She stepped into the room and smiled as she slowly walked toward the bed. Sarah looked like a woman in her late twenties, give or take. Her shoulder-length brunette hair was stringy but finally drying, and her big brown eyes stared up at Autumn when she walked into the room and widened in surprise as if she hadn't expected to answer questions about her near-drowning. Autumn's gentle query was nothing more than to confirm Sarah hadn't tried to commit suicide. But what had happened?

"Hi, Sarah. I'm Chief Long. You got lucky today."

Sarah swallowed but said nothing.

"I was flying in from Juneau when we saw you. Of course, the real hero is Grier Brenner, who happened to see you too. He had to dive deep for you because you went under. We landed on the water and flew you back to town." Autumn studied Sarah as she listened. How much did she remember about what had happened? Sarah Frasier—the name she'd given—wasn't a resident. She had no ID on her, and she hadn't given her address or filled out any paperwork yet, Autumn had been informed. "Is there anyone I can call for you? Family? Friends?"

Without hesitation, Sarah shook her head. Autumn found that hard to believe. Who didn't have at least one friend, if not family? Even those who lived off-grid in Alaska had an emergency contact.

"What do you remember about what happened?" Translate . . . why were you there to begin with?

Sarah's gaze shifted from Autumn to stare out the window as if she was remembering, thinking, and measuring how much to say. Before his big fall into insobriety, her father had taught her to listen to her instincts. To listen to what people said, and to what they didn't say. Sarah hadn't said anything yet, but she was already speaking volumes with her body language—she was scared.

Of what or of whom?

"I was out on a boat. It sank. End of story."

That could happen. And while it made sense, Autumn didn't believe her. She couldn't explain why, other than intuition and the fear Sarah tried to hide. She could have died, and Autumn didn't want to push her for answers just yet. She'd let her recover and return later. The doctor had said he would keep her overnight for observation.

Then, of course, she'd decided she wanted to look for the sunken boat. When she returned to speak with Sarah, she would have enough information to press her for answers. Autumn rubbed her eyes as images of Grier flitted across her mind.

When she asked him to dive with her, he seemed reluctant, and for her part, she would have preferred to ask someone else. *Anyone else.*

But if she wanted to dive quickly so she could be ready to question Sarah again, Grier was her man. She didn't know him well and sensed he hid something, but at the end of the day, here in Alaska, who wasn't hiding something? But he had proved himself before when he'd brought her drunk father home rather than letting him drive, and then again today when he risked his life to save a stranger. His actions only confirmed what Autumn already knew—she could trust him on the dive with her. Better him than a stranger out of Anchorage who could have connections to Wally. She rolled her eyes at the paranoid thought.

Besides, she preferred to think about Grier. He wasn't from around here, but he'd quickly fit in with the locals. Autumn got mixed signals from him, though—like he kept to himself, or wanted to, but was ready to help when needed.

She had a feeling about him . . . an idea about who he really was—

The door to her office opened, and Tanya stuck her head in

and smiled. With her Tlingit ancestry and long black hair, Tanya was beautiful and never seemed to age. Autumn could only hope she would look that good at fifty-three. Tanya worked as the all-around office administrator and on-call dispatch when Kelly Jeffers wasn't around for the night shift. The five of them—counting her three officers, Ross, Craig, and Angie—managed the Shadow Gap PD.

Shadow Gap might be a small town, but crime still existed.

Tanya handed off more reports to add to the stack on Autumn's desk to prove it. "Here you go. They're from the last two days, Chief." While Autumn wanted to think of the police department as one small, happy family, at least one of her officers—Craig, Wally's nephew—wasn't keen on her being head of the department, and so the rest of them called her Chief as a reminder that she was the one in charge. Sure, she got her hands dirty—she literally got out there to investigate alongside her officers—but she didn't want to give anyone the idea she wasn't also in charge.

Especially now that she was no longer certified through the state of Alaska. A pang ricocheted in her chest. She couldn't deny their decision had hurt. But Tanya didn't need to know that.

The woman winked and closed the door. Having Tanya as the office encourager, and knowing the woman had her back, went a long way to bolster Autumn's confidence, except when it came to her father. She really needed to check on him but instead procrastinated in her office.

For the rest of the afternoon, she kept her head down and focused on reading through and signing the reports—and ignored the remorse that kept cropping up at the fact that she hadn't gone home to see Dad earlier in the day after she returned from her trip.

When Tanya finally opened the door again, it was dark outside.

Autumn caught the keys that Tanya tossed. She'd taken the Interceptor to get supplies when her Ford Explorer wouldn't start. "Almost forgot to return these. I had to park it in the back, by the way. Listen, Ted and my granddaughter Kimmie are waiting on me outside. He tried to start the Explorer, then looked under the hood and decided he can't fix it, so it'll sit there until he comes back to tow it later tonight or tomorrow morning." Tanya frowned. "You look tired. You should call it a day too. I bet your dad is wondering about Anchorage." A look of compassion crossed her face, and she shoved a strand of her black hair back. "I know it's hard."

She didn't add "to face him."

Autumn might have responded with, "You have no idea," except if anyone knew, Tanya was that person. She understood Autumn too well and had also worked for Dad when he was chief, so she knew him equally as well. And maybe she understood the pain that followed his accident, along with his downward spiral.

Autumn dragged in a long breath of stale office air. She needed to go home but first had to work up the courage.

"You're right. I'll take him some supper." She could lead with that and maybe head off a bad night.

It shouldn't be so hard to face Dad, but oddly, he was her biggest problem.

SIX

G rier entered his private wilderness getaway—a 530-square-foot rustic cabin with one bed and only one bath, but, hey, this was Alaska and he was surrounded by a beautiful rain forest on two acres almost four miles out of town. That was about as far as the road went or the electricity extended. In his mind, this place was as far from civilization as he could push himself to stay for any length of time beyond a day—at least by choice.

Cap jumped off the old sofa that had come with the place, and Grier rubbed the thick white-and-black fur on his head and ears. "I missed you too, buddy."

He let the dog outside to run around in the fresh air. He and Cap had become fast friends just like he had with the others he'd met in Shadow Gap, and he loved the dog. He suspected Cap wouldn't be outside long, because while he liked the snow, he hated the rain.

Grier shared the sentiment, and since he'd had enough rain and water today, he shut the door. Cap would let him know when he wanted back in. Pressing his back against the cold wood surface, now, finally, Grier could let himself breathe. He might have been holding his breath ever since the chief asked him to dive with her. Of course, that couldn't be true, but it felt real enough, and his heart rate finally settled to a normal-ish, steady rhythm.

Grier pushed off the door and in four strides was at the woodstove. He opened it and stoked the fire to warm the cabin, thinking over the day's events. One simple act of kindness. But because he rescued Sarah, he now had to dive with the chief tomorrow morning. One thing had led to another. A step in the wrong direction or veering off the trail even a little could land a traveler far from his destination.

Grier had burrowed deep in this small town lost in Alaska, his only intention to remain under the radar until he didn't have to disappear anymore. Over the last several months, he'd almost started to believe he might live here forever, because he had no plans to leave until it was safe.

So he'd stayed hidden in plain sight. Only a fiery woman with odd eyes could bring him out of his hole, and that's exactly what was happening now. She was the police chief, after all, and any relationship with her on the friendship spectrum wouldn't end well no matter how many ways he considered it, especially since she not only had a big brother, but *he* was an Alaska State Trooper.

But admittedly, Grier was stuck on her. And when she got that distant look in her eyes, he instantly connected with her because he knew that look all too well. Felt it prick his soul.

She has secrets.

But what did it matter? Everyone had something they held close, including Grier.

Like the fact that he wanted to know Chief Autumn Long. He never called her by her name for fear she might hear something in his voice that told her too much. He couldn't afford to take the risk of getting to know her better, even though he was desperate to do just that. She'd asked him to dive, and he couldn't say no. At the end of this long, dark cave, he should consider that he could use a friend on the inside of a law enforcement agency, but he recoiled at the idea of using her friendship in that way.

The fire in the woodstove crackled, burning hot, and pulled him from his thoughts. Grier set bear stew to warm on the propane stove. After the chief's request, they arranged to meet on the boat in the morning. Grier had secured her tanks, along with his own, and borrowed a friend's boat, heading across the Chilkoot Inlet to Haines where his friend Tex, who owned the expensive and necessary equipment, could fill them. The nearest dive shop was in Juneau—about forty minutes by plane.

Grier realized that Cap hadn't barked to be let in, and the slightest concern raked up his spine. He moved across his small cabin in socked feet to open the door and call his dog, though he really couldn't think of Cap as belonging to him. The intense darkness overwhelmed him, along with a cold gust of chilly night air bursting down off the mountains of the Kakuhan Range.

Fortunately, Cap raced through the door and Grier crouched. The dog could well enough live outside with his layered fur, perfect for Alaska or Siberia, but Grier welcomed his furry friend's company, and Cap seemed to want to stay inside.

"You really are a godsend, you know that?"

Cap responded in that way of his, making funny dog sounds that weren't quite barking but almost sounded like he might speak English if he practiced enough. Grier stood and filled Cap's food and water dishes, then ladled bear stew into a bowl for himself and they ate in comfortable silence.

This was the life—almost.

After both Cap and Grier had eaten their fill, Cap fell asleep next to the fire and Grier went to the far corner of the small space where his laptop sat. Lucky for him the cabin wasn't so far out that he didn't have electricity or access to the internet via a low-earth orbiting satellite. His palms slicked as he sat at the desk he'd cobbled together from a board and a few blocks he'd found in the outbuilding next to the cabin.

He hadn't wanted to think about what he would find when he opened his email, yet he needed to hold on to hope—it was all he had. Unease coiled in his gut when he confirmed his in-box was empty and he still hadn't heard from Krueger—the one person who could help him. Krueger updated him once a week, on Tuesdays, and it was Thursday night. Two days late.

Why hadn't Krueger contacted him?

Grier could think of no good reason for the man's silence. He hung his head and tried to grasp what little hope someone had offered today.

"God brought you here for a purpose greater than your own."

He wanted to cling to the words, but Otis was a crazy old man and Grier was a fool to believe him.

 # SEVEN

As Autumn crossed the street, she knew she'd waited too late to offer supper as a peace offering, but she'd texted Dad she was bringing food, so that would have to do. She entered the Lively Moose and made her way through the dining area, nodding at anyone who happened to glance up and see her. During the evening meal, the lights were dimmed to project a quiet ambiance, and the patrons stayed longer and ate more. Autumn had already called in her pickup order, and she walked around the long counter to enter the back of the house, then through the kitchen, where she found the office and her grandmother sitting behind a desk.

Pearl Lively was in her early seventies, but with her shiny auburn hair and big hoop earrings, she might as well have been in her forties, ten years older than Autumn. Running a successful restaurant in nowhere Alaska kept her young, she always said. Pearl and Autumn's grandfather, Ike, founded the restaurant long before Dad moved Autumn and Nolan to town from Topeka, Kansas, twenty-plus years ago when she was only ten. At the time, her grandmother had instructed Autumn to call her Birdy, her preferred term of endearment regarding her status as grandmother. Pearl was a nature lover and birdwatcher, and especially loved the local eagle reserve. So Birdy it had been ever since.

Birdy stared at the computer, working on the books she always did herself, or at least ever since someone embezzled ten thousand dollars from them in the early years. From then on, she trusted only herself with the money—not even Grandpa Ike. He managed the restaurant, and she kept the books, and together they'd grown the popular place that drew the tourists across the inlet from Haines. Autumn was glad they'd found success here, but she was more grateful for the chance to get to know and love them after Mom died.

She could thank her father for at least that one thing—bringing her and Nolan to Alaska.

On the wall above where Birdy sat, a placard was painted with Scripture: "But the path of the righteous is like the light of dawn, which shines brighter and brighter until full day (Prov. 4:18)."

"Nice to see you back, Autumn. Glad you got that nasty business behind you." Birdy didn't pull her eyes from the computer. "I heard about that woman who nearly drowned today. I'm so relieved that help arrived in the nick of time." Birdy shook her head. "Grier is such a nice young man."

Birdy waited until that moment to grin and wink at Autumn, and she couldn't possibly miss the meaning behind Birdy's "nice young man" comment. But she could ignore it.

Autumn took the chair across the desk. "Yeah, don't get any ideas. I'm not looking for a nice young man. Especially someone I know so little about."

"And why not? Oh, if I was young and single, you can bet I would be searching for a nice young man. The day I met your grandfather was the best day of my life. After fifty-five years together, we've had our ups and downs, but that hasn't diminished our love for each other. In fact, it only gets better with time."

"I'm glad to hear it," Autumn said.

Birdy poured tea from a thermos into a teacup. "You want some?"

"No thanks. I'm just waiting for the takeout dinner for Dad."

After drinking from her teacup, she said, "Sometimes you only need to know what a person is made of. Their mettle. And I'm referring to Grier here, in case you were confused."

Dad had courage . . . at one time. The thought lodged in her gut and sparked disappointment.

"How *is* your dad?"

"I hope he's the same as he was when I left."

"You haven't seen him since you got back?"

"Nope. I came straight from the airport to the office to review incident reports—well, after Carrie and I helped rescue the girl. I was on the plane, and we landed, and then the ambulance took her to the hospital. I took Grier back to his truck." She instantly wished she hadn't added that part. "I've been busy and haven't been home. You know I can't afford to let anything fall through the cracks." Or she would lose her job.

She was hanging on by only a thread. Autumn shook her head, her loathing of politics growing by the minute.

"You're worried about Wally, but don't be. He's had it in for your grandfather for years. Then your father. And now he's taking it out on you. He's just making noise."

"Sitting at that table in Anchorage, facing a committee, didn't feel like noise, and now I've lost my certification."

Her grandmother set her teacup down. "You don't need it here. Besides, we're a small town with not much crime to worry about."

Autumn considered the incident reports she'd read that covered the last two days she was gone.

Area caller reported slick roads.

Officer responded to a disorderly male.

Officer assisted a citizen in retrieving personal property.

Report of suspicious activity. And then Hank Duncan . . . Bigfoot could have taken his dog.

And on and on it went. Small crimes still took time.

Autumn scraped a hand down her face and stood. "Night, Birdy." *I'm going home to face the biggest threat in town. My father.*

Holding the bag with the boxed-up dinners—Dad's favorite, Alaskan king crab—she headed across the street, quiet this time of evening except for the local bar, aptly named the Rabid Raccoon, a block down. Raccoons weren't native, but someone had tried to introduce them a few decades ago and it didn't take. The Rabid Raccoon was where she'd picked up her dad, drunk, after he'd gotten entirely too rowdy and blasted the town—probably didn't even remember what he said. Though the trouble with Wally hadn't started there. The incident was one more misdeed, one more mark against *her*, not Dad.

She angled for the back alley where Tanya said she'd parked the Interceptor. One of the security lights had gone out, leaving the alley entirely too dark. A dog barked, and she glanced up and down the street, taking in her surroundings. A raucous group spilled out of the Rabid Raccoon, and a young couple exited the Lively Moose, their daughter between them, and climbed into their four-wheel drive. The child yawned.

Yep, it was definitely time to head home and face what came next. She stepped into the alley. A man exited the bar and headed down the boardwalk. She caught a glimpse of his sweatshirt and blue jeans and stopped in her tracks. She stepped out of the alley to get another look at him, but he was gone. A sense of familiarity washed over her—and not in a good way—but she shook it off.

Even so, unease crept over her as she entered the alley and rushed to her vehicle. Autumn was glad nobody was around to watch her fumble with her key fob. So un-police-chief-like of her. She almost dropped the boxed dinners. Finally settled in her vehicle, she drove through the alley and onto Main Street and drove slowly, letting her gaze shift back and forth, searching the shadows, but she didn't catch sight of the man again.

Then she accelerated and drove three miles out of town, turning onto the drive to the house she shared with her father that overlooked where the Goldrock River spilled into the Lewis Inlet. At least she had one thing to look forward to—the home had a million-dollar view and Dad had gotten a deal on it. From the wraparound deck located on two hundred feet of waterfront, she could watch the sun set, the clouds gather, and fishing boats and sometimes cruise ships pass by, along with sea life. The thoughts helped her relax, and once inside the house, she set the bag holding their dinner on the kitchen counter, then glanced around the living area, dining room, den, and up the staircase, hoping she'd see her father standing there with a smile. But she was asking for too much.

Miles Long—his parents had a terrible sense of humor— was the Shadow Gap police chief until two years ago when an accident left him with a mangled arm. Autumn had taken his place in the interim until she was officially put in the position a year ago.

Dad had been her rock, holding their family together after everything that happened surrounding Mom's death. She'd been an attorney, and Dad, the Topeka police chief. He'd whisked them away, leaving his job to move them to the farthest place on earth. At least in her child's mind, Shadow Gap, nestled in a secluded fjord in Southeast Alaska, had been at the ends of the world.

He'd claimed that Topeka held too many memories. Now that he was no longer chief, something was eating him alive, and every day she watched him sinking deeper into the mire.

Autumn made coffee, just in case, and plated their dinners.

Now she would go in search of Dad. Once she found him, she would use Alaskan king crab as a peace offering for a thousand mistakes, especially not rushing right home after she landed today.

Dread built in her gut at what she might find.

Please let him be sober.

She moved through the house, then finally walked out onto the deck and spotted him sitting on the last step near the rocky beach. She hiked down the steps and eased onto the one just above him. A chilly gust whipped past her, bringing with it the hint of alcohol. While she wasn't surprised, her heart sank.

They sat in silence for a few minutes, watching the strokes of magenta in the sky dipping down between the purple mountains, and beyond those, the snowcapped peaks—miles and miles of them.

The view took her breath away every time, and truly, she had nothing to complain about. Only blessings, really.

Soon the stars would come out, and if the conditions were right, the aurora borealis would mesmerize her. The beauty of Alaska had reached into her heart and grabbed her soul years ago, and it made her want to weep, right here. Right now. But more than that, as the night sky settled in and stars teased her with promises . . .

All of it reminded her of—

No. I'd better not go there. "I brought your dinner. It's probably cold now."

"When did you get back?" His voice was gritty.

"Earlier today." Guilt suffused her that she hadn't rushed home to check on him. If only Nolan hadn't gotten assigned so far away last year, he could help. "There was an incident I needed to check into." A few, actually.

"The girl on the boat," he said.

Right. News traveled fast in small towns. "I'm going out tomorrow to look into it."

Dad slowly turned to her with his bloodshot eyes, the sadness reaching into her chest and squeezing her heart. "Your mother—"

Please . . . I want to know. Pain ignited in her chest. She couldn't stand to watch him break tonight. Nor did she want to be crushed under the pain either. "Don't, Dad. That was a long time ago."

Autumn stood and offered her hand. She didn't want to know, after all. She would eventually, but not tonight. Maybe tomorrow.

But never tonight.

"Let's go eat. I made you some coffee too."

She'd been so torn about what she wanted. Did she really want to hear what he might say and stir up the horror? No, thank you. Still, she hadn't stopped thinking about her mother since watching Sarah nearly drown today, and she would be dead had Grier not been there.

Mom had drowned twenty-two years ago after swimming Autumn to shore.

"Memories made on the water last forever." Dad had loved the saying and had tried to make those memories.

She wanted to push the thoughts aside, but unbidden, the images flashed through her mind as if they'd happened yesterday. She and Mom on the boat, waiting for Dad and Nolan, when the strangers showed up. Squeezing her eyes shut, she shook her head. *No, no, no . . .*

Autumn held back the flood of memories that would hollow her out if she let them.

 # EIGHT

G rier arrived early at the marina situated at the edge of
town along the Goldrock River and boarded the *Long
Gone*, an old twenty-eight-foot Carver Riviera cruiser.
He stomped onto the deck, admiring the loving touches someone had put into updating the 1980s boat. While he waited on
the chief to show up, he loaded the tanks and his gear, making
two trips from his truck to the boat.

He'd almost finished preparing for the dive when he realized
she should have been here a few minutes ago. He tried to dispel
that prickly sensation that someone was watching him. He
never ignored the well-honed instinct, and wouldn't start now,
so he walked the pier and searched for the source but found no
one lurking in the shadows.

Maybe his rising apprehension over the upcoming dive with
the chief had heightened his senses and made him feel "watch-
ers" when he was practically alone at the dock. He was over-
reacting. Either way, he'd maintain situational awareness at
all times.

Per usual, the sky was overcast and the temperature in the
midfifties as the drizzle continued. With the wind at fifteen
knots, the water had a one-foot chop to it—not ideal, but then

again, they would be spending their time beneath the surface. Another group of storms was forecasted to push through the area today, so Grier hoped to go down, take a look and see what was what to satisfy the chief, then head back up and get off the water pronto. When he dove with Tex yesterday, the water was murky in the shallows, but once they got below twenty feet, the view cleared up and visibility was excellent. Grier hoped for good visibility again today.

Cold-water diving in Alaska was some of the best in the world, in Grier's opinion. Tex agreed. But it was also more complex than diving in warmer waters. For obvious reasons, exposure protection was important, and decompression limits changed because one's body reacted differently to the cold temps and burned more calories to stay warm and therefore also consumed more air. The correct regulator was necessary to handle the buoyancy control device, with all the additional layers beneath the dry suit. The shock of the cold added another set of problems, but one big difference made him smile—the marine life. Mammals preferred cold water, so when Grier went diving, he hoped to see seals, porpoises, and whales, though from a safe distance, along with kelp forests, which thrived in cold water.

He would love to explore all this with the chief. He was surprised when she asked him to go with her but was more surprised to learn she was a diver too. He wanted to know more about where she'd been diving and pictured them sitting at a café talking about their adventures.

Otis's words came back to him . . . *"I see how it is."*

Grier had to get a grip. The chief might be something special, but he couldn't let her become something special to him.

Another glance at his watch told him that she was a half hour late. He frowned. Had she changed her mind? He reached to check his cell but froze when planks creaked behind him. Could be another boater, but he couldn't be sure and would remain cautious. He slowed his breathing. Listened. Braced for anything.

And pressed his hand to the 9mm pistol in his holster . . . just in case. You just never knew who might sneak up on you. Only in his case, he had an idea.

"You gonna shoot me?" the chief teased, but apprehension was in her voice somewhere.

Tension stayed in his shoulders as he dropped his hand and turned to face her, shooting her a smile instead. "You're late."

She tried to keep her serious expression, but amusement danced in her eyes. "Did you think I would stand you up?"

"The thought crossed my mind. After all, Shadow Gap keeps you busy," he said. "Then again, this is *your* boat."

She hopped onto the deck, lugging a large duffel with her, then gently lowered it.

"It's a nice boat, by the way."

"Dad got a good deal on it. It was a fixer-upper, and he threw his energy into it before . . . well . . . that doesn't matter. Anyway, thank you for the compliment and for going with me today. The official police department boat motor has an issue, so the *Long Gone* it is." She turned her attention to unzipping the duffel, then fished around inside and retrieved sunglasses, which she placed on top of her head.

And that gave him another chance to look at her irises. She was probably accustomed to people staring, but gawking was rude. He found his jacket that he'd removed when he worked up a sweat and donned it again. The wind and rain would be colder once they got out on the water.

While zipping her jacket, she said, "The boat was originally named after my mom—the *Jessie Lynn*, but she died." Frowning, she shook her head and gave him the feeling she hadn't meant to share that much.

"I'm sorry." But now he knew why it was called *Long Gone*. He wouldn't press her for more about her mother, but he wanted to know more about this dive. "You never said why you thought Sarah was lying."

"I didn't say I thought she was lying."

"But you suspect she was."

Autumn shrugged, apparently not wanting to commit.

"I get it. I'm not working for you. And yet, I'm diving with you today." This could have fallen to the Coast Guard, at least, but she had her reasons for looking into things herself, and he didn't blame her.

She smiled. "And I appreciate your assistance. I need to check out her statement, that's all."

The chief released the mooring, moved to the helm, then started up the boat. She slipped her sunglasses onto her face, then skillfully maneuvered out of the small marina and the wake zone before accelerating into the Goldrock River a short distance, until it spilled into the Lewis Inlet. He stood next to her as they headed down the Lewis Inlet to where it connected with the Chilkoot, one of the many intracoastal channels of the Inside Passage. Mountain ranges and steep cliffs lined the waterways on either side, creating the fjord.

"I hope we'll be done before the storms move in," she shouted. "With mudslide warnings already in place, we sure don't need more rain."

The boat bounced over the waves, which had more chop to them than an hour earlier. Grier took a seat and watched the scenery, which included Chief Long, her curly hair whipping behind her despite the windscreen. He trusted she knew where she was headed and simply enjoyed the ride. She finally slowed the boat as they neared the location where he'd rescued Sarah.

He stood and moved next to her as she circled the boat around.

"I think this is about it. I'll drop anchor. And we can gear up and get to it."

"Aye, aye, captain. I'll set up the dive line to be safe." Visibility could be an issue, as could the current. He wanted to ask her about her diving experience. Her diving buddies. And why she'd asked him to go with her today. Instead, he said, "You realize I pulled her up right above where the SS *Tate* sank. It's an old Yukon gold rush shipwreck."

The chief's eyes widened as if she didn't know.

"What? You're a diver and you haven't been shipwreck diving?"

"Not here, no."

"We'll have to remedy that one day."

"Today is not the day. Let's stay on mission."

"Where then?"

"What do you mean?"

"Where have you been diving if not here?"

She froze and stared right through him. "It doesn't matter."

"Just making conversation, Chief. You don't have to tell me."

"One day, Grier. I'll tell you one day."

One day, then. He doubted that day would ever come. Still . . . "You never said if you had the required certification . . . in our conversation yesterday."

"I wouldn't be here if I didn't."

"That's what I thought." The certification to dive at certain depths was one thing, but it was about much more than deep diving. Experience meant being more relaxed, and that meant needing less air. Maybe they should have had a practice dive first, but he was here and this was happening now. All his second-guessing was only increasing his heart rate.

Way to go, Grier.

They got into their dry suits, geared up, and assisted each other with tanks—nothing he hadn't done too many times to count, but never had his breathing hitched so much before diving. Chief Autumn Long had a deleterious effect on him, which wasn't good when he needed to be at the top of his game.

He handed over a communication device. "Here, we can use this to communicate."

She glanced up at him and smiled. "I've never used one of these before."

"Since you have a full face mask, that's a little surprising."

"I'm used to the customary hand signals."

"Good to know. Well, this is a mic and earpiece. It's basically just an underwater walkie-talkie. You attach it to your head via the straps. If you want to talk, you have to press the button. After you hear the activation beep, then you can speak. Just remember, talking uses up oxygen too."

He was adjusting his mask when the chief made an entirely girly noise. A squeal? She pointed across to the port side where a pod of orcas, or killer whales, swam through the water.

"There must be more than thirty of them!" She stood taller and waddled over to the port side in her fins, not an easy task.

He chose to keep his position and secured his Olympus Tough waterproof camera. "We should wait until they pass if they don't stay around too long. I hope they don't mess with my line."

"Oh, I think it would be amazing to see them in the water."

It is. "Amazing and *dangerous*. So we need to be careful. I don't know about you, but I don't have a SeaWorld certification. Sorry."

A few minutes later, she maneuvered back to sit next to him on the edge of the boat. "They've gone up the inlet. You ready?"

He nodded, positioning his mask with the incorporated regulator while she did the same. Together they rolled back into the dark, cold water. He led them down, pacing them as they followed the dive line, descending deeper into the cloudy water, counting on it to clear up any minute now. Grier slowed at fifteen feet to wait a few minutes.

"Good thing this isn't the Lynn Canal." His voice sounded strange, and the comms crackled. "At over two thousand feet deep, only Greenland has a deeper fjord in North America."

"Thanks for the intel. You're a regular walking—or I should say, diving—encyclopedia."

"Funny. My point is that you and I wouldn't be confirming Sarah's story at those depths."

They continued descending the line another fifteen feet, waited for the nitrogen to clear their blood, then continued on.

Grier was relieved when visibility finally opened up at thirty feet. "I see the SS *Tate*."

He left the line and headed toward the old shipwreck.

"What are you doing? We have to stay on mission." The chief moved next to him. "Grier, please. This isn't a pleasure dive for me."

"I can't say that doesn't hurt a little. You don't enjoy diving with me?" He injected teasing into his tone. "Relax. We're still on mission. Sarah's boat, if it exists, would be around this area. The current tends to push things near the shipwreck. In 1892, the ship sank exactly three quarters of a nautical mile west, and the current pushed it here. This is our starting point, and we'll work our way out."

"I knew I got the right person."

"What was that you mumbled?" Her comment was telling that she had been sizing him up. "So far, I don't see evidence of another boat, and visibility is good for almost fifty yards down here."

In the near distance—maybe fifteen yards away—he spotted something of interest and kicked harder, assuming she would stick close. He didn't have to say anything to draw her attention. The chief easily spotted the Alaskan king crab holding a smaller crab. There could be more along the wreck, so Grier swam around, taking in the two-hundred-foot broken hull of the steamer covered in anemones as rockfish swam in and out. The chief gazed upward, backlit by the bright green water, and behind her, a school of fish circled. A stunning sight. He lifted his camera and captured the image.

Frowning, she glanced around and saw him, then offered a smile that made his heart jackhammer. Not good when diving. He turned his focus on the shipwreck and the area surrounding them—he could see the sandy inlet bottom. Still no sunken boat besides the old shipwreck.

"Let's start looking in earnest for Sarah's boat." Worst case, they could use sonar to find it. Grier headed west, and she followed.

Her voice crackled over the communicator, but he couldn't understand her. He shook his head and motioned that he needed a gesture.

She lifted her hand with an "okay" signal. At least she'd understood him, but apparently, he couldn't hear her. She swam next to him as they perused the bottom of the inlet searching for evidence of a sunken boat but found none. He couldn't say that he was surprised, and he doubted she was either.

So why had the woman lied, and why had she been out on the water as if someone had just dropped her there? All questions for the chief to answer. Grier should mind his own business.

He signaled that they needed to start back. She swam toward the shipwreck, and he followed her lead this time. Passing the bow of the shipwreck, she paused and then suddenly turned back to look. She stared past him at the boat behind him, and her eyes suddenly widened. If he could have heard her comms, he thought she might have screamed. Bubbles erupted, too many bubbles, as she jerked backward and turned, swimming chaotically away from the boat.

Panic could kill.

He caught up and turned her around to look in her eyes, willing her to slow her breathing. Maybe she could still hear *him* through the comms. "Chief . . . relax. Slow, even breaths. At this temperature and depth, you'll burn through what's left too quickly." But she knew that already. He stayed with her until she got her breathing under control.

She kept her gaze focused on him, slowing her breathing. Life or death stuff. But the terror remained behind her stunning eyes, and seeing this experienced law enforcement officer so rattled unsettled him. But calm first. Questions later.

"Good." He was glad she'd invited him along. This was why buddy diving was the only way to go.

Her gaze shot past his head, locking on something behind him. Her frown deepened and her complexion looked almost green, but maybe that was just the reflection of the water down here.

Then she pointed behind him and freed herself from his grip, swimming toward the shipwreck. He almost made the mistake of trying to stop her—his protective instincts kicking in. But she was the Shadow Gap police chief on an investigative dive, and he shouldn't forget that she could handle whatever she'd seen, though she was startled at first.

He followed her back to the shipwreck, gripping his diver's knife just in case. As they swam, he looked beyond the anemones, the king crabs, the fish, and a veritable coral reef.

"Look." Her communicator crackled as she pointed. Her comms were working again, at least.

Grier swam closer to the bow and peered through the opening into what was left of the helm. Arms floated upward, attached to a still-clothed body. By the short, dark hair, he would guess it was a man's body. Though the chief remained where she was, he swam around to see the body from a different angle. Now he fought to control his own breathing as he took a few pictures. They hadn't expected to find a body, and her reaction made a lot more sense now. But what didn't make sense was finding the body in the remnants of the SS *Tate*.

He suspected the chief was still breathing too hard. He

certainly was. With their increased heart rates, they were sucking oxygen much too fast.

He turned to find her watching him. She gave him a thumbs-up, presumably appreciating that he'd brought a camera. Then he led them away to search for the dive line.

"Grier, look."

The dive line was coiled at the bottom in the sand.

NINE

O n the boat deck, Autumn dropped to her knees and removed her face covering, cold water dripping from her body. She felt like she weighed three hundred pounds. "The orcas . . ."

"They're gone. They probably got briefly tangled in the line, and that's why it severed. Better than one of them remaining tangled."

"Right. You're right." She gasped, sucking in air. She'd never experienced claustrophobia while diving, and it seemed odd, but with her oxygen levels diminishing, she'd felt trapped and feared she would run out of air. She'd been breathing too hard the entire time, and seeing that body hadn't helped.

They'd made their way slowly upward, stopping in the cold and cloudy depths to decompress as they ascended. She couldn't be more relieved to be out of the water. The image of the body trapped in the shipwreck was seared into her mind.

Grier hadn't missed a thing, though—from her reaction to her near panic as they ascended. She had to get her act together.

Starting now.

A gust of wind and the rock of the boat brought her back to the moment. Grounded her.

"Let's get out of this gear." Grier's voice sounded strong and sturdy.

Autumn climbed to her feet, and he assisted her out of the tanks as the rain lashed them, then she returned the favor. Free of the gear, they stowed it below in the forward cabin. After getting out of her dry suit and pulling on a sweatshirt, she helped Grier when the zipper stuck on his suit, then threw him a blanket to put over the thermal shirt he'd worn underneath. Even with all the layers, the cold could find its way through and seep into your bones.

Autumn sat on the cushioned seats in the berth. She needed . . . a moment.

Grier eased into the spot across from her at the table. "We should get going."

"Not yet. No. We're anchored. The storm won't be that bad." Of course, belying her words, the wind howled and the boat swayed.

Grier's eyes turned the dark, mossy green of an eerie, forbidden forest. His commanding presence seemed to fill up the entire cabin. She wanted to know more about this stranger who showed up in Shadow Gap a few months ago. Without a legitimate law enforcement reason to look into his background, she had no business checking on him. That would not only be overstepping her authority, but it would also give Wally another item to add to his list.

All she knew about Grier was what she could find via the state database check for his driver's license and any possible warrants. Her curiosity had gotten the best of her and she'd searched him on the internet but came up empty. He wasn't even on LinkedIn. She would just have to find out more about him the old-fashioned way. Either he would tell her on his own, eventually, or she'd ask.

She needed to give Grier space to breathe, because that's why outsiders came to Alaska. And like everyone else here, Grier had a right to his privacy.

Uncomfortable under his gaze, she got up. "I'll make us some hot chocolate. Or would you prefer coffee?"

"I'll have whatever you make."

Giving herself time to think about their dive, she turned to the small kitchenette and focused on getting them something warm to drink. She'd seen plenty of grisly sights, mostly while on the job. No heinous murders had occurred near Shadow Gap. No serial killings, that sort of thing. Not yet. But what an animal could do to a man's body wasn't something she wanted to see again. She hadn't looked at the body in the shipwreck too closely and had avoided even trying to get a look at his face. Sea critters had probably made him unrecognizable anyway.

Nausea rolled through her, along with a chill that crept into her soul. She put the teakettle on the small stove and started heating the water. *Dad should put a microwave in here.*

"Are you okay?" Grier's question pulled her from her morbid thoughts, his gentle tone sending warm currents curling around her anxious heart.

"I think we're both shaken." Time to pull it together. "I've seen a lot, but usually when I've been searching for a missing person or called out to a situation for which I'm mentally prepared. I wasn't expecting to see a body today, and it jarred me." Too much. She was sharing too much. She should have been prepared for anything.

"Don't beat yourself up. It means that behind that uniform and badge, you're human. You're not immune. Your heart hasn't grown cold. It shocked me too, but to be fair, I knew to expect something gruesome after seeing your reaction."

"So we weren't able to confirm Sarah's boat sank and instead we found a body in an old shipwreck. A body that wasn't there when the boat went down."

The water from the teakettle had to be hot enough by now,

so she turned off the stove, then poured the steaming liquid into the cups, dumped in the hot chocolate powder mix, and stirred it with a spoon. She stepped to the table and slid Grier's mug over to him, then sat and wrapped her hands around her own warm mug.

"What's the next step?" he asked. "Are you going to call Alaska Dive Rescue?"

"Yes."

Given the political pressure she was under, she didn't want to make any mistakes. This was simple enough. Recover the body. Take one thing at a time. "Let me see the pictures you took."

"Sure." He got up and moved to his duffel, grabbed the camera.

"Smart thinking, taking your camera."

"I take it on every dive." He pulled up the images for her and showed her how to scroll through.

She found the pictures he'd taken of the fish swimming behind her and remembered that moment. She felt him looking at her, even now, and somehow had to ignore the heat surging through her.

When she found the images he'd taken of the body, that did the trick.

"About six weeks ago, I went diving here to see the shipwreck," Grier said. "There wasn't a body."

"Makes me wonder what Sarah has to do with it, if anything. I don't believe in coincidence. But if she's somehow involved, it doesn't make sense to me."

"It could be a simple case of searching for answers and landing in a new investigation altogether. Like when a search-and-recovery group goes out to find a body and locates remains, just not the ones they were looking for. It happens. Doesn't mean the cases are related."

Was this a hint into his background? "Were you a cop before you came here, Grier?"

His eyes widened, then narrowed slightly. "Me? No."

"A volunteer on a SAR team, then?"

He stared into his cup of hot chocolate. "I've read my share of mystery novels, Chief."

He hadn't denied anything with his answer. Why so mysterious? It only made her more curious.

"If you want to confirm another boat, Sarah's boat, you'll have to use sonar."

"That's not in the Shadow Gap budget."

"I'm going to go out on a limb here and say that there's probably not a boat and your instinct about Sarah lying is correct. Like a lot of law enforcement officers, you've got that uncanny sense about people."

That forbidden forest green again. Was Autumn imagining it, or had fear flashed in his eyes? There one second, gone the next.

"Let's talk about the body." She grimaced. "You seemed to know a lot about the current surrounding the wreck, so I'm going to go with that. The current could have carried the body there, but I don't know that it would have lodged in the wreck, in the helm, like that. What do you think?"

"It's possible. Anything is possible. But you won't know until someone gets a closer look."

"Did you see anything that would suggest foul play?" She stood and stepped to the kitchen, then leaned against the counter.

He shook his head. "I saw what you saw. Is it a crime scene or a secondary crime scene? Was he murdered and stashed in a shipwreck, which . . . why would anyone do that? If you want to handle it as a crime scene, that's your call. But since it's recovery and not rescue, it could take the dive team a couple of days or more to get out here. They're busy rescuing people all over Alaska."

Autumn lifted her mug but stopped, pausing at Grier's contemplative, distant look. "Why do you bring that up?"

"They're all capable volunteers with the right check marks in the right boxes."

And activated by the state search and rescue coordinator. "I know this, Grier."

"It's helpful when communities can have their own water rescue and recovery teams, that's all." He frowned and stared hard into his mug.

The boat swayed and rocked, and she tried to ignore the roll of her stomach. "You're the only diver I know locally. I'd rather hand this off. Unless you know someone else who's experienced in recovery and investigation, if this turns out to be a crime scene. But I'll still contact Alaska Dive and run this scenario by them. They might defer to the Coast Guard, for all I know."

His expression softened, and amusement surged in his eyes. "I see what you're doing here. You're trying to get me to put together a small dive recovery team."

"Me? What?" *You're the one.* She shifted forward, wanting to know more.

"I think it's a good idea to build up your own resources, despite funding issues. Show them what you're made of, with or without the state's help. Maybe you feel the sting of betrayal, but you're still in charge." He drank from his mug, his eyes snagging hers over the rim.

Her heart spasmed at the connection. The emotion that flashed. *The sting of betrayal.* He'd said the words as if they meant something personal to him. Like he'd gone through something similar.

"What do you think? Should we keep this local?" he asked.

We? And then, suddenly she got the impression that he had his own reasons for wanting to keep this local. Or was it her imagination again? Maybe she dove too deep today and her brain was fuzzy.

She dumped the remains of her cup into the sink, then rinsed it out. Think, she had to think. "Let's say I said yes, then who do you know who's qualified for a recovery?" Because for whatever reason, she had no doubt Grier had resources. "I can't afford any mistakes."

Maybe asking Grier for help in this would be her next misstep.

But she didn't think so.

"A friend in Haines is trained in underwater investigation and recovery. Tex is a volunteer on the Alaska Dive Rescue team, so I'd start with him."

"Tex?"

"Yep. His real name is Blaze Johnson, but I just call him Tex."

"I assume he's from Texas."

"He is."

Okay, then. "And you think he'll do this for us? Because I'd really like this taken care of as quickly as possible."

"I figured you might not want to draw negative attention to the community."

Or myself.

He hadn't added that last part, but he'd pegged her motivations. And that was part of why she was talking it over with him first—someone who wasn't in her police department. If possible, she wanted to keep politics out of it.

If only she could talk to Dad.

"Not that my opinion matters, but you can do this." He rose from his seat and followed her lead, dumping the contents of his mug into the sink, then rinsing it out and putting it away. "You have the right people here locally, and you can keep it close for now. Really, the Alaska Dive group exists because communities don't do this themselves. If it turns out to be more than a simple drowning, then you deal with one thing at a time. Not that you asked, but . . . I'm leaning toward criminal activity."

"Because?"

His frown deepened and he hesitated. "I couldn't recognize the face."

Nausea erupted at the thought of the images Grier had captured. "Sea creatures, Grier. They pick and nibble away. But I hear you. This needs to be handled as an investigation in case it's more than simply the current washing a body into a peculiar place. But we're using an abundance of caution, that's all. Let's hope no crime was committed, and then once we identify the body, we'll have one less missing person in Alaska. This will bring closure to loved ones."

Closure was something she'd personally longed for since Mom drowned and her body was never recovered.

Grier nodded. "I'll explain to Tex that this needs to happen quickly and quietly, and that we're possibly building a community team. Another friend is out of Skagway. This could be the start of something great for you, Chief. I'll make the arrangements."

"That's all good and well, Grier, but . . . who are you?" She stood entirely too close to him in the small space, but she wouldn't step away as she looked up into his eyes. "Really?"

Because she was trusting him based on those instincts he'd mentioned earlier. But maybe he'd gotten on her good side, her best side, when he rescued her father from the bar that night and helped get him home.

Then yesterday he rescued Sarah. She knew deep down he was a good guy, but even good guys carried baggage.

"I'm the guy helping you build a local dive and recovery team."

 # TEN

The next morning, Grier stood on the deck of Tex's boat. The gray skies and relentless rain might get him down if he weren't getting ready for yet another dive and setting some kind of personal record by diving three days in a row.

He'd never needed a reason to go for a dive. Didn't *want* one now. Hadn't wanted one yesterday, but for some inexplicable reason he couldn't turn down the chief. He should have told her no when she'd asked him to dive with her. Another good deed for which he was suffering punishment. Hadn't saving Sarah been enough?

No. Saving her had only led to the invitation to dive.

And while he enjoyed the occasional pleasure dive, this was a different scenario completely—and one of his own making. While he should keep his head down and stay in the shadows, instead he'd suggested she build her own local rescue and recovery dive team, led by him.

Brilliant, Grier. Brilliant.

He recognized when someone needed help, and he couldn't stand by and watch her being pulled down by a bunch of nitwits on the city council.

So he'd been a nitwit yesterday too.

Why hadn't he kept his mouth shut and let her call the state dive team? But all she had to do was look at him, and he wanted nothing more than to please her. To spend time with her. He wasn't sure if he could ever shake the power she had over him, but he would have to try.

So what if the recent loss of the chief's certification coupled with finding a body in a shipwreck prompted a news story? It would be gone the following day, replaced by the next big story, and he wouldn't need to worry about his face showing up in the news either.

He'd chosen Shadow Gap for a reason. Well, Krueger selected it, but for all the right reasons. Like so many towns that barely survived, Shadow Gap didn't have surveillance cameras on every corner, which made it more difficult to find people using facial recognition software.

Whatever. He was here now and had to see this through because he'd gotten involved in a big way this time. That decision could come back to bite him. He couldn't seem to think like a rational man when he was around the chief and was glad he would be with his diving buddy today instead.

Tex's boat—the *Black Pearl*—was a nice Munson 36–8 dive boat with a dive entrance on the port and starboard sides, ladders, and dive bottle shelves. Tex had also invited along his friend Maggie King, whom Grier had gone diving with a couple of times. Maggie adjusted her face mask, ignoring Tex's failed attempts at flirting.

"I never could understand what a former Texas Ranger was doing all the way up here," Grier said. "I've never been to Texas, but the way I understand it, Texans love their state."

"The great country of Texas, you mean. Nah, man. We love the salsa." Tex's eyes crinkled. "Okay, the state is great too."

Tex winked and positioned his full face mask, then hopped into the water along with Maggie, in perfect sync as if they had practiced. Grier released a sigh of relief after he realized his mistake. He and Tex had never discussed what brought them to Alaska, and he shouldn't have a conversation that could take them down that road.

He secured his mask and joined them in the cold water. Together they descended along the dive line, waiting at the proper intervals, and then Grier led them over to the SS *Tate* and the body.

He took more pictures while his friends carefully extracted the body from the shipwreck, then bagged the hands, head, and feet to preserve trace evidence. Finally, they secured it in a specially designed bag for underwater recovery before transporting it to the surface. Eventually the ME would identify it and a family would learn what had happened to their missing loved one.

People went missing all over the world, but Alaska set records when it came to missing people. And drownings were a big part of those statistics.

Either no one knew this guy had gone into the water, or maybe they did, but, like the chief had suggested, the current had carried his body miles away from the search area. His disappearance, his death, probably had not been intentional.

However, some people went missing by choice. Disappearing in Alaska was part of their grand scheme.

And others were forced into hiding to survive.

 # ELEVEN

While Grier and his volunteer dive team set out to recover the body this morning, Autumn remained in the office and worked through the stack of paperwork.

This morning she'd also checked on Sarah, who'd had to stay another night at the hospital until her lungs sounded good. Dr. Combs had been worried about pneumonia developing, but she would be good to go later today. Autumn wanted to talk to her more but was waiting to hear from the Shadow Gap dive team first.

She glanced at the clock on the wall. 2:30 p.m.

Shouldn't she have heard from Grier by now?

The more she knew when she questioned Sarah, the more she could learn about whether the woman's incident was connected to the body found in the shipwreck. Perhaps Autumn and Grier had missed Sarah's boat, and the dive team would come across it.

Shadow Gap Dive and Rescue.

A smidgeon of pride swelled at what could be a good thing, and she definitely needed something good going for her. The whole town needed it.

Could she really give the loosely cobbled group a name yet, since at least two of the volunteers hailed from across the water and not Shadow Gap at all? Still, the idea excited and scared her at the same time. She'd taken off on this endeavor without talking to the city council, but who had time to wait for every decision to go before a committee of controlling, small-town politicians?

Exiting her office, she stopped at Tanya's desk. "I'm heading out, but I'll be back shortly."

Dad had called her but hadn't left a message and now he wasn't responding to her calls. She needed to check in on him, but she wouldn't broadcast that.

Stepping onto the boardwalk and into the rain, she drew in a deep, calming breath to steady her nerves. Seeing the body in the old shipwreck had affected her more than she'd thought. The image of the drowned body stuck in the helm, arms up and waving in the current, had collided with her memories of her mother missing . . . drowned . . . forever lost to her. Another gulp of air and she pushed past the gruesome images and deep remorse.

One thing at a time.

She could do this. No matter the trials of policing a small town, she was blessed to live here with the Goldrock River ahead of her, mountains at her back, and good people she'd known for most of her life by her side. She hiked over to her vehicle and gave a cursory glance at her surroundings. Across from her vehicle on the southeast street corner—there he was again. His eyes flicked away from her.

He'd seen her too, which didn't mean anything, except— Did she know him? The man was somehow familiar. She rushed back to the boardwalk and started toward him. A shop door opened, blocking her view. Hiding her frustration, Autumn smiled and said hello as she passed a family of five as they exited the store. When the door closed, the man was gone. Autumn continued her purposeful hike to the street corner. She kept a calm expression and waved at Leslie Crank as he loaded supplies he'd purchased at the local outfitters.

At the southeast corner of Main and Spruce, Autumn paused. She knew most of the residents, but tourists often found their way here, coming across the Chilkoot Inlet from Haines when the cruise ships docked. So she didn't know everyone, but never before had a face seemed so familiar—one she couldn't place.

But it was much more than that. Her gut had twisted and tightened when she saw him. Why that reaction? Autumn wanted to know who he was. But after walking up and down two blocks, she hadn't caught sight of him again. She didn't have time to chase shadows, so she gave up the hunt and climbed into her vehicle, thinking about what she would say to Dad when she got home.

After diving with Grier yesterday, she'd wanted to talk through their discovery with Dad, but he was in no place for a serious conversation. She needed his advice. Longed to connect with him—the *old* him. She wished he hadn't retired and that she was still working under him, but that was no way to think. She hoped when she got home she wouldn't find him on a binge already.

Lord, help him to pull out of this!

Watching him broke her heart, and really, he was no longer anything like the father she'd known growing up.

Tanya's voice squawked over the radio. "Chief, Hank Duncan is asking for you. It's about his dog again."

"Didn't Ross go out to talk to him?"

"He did, and they searched for the dog but didn't find him. Ross left to look into a more urgent call, but now Hank is demanding to talk to you."

She didn't have time for this and inwardly groaned. Hank was the local cryptozoologist, but he wasn't a Bigfoot believer when he first arrived—at least Birdy had shared that much.

After attending an expo in Fairbanks, Hank had become obsessed with Bigfoot or Nantiinaq—big, hairy creature—not to be confused with the Tlingit tribe's Kushtaka—land otter man. He'd then become an official member of several Bigfoot societies. Odds were that he now blamed the mythical ape-man for his missing dog. "I'm on my way."

"Ross said he'll meet you there. He's just leaving an accident site. Everyone's okay. Lander's car rolled in the ditch, and the tow has already pulled it out."

"Glad he's okay. Can I get more details on why Hank needs to see me? Is there something more besides his missing dog?"

"If I had any to give, I would. Sorry, Chief."

Every time Tanya called her Chief, she thought of her dad, because he'd filled that role for the better part of Autumn's life. Now she'd have to put off checking on him.

Later, Dad . . .

Two miles out of town, Autumn turned off what could barely be called a road, then followed the muddy ruts up a steep hill that led to Hank's cabin, the lush Tongass growing thicker around her and filling her vision. Maybe if she lived in the dense part of the forest, she'd search for Bigfoot too. She steered right and onto the edge of the one-car road, then parked behind Hank's old truck, which he'd left sitting as far off the road as possible. The path ended a few yards ahead.

Autumn got out and eyed the forest around her—evergreens mixed with the bright yellows of the cottonwood and birch trees. For a second, she was reminded of Grier's eyes and how she'd compared them to an eerie forbidden forest. Rain dripped from the leaves and the needles, but other than that, the forest was quiet.

Yep. Eerie.

Getting to Hank's cabin required a good, exhilarating hike. Fortunately, his trips to and from his truck had created a decent trail, and she wouldn't have to fight the underbrush along the way. His cabin was about a quarter of a mile in. He lived outside the city limits, and his troubles—technically—fell within the Alaska State Troopers' jurisdiction, but she considered Hank part of the Shadow Gap community all the same. Wally would probably call her out on having the police department answer such calls. But seriously? This didn't warrant calling in the Alaska State Troopers, who covered the entire state. Too few of them for too many acres.

Approaching Hank's dwelling, she again noted the beautiful but eerie quiet. Hank's cabin was small but included an attached lean-to under which he kept a snowmobile, firewood, and a generator along with other tools required for living in the Tongass.

She knocked on the door. "Hank. It's Chief Long." Waiting, she listened, but no sounds came from the cabin. Interesting. Hank knew she was coming, didn't he?

Ross emerged from the woods, hiking from the trail, and headed toward her.

She smiled, glad to have him join her in talking to Hank. "You must have been right behind me. What's Hank—"

Gunfire rang out, echoing off the mountains and through the forest. Autumn tensed and grabbed her firearm—a Staccato P4.4 9mm pistol. Ross his Glock 9mm. The sound of gunfire was familiar in Alaska, and guns were discharged for many legitimate reasons, but the gunfire sounded close. That set her on edge since Hank wasn't where he should be. She'd try his cabin one more time.

"Hank, you in there?" She raised her voice this time. "You wanted to talk to me, remember?"

"Hank. I got the chief out here like you asked," Ross said.

Shouts echoed through the forest to the west of the cabin.

Autumn shared a look with Ross. "Let's go," she said. "I think one of the voices belongs to Hank."

"What has he got himself into now?" Ross growled and followed her into the woods, rushing through the underbrush, Sitka spruce, cottonwood, birch, hemlock, and cedar trees as they hurried toward the voices.

"Be careful. We don't need to get accidentally shot by poachers." Or intentionally shot.

She led Ross, cautiously weaving her way through the foliage but rushing all the same. The shouting died away. She paused to catch her breath and looked at Ross. "There's another cabin not too far if we continue this same direction."

"The way sounds echo in the mountains and woods, the gunfire could have come from miles away. The shouts too."

"Agreed, but we'll check that cabin first," Autumn said.

The angry voices started up again.

Ross huffed. "My guess is that someone could have taken up residence there, and Hank has a bone to pick with them."

"Maybe he found his dog," Autumn offered. Since she didn't hear any barking to accompany the voices, she hoped not.

Weapons drawn, Autumn and Ross continued cutting through the woods toward the cabin, and once they neared the dilapidated structure, they slowed their pace and approached with caution. Ross crept behind her as she slowed to a stop, taking in the surrounding woods and the cabin about twenty yards ahead through the trees.

"The chief'll be here soon. Come on out." Wearing an old green Army jacket and a knit cap over his long, greasy gray hair, Hank stood behind a tree, holding his hunting rifle.

From behind another tree Autumn spoke up and made her presence known. Surprising Hank or the man in the cabin could get her or Ross shot. "What are you doing taking the law into your own hands, Hank?"

Now that he knew she was here, she peered around the tree. Hank acknowledged her, so she crept up beside him.

He turned his attention back to the cabin, which had deteriorated into nothing more than old rotting logs cobbled together with the roof caved in on one side. He didn't take his eyes off the cabin as he answered. "He started it."

"Right. Looks like you're the one to me." Ross remained behind a thick spruce trunk near them, though Autumn could see him.

"Doesn't matter who started it. We can sort it out later," she said. "Hank, what's this guy's name?"

"No clue."

Great. Autumn raised her voice as she informed the man in the cabin of her presence. "This is Shadow Gap Police Chief Autumn Long. I think we have a misunderstanding and nothing more. Please set your weapon down and come out of your cabin with your hands in the air."

"I didn't kill nobody's dog." The guy had the hint of a foreign accent, though he tried to hide it.

She eyed Hank. "Do you know if your dog is dead?"

"Bear is missing. Only thing to keep him from coming home is death."

"What makes you think this guy killed him?"

"That doesn't work for me." The stranger shouted through the window in answer to Autumn's request.

Seriously?

"You need to set your weapons—all of them—down and walk away," he shouted again. "I'll disappear. I haven't committed a crime. Didn't kill a dog."

Autumn shared a look with Ross, then whispered to Hank. "Hank, put down your rifle. I'm not so sure you won't be charged, especially if this thing escalates."

"I was defending myself," Hank said, raising his voice.

Ignoring Hank, she said to Ross, "You keep him talking and try to de-escalate. I'll go around back."

"Careful, Chief." Ross cleared his throat, then shouted, "That isn't how law enforcement works, friend. If you haven't committed a crime, you have nothing to worry about. But we still need you to come out with your hands high so we can see you're unarmed, and then we can clear this up."

While Ross talked to the man, Autumn slipped between the trees and made her way around to the back of the dilapidated cabin. It wasn't unusual for transients or squatters to take up residence when a place had been abandoned. She could hear Ross's voice as she crept up to the back door. It didn't sound like he was making any progress or that the stranger was going to give up, which led her to believe he was probably hiding. From what or whom, or if he feared the law, she didn't know. But she intended to find out.

A gunshot echoed, loud and harsh and much too close, but where had it come from? Inside the cabin? Outside? Heart pounding, she peered through the dirty back-door window. She quietly opened the door and led with her pistol, clearing the spaces as she moved in case the man wasn't alone and someone approached her from behind.

When she spotted him standing at the window, his back to her, she made her move and pointed her gun at him. "Police. Freeze."

He remained stock-still, but his shoulders inched up—stiff and tense. He had the bearing of a trained fighter. Her gut tightened. She sensed he had every intention of turning on her.

"Toss your gun aside and lift your hands over your head now!"

"Or what? You going to shoot a man in the back?"

Hank's shouts came through the open window. "Officer down. Officer down."

"You shot a cop?" Before he could answer, she closed the distance, fury and panic blasting through her. Still, she didn't get so close that he could disarm her. "Give me a reason. Just one reason to put a bullet in you!"

He tossed the gun to the side and lifted his hands above his head.

Her most dangerous task awaited—searching and cuffing.

"Place your hands behind your back."

When he complied, she was honestly surprised. But she would remain vigilant, wary, not letting her guard down for a moment. After cuffing him, Autumn pushed the man through the front door, then forced him to the ground, facedown in the muddy loam. The area around the cabin was clear, so no trees blocked the drenching rain.

But she didn't care.

Ross!

Her heart jackhammered when she eyed her officer on the ground, blood seeping into the earth, mingling with the puddles. Anger and grief surged in her chest. No! Disbelief shattered her.

This couldn't be happening.

Lord . . . save Ross!

Hank pressed his hands against Ross's midsection, blood seeping through his fingers. "I got Tanya on his radio. She's sending a life flight. I told her to hurry. She's sending an ambulance too and said Atkins and Greenwood are on their way. I don't want to move my hands, even to take off my jacket to use."

Her two other officers—Craig and Angie. Pulse soaring, Autumn didn't want to focus too hard on the man who just shot Officer Ross Miller, because she wasn't sure she was in total control of her actions.

"Thanks, Hank."

Sending a barrage of silent prayers to God, she stood guard over her prisoner but looked at Ross, wanting to be there by his side instead and help Hank staunch the flow. "Ross, how you doing?"

He didn't respond. Face pale and lips blue, he was losing too much blood. Hank held her gaze and subtly shook his head. His efforts to slow the bleeding weren't going to be enough while they waited for help to arrive.

I need my medical kit!

Autumn radioed dispatch and steadied her voice. "Tanya. How long for the helicopter?"

"Coming out of Haines. Fifteen minutes. Ambulance coming out of Shadow Gap, but also fifteen minutes out."

She ended the communication and looked around, shaking her head in dismay as the rain soaked her hair, her face. Nausea ripped through her.

"I'll take this guy and stash him in the Interceptor and come back with the kit." She quickly removed her jacket and tossed it to Hank. "Use that to help slow the bleeding."

Hank quickly went to work pressing her jacket over the wound.

To her prisoner, she said, "Get to your feet." Though her insides quaked with fear for Ross, she injected authority into her tone.

"How am I supposed to do that with my hands cuffed behind my back?"

"You'll figure it out. I'm sure you know that if this man dies, you'll be charged with his murder."

The man got to his knees, then stood. Getting him to her Interceptor would be tricky. She had no doubt he would give her trouble. He was just waiting for an opportunity to escape.

But with Ross's life on the line, she'd take her chances. "Let's go." She gestured toward the northeast, and he started forward. Gripping her pistol in her right hand, Autumn kept a firm grip on his bulky bicep with her left.

When footsteps pounded through the forest, she tensed, ready for anything.

Except for Grier.

He emerged through the trees, carrying a medical supply kit. Confusion stunned her, but relief blew through her. Supplies in the kit could potentially buy Ross extra moments of life while they waited for the helicopter.

"What are you doing here, Grier?"

"You still need help with Ross?"

"Yes."

He slowed as he looked from her to her prisoner, appearing to consider if *she* needed help.

"Please, hurry," she said.

Grier took off toward the cabin.

She steered her captive after Grier. She'd wait for Angie and Craig to escort him all the way to a jail cell.

"Get on the ground on your stomach."

"What?"

"Do it," she ordered him, and he got on the ground.

Grier dropped to his knees next to Ross and quickly pulled items from his orange bag. "I've got this."

"What are you doing?" Hank asked.

Grier opened a packet and applied powder to the wound. "Celox granules clot blood. The main reason people die from gunshot wounds is that they lose too much blood."

Grier's grim expression didn't offer much hope—had Ross already lost too much?

Autumn couldn't think about it. She had to keep praying. Keep the faith. Hold on to hope.

"Should we move him into the cabin?" Hank asked.

"No." Grier pulled out a shiny solar blanket and unfolded a tarp to protect Ross from the elements, and himself while he took care of him.

Where was that blasted helicopter? She wanted to search the skies and will the air ambulance to get here faster, but she couldn't afford to let the prisoner out of her sight.

"I'm sorry, Chief." Despondency surged in Hank's eyes.

The cop shooter twitched, drawing her attention. He probably wanted a blanket too, but he could suffer in the rain with the rest of them. She held back her anger and would conduct herself professionally, but deep inside, she wanted to punch something.

"This wouldn't have happened if you had just walked away like I said." He coughed as if choking on rainwater.

His words surprised her. "What was so important that you had to shoot someone? Maybe you didn't kill Hank's dog, but the consequences of your actions today are far worse now."

And *her* actions? If she'd been in that cabin sooner, maybe she could have prevented this from happening, but she wouldn't carry the weight of "what-ifs" as her father had. She'd seen what it had done to him. What it was doing to him.

God, please let Ross live.

"Chief," Grier called from under the blanket, urgency in his tone. "The wound is a through and through. The front is the exit wound."

Autumn took a few seconds to comprehend what that meant.

She jerked her gaze to Hank. "Was Ross facing the cabin when he was shot? Tell me what happened."

"Ross stepped into the clearing to approach the cabin. He was heading forward. I reached down to grab my rifle. I heard the gunshot. When I looked up, Ross had collapsed." His brows furrowed. "He was facing the cabin before the shot, as far as I know."

"We could have another shooter. We need to take cover! Grier," she said, "we need to move Ross."

"Not happening. But *you* should take cover."

Man, she hated this.

"On your feet."

Once again, her captive got to his feet, soaking wet, his face muddy. She ushered him to a tree trunk. "Slide down to sit."

"What about the cabin?" the prisoner asked.

She didn't answer as she took cover next to him. Though at this point, no telling where the shooter had changed position, but she wouldn't leave Grier out here alone. Hank had hunkered down behind a nearby tree as well.

Autumn radioed dispatch again. "Tanya, have Angie and

Craig search the woods for another shooter before coming in. We need to secure the whole area."

Now was a moment they could really use that Alaska State Trooper they had lost due to budget cuts and lack of need. Right.

She blinked a few times to clear rain from her eyes. "So what's your story? Why did you let me believe you shot my officer?"

Sitting against the tree, the man hung his head and said nothing.

"Maybe his buddy wanted to cause a distraction so he could get away, but it didn't work out. Just a theory," Hank said. "But we've been standing here long enough. He would have taken another shot already if he was still out there."

"Too risky, Hank," she said.

Ten more minutes ticked by.

Whomp, whomp, whomp. Relief washed over her. The helicopter was finally here for Ross.

But if they still had an active shooter in the woods, this was a dangerous scenario.

Angie and Craig rushed forward from the forest, their faces awash with horror and anger.

Angie gasped for breath. "We were already in the woods headed to you when we heard from Tanya about another shooter. We searched as best we could, Chief. Lots of places to hide. That said, I think he's gone."

"Good work," Autumn said.

Grier stood near Ross, holding the tarp and staring up at the sky. A medic secured to a basket was being lowered for Ross.

Craig marched toward her, drawing her attention. He stared at the handcuffed prisoner, who remained on the ground by the tree. "That's him?"

She gestured to him. "Both of you, get him out of my sight. And watch your step with this one."

He may not have shot Ross, but he knew who did.

Angie and Craig shared a look.

"What's the matter? You heard me. Do it now. Then get back here to collect evidence."

The officers assisted the man to his feet, and though he didn't resist, he speared Autumn with a glare.

Autumn called Tanya again and asked her to secure assistance in a manhunt for a cop shooter. Law enforcement from Haines and Skagway would join in, as well as the Alaska State Troopers—but it all took time. Maybe too much.

Now that the stranger was on his way to incarceration, she could breathe—just barely. She stood back to watch two paramedics, along with Hank and Grier, secure Ross in the medical basket. The local ambulance crew had finally gotten here too.

Autumn's throat grew tight and she swallowed, searching for the words. Grier . . . He'd shown up—again—to save the day. How did he do that? Grier and Hank stepped back from the basket as it was hoisted up to the helicopter. When Grier glanced at her, she searched for hope in his eyes, and instead disappointment lodged deep in her heart.

 # TWELVE

G rier stared at the sky and the silhouette of the basket being lifted, winched up by the medical crew on the air ambulance helicopter hovering above them. The chief came to stand next to him, and anxiety rolled off her. Tension, mixed with fury and grief. He'd seen fear in her eyes for the police officer for whom she was responsible. Grier had wanted to give her hope, but her man was hanging on to life by a thread. He was in God's hands now, as it were, but then he had always been in God's hands, hadn't he?

Grier didn't have the emotional energy to sort through faith issues at the moment and could barely squash his need to pull the chief into his arms. Hold her. Reassure her. He doubted she would go for that—at least while she was still in uniform.

Hank still lingered as well, and the three of them waited as the basket was hoisted into the helicopter. Then the chopper took off, heading to the nearest trauma center—likely Bartlett Regional in Juneau, which was only a level 4 trauma center, but it was the closest.

Watching the young police officer fighting for his life left Grier shattered as memories from his recent past hit him like shrapnel. Somehow he had to pick up the pieces. Stay strong and keep breathing. Keep moving.

Keep living.

He sucked in air. He should say something to break the morbid silence.

At this point, the officer's life could go either way, but it was better to remain positive. "He's alive, and they'll keep him that way. We have to believe it."

"Thanks to you, Grier." She shook her head. "Why were you even here? I thought you were assisting with the dive for the body."

"Body? What body?" Hank stepped up.

"It's none of your concern." She didn't look at Hank as she answered, her tone reflecting the stress she was under and her concern for her officer. "Well?" She wasn't going to let it go.

Telling her about what they'd learned had been his intention, but now wasn't the time to go into the details. "We finished up, and I was heading home when I heard the police scanner."

Her eyes narrowed. "So you thought you'd drive on out to help? Remind me again, why aren't you working for me?"

Though grinning felt entirely inappropriate, he cracked a tenuous one—they both needed levity. "You can't afford me."

Oh, but that was the wrong thing to say, after all, and he felt the pang shoot through his chest. She was down one officer for the foreseeable future.

Without further comment, Autumn headed into the cabin and Grier waited outside. He knew better than to trample on a crime scene. When she returned, she held up a pistol in an evidence bag. "I wanted to at least secure this. Angie and Craig will be back for the rest of the evidence."

Fire and anger sparked in her eyes as she started toward the woods.

She brandished her own pistol again. "Let's stay alert. Until we find the other shooter, we can't let our guard down."

"You don't plan to start your search for him alone, do you? Hank and I could search with you."

Her frown deepened, and she spared him a glare. "I appreciate your help with Ross and your observation. I've already asked for backup in finding the cop shooter. Help is on the way."

The chief looked at Hank. "Come on, let's go."

Grier followed as she pushed the underbrush aside, carving out a path in the woods, a chorus of pine needles and leaves dripping with water adding to their soft steps.

"Let's stick together as we walk back to the vehicles, then you and Hank go home and lock your doors."

"I'm not leaving you out here alone."

"I'll wait for my officers and hopefully some additional assistance from Haines and Skagway," she said. "Unfortunately, by the time troopers arrive, the shooter could be long gone. Then again, he has a lot of territory to cover to escape. Could get trapped between the river, the inlet, and the mountains."

And that was the way of it in the wild expanse of Alaska. Grier hiked next to her, his own weapon out and ready. Hank had his rifle. Together they kept a sharp eye out.

Grier was still trying to figure out why someone had shot Ross. Hoping to save his friend in the cabin? Too many scenarios played through his mind. They were all lucky to be alive—someone could have taken them all out and dumped their bodies where no one would find them.

Even though Angie and Craig claimed the shooter had left the area, the chief continued zigzagging as she led them so she didn't make them more of a target in case the shooter had remained.

"If Bear was here," Hank said, "he'd let us know if someone was still out there. And that's why he's gone now. They didn't want him alerting others to their presence."

"We're going to find the truth, Hank. Don't you worry."

Frustration edged her tone as she pushed through the woods, Grier and Hank sticking close. "Do you happen to know if more than one person was living in the cabin?"

"No," he said. "I don't know."

"We'll find out once we go back to look."

"Grier and I can help you search," Hank said. "We're just wasting time now, Chief."

"As I already told you, get home and stay safe. Lock your doors."

Grier considered the man the chief had handcuffed, though he'd been more focused on keeping Ross alive. The guy was big, stout—muscular, not chubby—and definitely had that tough-guy military demeanor about him. But whose military? He'd heard a subtle foreign accent in the few words the man uttered.

And as the officers ushered him away, the man had flicked his gaze first to Autumn and then to Grier. The fact that he went willingly surprised Grier. Someone who partnered with a cop shooter likely wouldn't have thought twice about getting the advantage over Chief Long and taking her down too.

He was putting too much thought into this. Grier should walk away—he had enough troubles of his own. But the sudden uptick in criminal incidents unsettled him. Through the trees, he spotted his truck, and they picked up the pace. At their vehicles, Hank headed in the opposite direction. His cabin wasn't too far, and Grier watched him hike home—without his dog.

The chief opened the door to her Interceptor and climbed in, and Grier joined her in the passenger seat. She gave him a quizzical look.

"I'll wait here with you." Though he'd prefer to be searching for the shooter, the chief wasn't going to let him get involved in a manhunt. Diving to recover a body was completely different.

She radioed Tanya again and learned that her officers had secured their prisoner in the small jail and were now a few minutes out. Tanya confirmed that the helicopter transporting

Ross was about twenty minutes away from landing at Bartlett, and Ross was hanging in there.

"Thank God," she said.

He joined her in relief that Ross was still alive. Now to hope and pray the doctors could save him or at least stabilize him if they needed to send him to a level 2 trauma center in either Anchorage or Seattle.

"How do I know you aren't the shooter?"

"What?" Her question shocked him, though it shouldn't have. "I think it's safe to say you don't believe that or you wouldn't be sitting in this vehicle with me." She sighed, and he could feel the weight of it.

"You have to have faith that Ross is going to be all right," he said.

Where were the words coming from? Because Grier felt hope slipping through his fingers.

"Did you learn anything definitive from the dive?" The change in subject startled him. He had to push aside images of Ross's life hanging in the balance and think about earlier today. So much had happened in just one day. Not his typical experience living in Alaska so far.

"I took pictures, but very little evidence could be gathered underwater. We preserved any trace evidence that might be found on the body. We did all we could to keep the recovery efforts local and timely—thanks to you—but Tex learned the regional ME out of Haines planned to send the body to Anchorage. Sorry, Chief."

She nodded. "Thanks for your help, Grier."

He rubbed his mouth, considering how much more he should say about what they found. But he would let the ME deliver that particular news about the body.

At least Grier had something he could share. "By the way, Tex took his boat out and used a sonar device yesterday after I told him about Sarah."

She twisted to look at him, her eyes wide. He loved surprising her.

"I . . . wow. Thanks. And?"

"No boat besides the shipwreck in that area. Sarah was lying."

His nerves on edge, he pressed his palm against his Glock 9mm that he'd rested on his lap. Grier wasn't sure how he'd gotten so involved and so quickly, but at the same time, he was glad to be privy to some of what was going on. Maybe it was the gray skies and constant rain. Call it a sixth sense, but something in the air had shifted—and not in a good way.

Did she sense it too? "Would you say this is more excitement than you've seen around here?"

She stared out the window and seemed to consider his words. "Two years ago, my father was the Shadow Gap police chief, and I worked under him. He was helping a family whose cabin had collapsed in a mudslide, and his arm was crushed. He never regained use of it. I know that seems like nothing, but it shook the whole community up. We know each other and care about each other. Then I became police chief. All that to say that I've worked in law enforcement here for a while, but even before that, I had a feel for what was going on because Dad was chief. To answer your question, sure, we have the usual crimes, but nothing like what happened here today, or yesterday when we found the body."

She had to feel like the forces of the universe had lined up against her.

"I'll be honest, I don't understand why this is happening." Then Chief Long turned to look at him, her blue-and-amber eyes sparking. "And I don't know why I'm telling you any of it."

Because to someone like Chief Long, Grier was probably transient. He'd come to town a few months ago, and for all she knew, he would leave in a few more. But he understood exactly why she shared—they'd connected months ago—when he'd brought her father home from the bar.

He'd come across the man fumbling to get into his vehicle late at night, well after the bar had closed, and Grier insisted on giving him a ride. Although the man had talked a lot during the ride, by the time they arrived at his house, he had passed out. Grier hadn't had any personal encounters with the local police chief, so he didn't know how she would react when he knocked on the door. Together they were able to get her hefty father into the house and into bed. Grier got the man settled for the night and covered him, tucked him in.

When he looked up, the chief stared at him, her striking eyes filled with unshed tears.

"Thank you," she barely croaked out.

But it was in that moment that she reached into his chest and touched his heart. He had no idea if she knew the effect she had on him, or if she realized that she had never let go of his heart. Or maybe it was Grier who wasn't letting go. He couldn't even explain what happened, the strangeness of it all. How did he begin to define the connection they shared?

All he knew was that, bottom line, one simple act of kindness had landed him here—hooked on Chief Autumn Long and up in her police business.

"I had hoped to keep the news about the body we found quiet and low-key, but it's going to get around. And the shooter out there too. All of it's going to draw attention. Really, media attention should be the least of my worries."

"No town wants that kind of news. It's bad for business and tourism." And made people question the authorities in charge. "That's why I hate to tell you this, but a reporter out of Juneau was at the marina when we arrived back with the body. Someone must have tipped them off."

Grier had delayed getting off the boat to avoid the reporter's questions while the ME's transport service offloaded the body.

Flashing lights reflected in the mirror. "Finally."

She started to get out, but Grier caught her wrist, half expecting her to throw a defensive move at him, but she simply hesitated. "What?"

"There must be others in town who can help with the search while you wait for the troopers. You have more than your fair share of people who know how to hunt, track, and look down the barrel of a gun. You get these woods crawling with them, and you'll flush this guy out." Grier was overstepping, but he wasn't wrong.

"I can't risk a civilian getting hurt. Tanya is putting out a shelter-in-place order. This isn't the first and won't be the last time a criminal has tried to flee into the woods. I have to do this by the book." Her gaze flicked to his hand on her wrist, and he quickly opened it up. "Go home, Grier. I need to set up a command center for this manhunt."

She got out and jogged to the back of her vehicle to meet with her two officers. More from Skagway and Haines were hopefully on the way, along with Alaska State Troopers.

Instead of getting into his vehicle, he hiked the rest of the way to Hank's cabin. Had the chief also briefly considered Hank could have shot Ross in the back? If not intentionally, his rifle could have accidentally discharged. But, clearly, she trusted the man. He was a little off. His perception, his truth, was probably different from the actual truth, but that was often the case with witnesses. But it was like that for most people, some more than others. Hank was in the more-than-others group. His biggest problem was that he claimed to have spotted Bigfoot on several occasions, and nobody believed him. His credibility on all things had tanked.

But Hank was a good guy. A solid man. Grier liked him. Trusted him.

Grier was about to knock when the door swung open, and Hank nearly barreled into him. "What are you doing here?"

"Checking on you."

"I don't need a babysitter."

Grier arched his brow. "Going somewhere?"

"To look for my dog, where else?"

He had a feeling Hank wouldn't stay home until he found Bear. "I'll help you find your dog, Hank."

"Maybe we'll get lucky and find that snake who shot Ross while we're at it."

He knew he liked this guy. If Grier was relegated to doing nothing officially, at least he could do this. "You misunderstand. I'll help you find your dog *after* they take down the shooter."

THIRTEEN

The next morning, Autumn and Craig slogged through the wet forest that was more than living up to its name as a rain forest. The hunt for Ross's shooter continued. She suspected Craig was the one who leaked the news about the body found in Lewis Inlet.

He was a troublemaker like his uncle, but beggars couldn't be choosers, as Birdy always said, and Autumn needed all the qualified officers she could get.

A mudslide had cut off a portion of the forest during the night, and the search had been called off. The Alaska State Trooper Special Emergency Reaction Team had joined the search this morning. She would have thought that her brother, Nolan, could have at least found his way to Southeast Alaska to help the people he grew up with, but he hadn't shown up.

She'd shoved past the disappointment and focused on finding a dangerous criminal.

At least Ross was in stable condition. She'd been able to confirm with doctors that he'd been shot in the back with a rifle. Since then, the spent bullet had been recovered near the cabin. It was a different caliber than the rifle Hank carried, which did little to comfort her since she hadn't suspected him, but others needed more than her instincts about the man to believe he wasn't the shooter. The information also confirmed that the man she'd arrested at the cabin, an Argentinian named Alberto Acosta, hadn't shot Ross and she hadn't needlessly called for a manhunt.

She had a sinking feeling the shooter had crossed the Lewis Inlet and been making his way through the Tongass National Forest long before the hunt had even started. Officials didn't know yet who they were searching for but had asked residents to contact police if they noticed any suspicious activity.

"You hear that?" Craig turned to glance back at her. "The creek is swollen, all right."

On the other hand, between the mudslide and the swollen creeks and rivers, maybe their fugitive couldn't have gotten far in this part of the wilderness. Either way, she was almost ready to give up the search, but she needed justice for Ross and to restore a sense of safety to the town.

Craig started toward the rushing water—a creek turned river. They'd circumvented the mudslide area that unfortunately cut off a few cabins to the north, and emergency crews had been called to rescue those who were trapped.

"Be careful," she said. "I think this is about as far as we can go. Besides, no way he could have made it across."

"You're right. He didn't." Craig glanced up at her, and she rushed forward at his pointed look.

Tangled in a mass of tree roots, a man lay facedown in the rushing water.

"We can't know it's him. It could be anyone." She stepped forward. "Here, help me get him before the torrent washes him farther down and out of our reach."

"I'll do it," Craig said. "You hold on to me."

She grabbed Craig's belt while he stepped into the water rushing toward the inlet and held on to a spruce for support. Craig worked to untangle the body, then yanked it toward him. Craig was a good fifty pounds heavier than Autumn, and when he stumbled backward into her, they both fell onto the water-soaked ground, the body on top of them. Craig moved off her, pushing the body away, and Autumn rolled to the right. Seriously—there had to be a better way. But they couldn't risk losing the body.

Catching her breath, she stared at the man who lay facedown in the mud.

Then she rolled him over to see if she recognized him as someone from the community. A local. She eyed Craig. "You know him?"

"Nope."

She tried her radio, but it wasn't working. Cell either. "Let's hope this is our man and this is the end of the hunt."

She took a picture with her cell and forwarded the image to Tanya, who could deliver it to the troopers once the image went through, and then Tanya could request assistance in retrieving the body.

"You think this is the man who shot Ross?" Craig asked.

"No way of knowing. Let's see if he has ID on him." She dug around in his pockets and came up empty. "If he can be identified as an associate of Acosta, then we can strongly suspect he took the shot. But that still leaves a lot of questions." She took a closer look at the body. "He has a knot on his head. He might have tried to flee but got caught in the mudslide."

She let her gaze drift to the surrounding rough terrain.

"In the dark," Craig said. "Maybe he slipped, hit his head, and drowned in the creek."

"I don't see another wound on him, so that's my assessment too," she said.

Fleeing into the wilds of Alaska on a stormy night had taken the man down.

"Fortunately for you, Chief, it's out of your hands. You don't need to worry about it anymore. The state boys will handle it all."

She cut a glance to Craig, then focused on the swollen creek. Had he been smirking? Autumn bristled at his words and his attitude. Whose side was he on, anyway? While, technically, Craig spoke the truth—her responsibility ended at the city limits—she wasn't about to let this go. Her job was to keep her community safe. She would get her answers, one way or another, and secure Shadow Gap while she was at it.

———

By the next day, any lingering outside law enforcement that had assisted in the manhunt had finally cleared out of town, and the shadows grew long in Autumn's small office as midnight approached. Exhaustion weighed on her as she sat at her desk and stared at the image of the man they had pulled from the creek. At first, Autumn wasn't completely convinced he was their guy. But they'd retrieved a rifle downriver from him and the ammunition to go with it—still, who in Alaska didn't carry a firearm? Ballistics would have to match his gun to the bullet that went through Ross and lodged in the ground near the cabin. Alaska State Troopers judicial services had also done her the favor of transporting Acosta from her small jail to Anchorage.

Like Craig had enjoyed saying—it was all out of her hands, including the body.

As for the man they'd found in the swollen creek, he was identified as Oscar Evans, a Brit and known associate of Acosta. She figured that was all she would get out of the troopers, but the two men from opposite sides of the world were found in her region of remote Alaska, so she needed to know who they were dealing with. Why had they been here? To find those answers, Autumn would continue to dig.

Now she understood how local police felt when the FBI swooped in and took over an investigation. She would keep her finger on the pulse of what was going on. She didn't believe in coincidence, and that philosophy solidified her feeling that the recent incidents were only the beginning and not the end. Her best option was to keep her guard up and be prepared for what could come next.

She'd carefully documented every facet of what had happened since the day she arrived back from Anchorage.

Tomorrow Autumn would follow up with Sarah, who'd been discharged from the hospital, so she would have to track her down. Catching the shooter took priority, so Autumn had been waylaid from her other investigations. Granted, if she worked in law enforcement anywhere else, the issues would be ongoing and her work probably filled with murder, domestic violence, and armed robbery every single day. She had long suspected that Dad had moved them from Topeka because he wanted a quiet, peaceful environment with less crime where he could enjoy more time with his kids.

She hoped that when she got home at this hour, she'd find her father asleep in his bed, snoring away. And if he wasn't? She wasn't in the mood for a confrontation, or to be his psychological crutch. Even if Dad was asleep, she wouldn't be able to sleep despite the exhaustion.

Birdy and Ike were always a soothing balm to her aching soul, and if someone was up at the restaurant, she could use encouraging words. Her grandparents were workaholics and went to bed late and got up super early, and they loved every minute of their lives.

Autumn hiked across the empty street, and just as she got along the boardwalk, she heard footfalls. She paused, the hair prickling along her neck. Pulling her weapon out, she held it at the ready and turned to take in her surroundings.

Again, she heard the steps. In the alley this time. She crept over to peek between the walls of the buildings. "Who's there?"

No one answered.

She shined her flashlight around. A ruckus came from the back of the restaurant. Someone in the garbage can. A bear?

Her grandfather? Heart pounding, she rushed down the alley, leading with her flashlight and Staccato P.

"Who's there?" she called again.

Autumn cleared the corner.

Her grandfather dropped the garbage but raised his .45 pistol, startling her.

She lowered her gun and gasped. "You scared me!"

"What are you doing back here?" His gravelly voice sounded breathless. She'd scared him too.

"I heard something—someone in the alley."

"It could have just been me. I heard something, thought it was a bear."

"Is that why you almost shot me?"

"I . . . no . . . your grandmother insists I take protection in case the bear that's been snooping around is out here. He comes out at night to avoid people."

"If you have a bear problem, let the wildlife troopers know. That's part of their job. And why don't you use bear mace instead? Or a paintball gun? Nonlethal and sends them running without hurting them."

"Or makes them angrier. Now, answer me—what are you doing out at this time of night?" He lifted a brow, but something in his wise old eyes told Autumn that he'd already heard about the day she'd had. He turned and gestured for her to follow. "You can tell me about it over coffee or warm milk. Your choice."

"Are you sure? I don't want to keep you up too late."

He chuckled. "As you can see, I'm already up, and you gave me such a start that I won't be able to sleep anyway. At least until you and I have talked." He winked.

"Sounds like you're saying I put you to sleep."

He chuckled and squeezed her shoulder as she entered through the back door, glancing behind her up and down the alley one last time.

No bear.

No two-footed creatures either—at least that she could see. She tucked away her gun while Grandpa Ike stashed his in a safe behind the counter.

Birdy was already upstairs in bed, so Autumn and Grandpa Ike sat in a booth and drank warm milk to "bring on the calm," as he put it. Autumn shared about the events since she'd arrived back from Anchorage, including her gruesome discovery on the dive with Grier, and then finding another body.

Grandpa Ike grunted. "And Ross is okay?"

"In stable condition. He's in Juneau. They didn't have to transport him to Anchorage."

"So you're down an officer."

"I am. And tomorrow I meet with the city council, and Mayor—"

"I'll speak to them."

"No, I don't want you involved. I can handle this." She didn't need her grandparents' political sway.

He leaned back and toyed with his napkin. "Your meeting is to talk about the Alaska Police Standards Council's decision."

"And now, the added criminal activity. This is a small town. Why do we even need to mess with politics?" She shook her head and stared at her empty cup, doubting warm milk would help her sleep once she finally got home. "I've been putting off talking to Dad about . . . his drinking." And what happened before.

"You're good to him. You and Nolan. He needs to recognize how blessed he is to have the two of you. I keep praying God will open his eyes. He's a good man. Honestly, sometimes I think my daughter didn't deserve him."

Autumn frowned at those words. How could he say that? But she didn't ask for an explanation. Instead, she hung her head.

"I miss her, and I'm sure he does too. It wasn't until the incident that left his arm useless that he just couldn't seem to rise above things. What else can I do besides pray and be there for him?"

"Prayer is everything, and don't you forget it. But you need to let go of the past too, Autumn. I can see it in your eyes. You've been through a lot, and you're here now, in this place and in this position, because God put you here. You need to believe that and know you're the exact person needed for this hour."

Grandpa Ike yawned, which Autumn took as her cue. "I appreciate the warm milk and good company. I think I need to head home and get some rest, and you're going to fall asleep on me anyway."

"Never." He winked and stood.

She had so much more she wanted to say to him and to Birdy too. She couldn't imagine her life without them. Autumn said her good nights and exited the restaurant. The sound of Grandpa Ike locking up behind her made her feel better. Times had changed. He never used to lock the doors.

The warm milk had relaxed her, after all, and she hurried across the street to her vehicle but stopped in the middle to glance up at the sky. With the sudden break in the cloud cover and endless rain, the stars shone bright.

The constellations had been different that night she lay on the beach waiting for help to arrive, her mother gone forever in the depths of the Caribbean. On starry nights, she could never escape the reminder, and that was one reason she loved Southeast Alaska's gray skies and rainy days and nights. No stars to jar the trauma back to life in her mind. Dad had loved the saying "Memories made on the water last forever," but for Autumn, the stars seemed to seal those memories—the ones she hadn't wanted—in her mind for eternity.

Maybe that's what Grandpa Ike was referring to when he said she needed to let go. She thought the memories from long ago held her captive, but she refused to let them go. It was all she had of her mother.

Once inside her vehicle, she drove slowly through town and spotted a man walking the boardwalk. She peered at him, and he barely glanced up. His face was in the shadows, but her heart lurched.

That's him!

She flipped on her lights and turned the Interceptor around. He'd disappeared into an alley, so she steered slowly between the outfitters and the IGA grocery. He hadn't committed a crime, at least that she knew about, but she wouldn't ignore her instincts either. But once again, he'd slipped away. Tomorrow she would find out who this outsider was—especially since she had the strangest sense that he was watching her.

She steered her vehicle up to the house and thought how nice it would be to finally lie down in her bed. The lights were out except for one on the porch. She breathed a sigh of relief. She loved her father, but his current state of mind drained all her energy. Still, he was her father—she would be there for him. She could do this.

Lord . . . help me.

Her cell buzzed.

She hadn't even made it to bed yet and wished she could ignore the text. She read the message from Grier.

The person found in the shipwreck was murdered.

The body had barely arrived in Anchorage, and the ME couldn't possibly know that yet. She considered her response. Why hadn't he told her earlier? Then again, she'd been busy.

How do you know?

Bullet to the forehead.

What was going on in her small, quiet town? Shadow Gap had never seen this kind of criminal activity. This couldn't be happening simply because Autumn was now chief, could it? People counted on her. She had to remain strong and stay on course. But Grandpa Ike had seen right through her when she hadn't even wanted to admit that she was having doubts about her skills as police chief.

"You're the exact person needed for this hour."

Another text came through.

You're doing great, Chief. Hang in there.

Did Grier somehow sense that she was sinking, so he was throwing her a lifeline?

FOURTEEN

As a fire crackled in the woodstove, Grier set his cell on the arm of the sofa. Cap liked to think he was a lapdog, and Grier didn't want to disappoint his only confidante.

"You're doing great, Chief. Hang in there."

He hadn't needed to add the last part, and it had sounded awkward. Earning points with the chief of police of small-town Alaska wasn't necessary, nor had it been his intention. He was just doing the right thing.

But Autumn Long wasn't just any chief, and he couldn't help himself.

As a kid back in Nebraska, where he attended a Sunday school class taught by his aunt who also raised him, always doing the right thing was drilled into him. What was that verse again? He snapped his fingers and Cap looked at him.

"It's okay, buddy." Grier rubbed the dog behind his ears, and the Scripture came to him. "See that no one repays anyone evil for evil, but always seek to do good to one another and to everyone."

And though keeping a low profile was in his best interest, opportunities to do good—to help people in need—kept presenting themselves. Like today when Ross needed help. After that incident, Grier had decided to wait and let the ME tell the chief the news. But sitting here tonight, he realized he'd been wrong to keep that from her. Grier didn't want her to be blindsided when she heard from the ME.

Texting wasn't the best way to tell her either, he knew.

He squeezed the bridge of his nose, then rolled his head back against the sofa. Maybe he should skip town altogether and start fresh somewhere else. But Shadow Gap was a place where he could practice being invisible.

At least according to Krueger.

He couldn't leave. Not now. And oddly enough, part of him was considering staying after . . . after he was free to leave. The town had become special to him. He hadn't imagined finding such resilient, down-to-earth people who cared. Had each other's backs. But that was only a small part of it.

What was the chief to him?

She was . . . beautiful.

Tough and determined.

And politics were working against her. On that, he could relate, and maybe that's why his heart went out to her. When he helped her, he crossed the invisible line he'd drawn to keep his head down. She needed to know about the body before anyone else so she could be prepared in case this, too, was used against her.

Why anyone would want to remove her as the head of police was beyond him. He would do what he could for her, but it was best for him not to get too embroiled in her issues or investigations.

At least he and Hank had found his dog—Bear. He'd been caught, tangled up in some old rope in the wilderness. Hank claimed the man at the cabin hadn't liked Bear coming around because the dog was interfering in his business, and according to Hank, the man had threatened to shoot Bear. That's when the dog went missing and things escalated. An officer was shot and nearly died. But that wasn't Hank's fault.

While Grier and Hank were hiking up the mountain looking for Bear, after the manhunt had been called off, Hank shared that he'd moved to Alaska because he'd been convicted of a crime. Missouri had a crime registry, and he couldn't get a job. But Alaska had meant a brand-new start. He worked odd jobs, and nobody cared about his past.

The man also loved all things Alaska, including the Bigfoot lore. He knew that made him the town kook, but he preferred it that way. Once Grier got to know Hank better, he realized the man was nothing like the persona he intentionally projected.

Grier could learn a thing or two from the man, and if he did leave and start over, Hank would be his model. He nudged Cap off his lap, and the husky lay by the woodstove. Grier shuffled to the laptop at the small table against the wall and sent an email.

Where are you? I need intel, ASAP.

No texts. No calls. Nothing remotely trackable or traceable. Their encrypted email setup was as secure as possible.

He got no response, and really, he hadn't expected any after the extended silence. He'd been praying for a miracle.

Elbows on the desk, he pressed the heels of his palms against his eyes. Soon he would need to move to plan B.

Plan B did not include Chief Autumn Long, but that was better for her.

———

The next morning, after a fitful night, Grier needed a good hot breakfast and a cup of strong black coffee that only Ike Lively could make him. He had just pushed through the door of the Lively Moose, looking forward to the food and the many metaphorical philosophies from his friends, when a round of applause caught him by surprise. The cheers warmed his heart, but even small-town notoriety was a risk.

He started to turn around and walk out, but that would only cause more commotion. More questions. He waved off any praise and made his way to his usual booth, where Otis and Sandford sat.

Otis patted him on the back. "You're a star around here."

Maybe he should have chosen a different booth and kept to himself, but he had a feeling that wouldn't have made a difference, especially when a few more people slid—more like squeezed—into the booth, packing him in tight. This was definitely too crowded when popularity wasn't part of his plan.

"After you saved that woman, you found a body . . . and saved Ross."

"And the most important part—you found Hank's dog."

"Are you Superman? Some superhero in disguise?"

Grier hung his head.

If only you knew . . .

FIFTEEN

After the last few days, Autumn found herself taking comfort in reading and signing reports. Who wouldn't prefer mundane tasks over bodies and shooters— murder and mayhem? Even though she lived with the former police chief and had worked under him, she hadn't realized the time demands required of her position. This was especially true considering the city council meetings and any other events happening around town, from volunteer assemblies to lunches to charity functions. And though it seemed that none of it had to do with policing or protecting the community, being a police chief was as much about communicating with the public as protecting them.

Autumn gathered her notes in preparation to speak with the city council and answer whatever questions Wally might throw at her. She opened her drawer and grabbed a couple of ibuprofens and downed them with the last of her soda. She straightened her uniform and badge and secured her hair back into a ponytail so not even one rebellious curl would get away. She knew some thought that she looked too young, *was* too young, for the job—and that worked against her when it came to the city council. She had no doubt they, Wally in particular, would grill her over the recent violence. The council knew the outcome of the meeting in Anchorage, and she could think of at least one reason they'd called this gathering—they wanted to fire her.

Autumn drew in a few calming breaths, then exited her office and headed to Tanya. She glanced around. The three desks at the back were empty—Craig and Angie weren't around—so she could speak freely.

"I'm heading over to meet with the council, then I'm going to talk to Sarah."

"Good luck with that."

"You think I'm going to need luck?" Autumn shouldn't overanalyze—Tanya hadn't meant anything.

Tanya's big brown eyes grew wide with her smile. "For the council meeting?" She waved her hand. "Pfft. You've got this. I was referring to Sarah. She left this morning."

"She left? How do you know?"

"I saw her getting on a boat when I was dropping off my brother at the marina."

"Well, I'll have to wait until she gets back. But just get me her contact information."

"I don't think she's coming back."

"How do you know she left for good?"

"She had bags with her. Since she isn't a resident, I imagine she left for good."

Autumn should have talked to her sooner. She pressed a hand to her temple. When would the ibuprofen kick in?

"Don't worry. I'll find you contact information," Tanya said. "In the meantime, you might want to see this before you go to your meeting, in case someone brings it up."

"What is it?" Autumn turned to stare at the television screen secured to the wall.

"KTOO-TV. The news out of Juneau."

An anchor offered details about the shooting and manhunt,

and tacked on to that story was a brief video of divers arriving back at the marina with the body they'd recovered. Normally people got excited when their community made the news—but that, of course, depended on the story. Autumn wasn't happy about this one. She caught a brief glimpse of Grier on the boat just before he ducked below deck. Then . . . another man's face in the background caught her attention.

She sucked in a breath. "That's him."

The news went to a commercial break.

"Grier Brenner?"

"No. Listen, Tanya. I need you to contact the station and get me the footage."

"What's going on?"

"I'm not sure, but just get me the footage, please."

Tanya stood and rushed around her desk. "I'm here to help. I've been here for decades, and believe me, I've seen it all. You can tell me what's going on."

"Nothing." Autumn headed for the door. "I'm not sure."

"Chief Long." Tanya's tone stopped her in her tracks.

She turned, surprised to see how intimidating Tanya could be when she decided to stare down her own boss.

The look broke through Autumn's resolve, and she blew out a breath. "I've seen a stranger around town."

Tanya arched a brow. "Nothing unusual about that, but if it bothered you so much, why didn't you say anything?"

"I'm saying something now. I've seen him at odd times. Late at night, I see the same guy." *I think he's watching me.* She'd keep that to herself for now.

Brows furrowing, Tanya moved around her desk again to answer the phone. "I'll get on it. Take a deep breath and re-member to take one day at a time. One step at a time. Just do the next thing. Go. Focus on your meeting."

Autumn thought of Birdy's words—the Scripture over her office walls—"The path of the righteous . . ."

Lord, help me to walk that path. Whatever it is, whatever it looks like.

She wasn't even sure.

Pushing through the door and into the drizzle, Autumn realized she was relieved that she'd told Tanya about the stranger. At the very least, she had taken her seriously and hadn't made light of it. And like Tanya had mentioned, strangers in town weren't unusual, but with two bodies now, and Ross getting shot, the Shadow Gap Police Department needed to remain on high alert and wary. Apparently not every stranger was a tourist simply out enjoying their time in Alaska.

Walking on the boardwalk, Autumn tried to push aside the feeling that danger was closing in. She needed to focus on the next thing—her meeting with the city council. But try as she might, she kept seeing the guy's face in the video. A shiver crawled over her. Where had she seen him before?

Autumn lived in Topeka until she was ten, and then they moved to Alaska. When she was twenty-one, she started going to the Caribbean every year, and then five years ago while there, she got her scuba certification. She thought by going back to the Caribbean, she could overcome her fear after what happened with her mother. So she'd traveled a little, but where had she seen this man in her travels? Why was he showing up here and now in her town? Even if his face hadn't seemed familiar in a disturbing way, she would have been suspicious of him anyway because of his nocturnal activities and the feeling he was watching her.

But enough about him—she was already late to the meeting. She hurried across the street and headed for city hall, only a block away.

The sky decided to open up and drench her right before she stepped inside. Of course.

She pushed through the last door down the hallway and into the conference room. Two of the five council members were already in the middle of a heated discussion bordering on an argument, and she couldn't have been more relieved that she was practically invisible. Mayor Cindy White sat at the end of the table and watched.

Autumn took a seat at the opposite end of the table and returned the mayor's apologetic smile.

Wally and Easton were arguing about how best to deal with the road damage after the mudslide, though they'd already set protocols in place. The conversation eased as Wally realized Autumn had arrived, and Easton stopped as well. Her palms slicked.

The mayor called the meeting to order.

Wally jumped right in. "You've lost your certification, and the trust of this town. We're going to vote about whether you should remain police chief."

"That's enough, Wally," Cindy said. "She isn't required to be state certified to remain our chief."

"Thanks for the vote of confidence," Autumn said.

"It's the council's decision—"

"I'm going to appeal the state's decision." Autumn stood. She wasn't sure where those words had come from or if she could actually appeal. All she knew was that she was fighting for a job she loved. Her place in this world. She refused to let them take it away from her.

She'd cut Wally off, silencing him for the moment, and before he found his voice, she would finish what she had to say. "But first I need to make sure the town is safe after recent events, including apprehending two strangers who were working together—one of whom was found dead. Ross's condition is improving, by the way."

Wally had gathered his words, it appeared, because he stood too, not to be outdone by Autumn. "Appeal if you want, but you'll be gone, so it won't matter. Craig apprehended that hoodlum, and he found the body in the creek. He should have been chief all along."

That wasn't how it unfolded, but apparently that was Craig's side of the story. She hadn't read his report yet. Autumn bit back her words, her confidence waning. Anger and determination warred inside. She couldn't lose this job, not after her father had been the head of this department for years. And what about Birdy and Grandpa Ike, pillars of the community? She didn't want to embarrass them. She suddenly wished she'd taken the help Grandpa Ike had offered when he mentioned speaking to the council. Then again, if she couldn't succeed on her own, what was the point?

What was it Grandpa Ike had said again?

"God put you here. You need to believe that and know you're the exact person needed for this hour."

She wasn't so sure. If God had put Autumn in this position for this time, then why was it so hard? Why did she have to fight to even be allowed to do her job?

"Fine," she said. "Vote. Make your decision. But in the meantime, let me do my job."

Fearing she might say something she would regret and dreading their reaction, Autumn turned and walked out. She pushed through the door. Exiting the building, she stepped out into the rain. Whatever the council decided, if it was the last thing she did, she would find out why Sarah had lied. Why had Autumn found a murdered man in a century-old shipwreck?

 # SIXTEEN

Grier exited the Lively Moose, suspecting that he might have seen the last of his new friends.

"Don't make friends." Krueger's words reverberated through his head. *"Hide out. Stay put. I'll fix this."*

Right. Nothing had been fixed.

Grier stopped at a gas station on the way out of town and had to pay cash before he pumped. And that was another issue—cash flow. He was going to run out soon.

Krueger, where are you?

Inside the gas station, he peeled the bills out of his wallet. While the twentysomething blond cashier took the money with a smile and a wink, Grier glanced up at the widescreen television and caught the video recording of the volunteer dive team—Tex, Maggie, and Grier—at the marina, handing off the recovered body to the two guys who transported it to the ME. He knew a reporter had been asking questions, but he hadn't realized the extent to which someone had recorded them until now. In the footage, he could be seen ducking out of sight into the bowels of Tex's boat. The camera zoomed in on him briefly. He'd suspected his image might have been caught, but he couldn't understand why the news continued repeating the footage.

Over and over and over.

Grier should have known better.

He wanted to punch something. Kick something.

The cashier looked at the television and then back at Grier. "What's with that body in the shipwreck?"

Great. She recognized him. Easily. "I don't know."

He took his change from her and exited. While he pumped the gas, he pulled out his cell to see what was on the internet and found the same footage he'd just seen. For some inexplicable reason, that interested people. He had no idea why, really, considering the many mysteries and murders occurring hourly around the world. The video hadn't gone viral, so it didn't have millions of views, but thousands were already far too many.

He ran his hand through his hair, then glanced around, taking in the snowcapped mountains; the forest of greens, oranges, reds, and browns; and the quaint little town. He never imagined he could actually be happy here, but over the past few weeks, he'd found himself relaxing in the slow pace, soaking in the beauty of nature, and enjoying those times when he got to look the chief in the eyes. But that feeling, that sixth sense that hit him a few days ago, was getting stronger. Grier might have brought trouble to town. What he couldn't know was if the recent uptick in criminal activity had anything to do with him. While it seemed unlikely, he needed to keep his guard up.

Finished pumping gas, he replaced the nozzle as a couple strolled out of the gas station and headed to their car on the other side of the pumps.

He climbed into his truck and heard their words.

"And that man the chief put in jail . . . I heard he was wanted by Interpol."

Grier froze at the words. His blood ran cold. The guy was on one of Interpol's wanted lists?

"What is that anyway?" the woman asked over the hood of the car.

"Some kind of international police agency. Fancy having someone like that here in Shadow Gap."

"Fancy isn't the right word at all. It's scary."

Grier didn't need to hear more. He closed the truck door, started it up, and sped back to town. Though he wanted to keep speeding, he slowed as he drove down Main Street, then parked at the police station.

He rushed inside and stopped at the counter meant as a barrier. Tanya, the black-haired dispatch/secretary, turned from her computer on a desk against the wall and smiled. "Ah, the town hero. What can I do for you?"

"I . . . uh . . . Chief Long. I need to speak to her."

"She's not in. I can leave her a message, and she'll get back to you as soon as she can."

"I can just call her." Text her. "What about the guy who was in jail here? Is he still—"

"He was taken to Anchorage, and then on to who knows where." She shrugged.

He glanced past her to look at the computer and the opened email. Though he couldn't read it from this distance, he recognized the logo of the state medical examiner's office.

"What did he have to do with Interpol?"

He not only wanted an answer she probably wouldn't give, but he also wanted to read that email because it might have to do with the recovered body.

"While I can't offer information about police business, I can say that we get all types here."

"Really? You've held a prisoner on a wanted list put out by Interpol in your small jail before?"

She shrugged. "Just another day on the job."

"You're kidding." *Come on, lady, give me something.*

"Excuse me?"

Oh, this woman was a tough one. She wouldn't be pushed to lose her cool or give him what he wanted.

"Shadow Gap is a small, quiet town. Surely you don't get international fugitives here often, and it's not just another normal day."

She laughed. "I worked for Chief Long's father, Miles, for twenty years, and then before him, I worked for the PD over in Anchorage. I've seen a lot, but you're right, it's quiet here and that's why I love it. Now and again, we get a crime wave, let's call it."

The main entrance door flew open, startling both Tanya and Grier, and the chief rushed in, her face flushed.

"The meeting went well?" Tanya asked.

Ignoring both Tanya and Grier, she passed them to enter her office, then slammed the door.

Tanya glanced at Grier, failing to hide her concern. Grier didn't see the other two officers around. Without asking permission, he walked past the counter to the chief's office and opened the door, ignoring the "Wait!" that Tanya called from behind him.

He didn't care. He, too, slammed the door behind him and took the seat across from the chief's desk, though she remained standing. Surprise widened her eyes, and her cheeks were red—but they'd been red when she rushed in. Her hair was pulled back but wet from the rain, and soft curls had escaped, framing her face.

She was more agitated than he'd ever seen. "What are you doing here?"

"I'm here to commiserate with you." He couldn't just walk out with the way she'd rushed past them, clearly upset. "You're down an officer. What can I do to help?"

"Nothing. I . . . I know nothing about you, Grier."

"You came to me asking for my help on the dive. You trusted me to put together a recovery and investigation team. You *know* me." He hated the way he sounded as the words spilled out. Why was he begging? He should shift gears. "Okay, you don't know me." Truth.

She stared at him and frowned. "Look, can we do this later?"

He'd never seen the chief so emotional. What had happened at the city council meeting? She wouldn't be here if she'd been fired—at least he didn't think. He needed to redirect, refocus her attention. Like he had any idea how to comfort her. But he could try.

"Have you heard anything about the body we discovered?" he asked.

Autumn dropped into the seat behind her desk and blew out a breath.

The tension in his chest eased, if only a little.

"Nothing," she said. "Why do you ask?"

Come on . . . check your email.

"And more importantly, why do you care?" She pinned him with her gaze.

And he loved it when she did that.

He shrugged, huffed, and grinned. "I don't know. Just . . . we found a body. There's been a lot of activity since then, and I just heard the guy you had in jail is an international fugitive. Was he on some sort of list?" Like a Red Notice to all law enforcement to locate and arrest the wanted fugitive and hold him for extradition?

"Grier, how did you learn that? Tanya didn't—"

"Come on, you know this town. I was getting gas when I heard that news."

"It's out of my hands now, and good riddance."

He didn't believe that for one second—the chief would want to know the truth, and she would keep tabs on the investigation.

"What is his name? Why is he wanted?"

She toyed with a pen on her desk and stared at it. Hard. "Look, Grier, what are you really doing here?"

"I told you already. Have you heard anything more about the body we discovered?"

"It's part of an investigation. We don't like to talk about investigations outside the office. And besides, you're the one who told me it was murder. You know more than I do."

"If you would look at your email, you might know more than me."

She narrowed her gaze.

"I couldn't help but see the ME sent an email. It was visible on Tanya's computer."

"They can't know anything yet. They're always behind."

But he could tell he'd stirred her curiosity. He wasn't sure why she was being so evasive now after she'd welcomed his help before. "Why don't you look and see?"

"You don't work for me, and I'm not at liberty to share." She lifted her chin.

He might be scaring her, pushing too hard and raising her suspicions. He abruptly stood, walked to the door, and pressed his hand against the knob—

"Wait." She sighed. "Grier Brenner. Why are you so secretive about who you were before living here? Why don't you tell me about yourself?"

And that was the crux of the matter. How could she fully trust him without knowing his past? He didn't blame her. His throat tightened. He wanted to tell her, but he couldn't.

He turned and jammed his hands into his pockets, that old cliché—*If I told you, I'd have to kill you*—running through his mind. Seriously, if he told her, that would only put her in danger. But he'd burst in here like a fool, and he had a feeling his time was short. Without Krueger to advise him, he couldn't know if his enemies were closing in.

"You asked me to dive and to help. Now, I'm asking you— what did the ME say?"

The door opened behind him, forcing him to step back.

Tanya pushed her way in and looked from Grier to Autumn. "Chief, you okay?"

She nodded. "Mr. Brenner was just leaving."

Brilliant. Grier bid goodbye to both women, then exited. She was right. He was just leaving. He would get in his truck and just keep driving, only he couldn't drive to escape Shadow Gap. He would have to fly or take the Alaska Marine Highway.

SEVENTEEN

G rier stepped out of Autumn's office and disappeared from her line of sight. Tanya held the door open as Craig walked by, heading to his desk. As he passed, he glanced at Tanya and nodded, then at Autumn and his head swiveled away, but not before she caught his smirk.

Fury could get the best of her if she let it, and as it was, Tanya probably thought the heat reddening her cheeks was because of Grier. But it was anger flushing through her at Craig's cocky attitude. Obviously, his uncle had notified him of the city council discussion. What she couldn't know was if he would go so far as to sabotage her efforts to prove herself. She couldn't imagine he would—because she believed he was a good guy. She and her three officers and two dispatchers were a team and had each other's backs. They'd worked well together even before she became the chief. It was only the last few months that her every move was watched and criticized.

If anything, Wally was fueling dissension.

Tanya closed the door, remaining in Autumn's office. "I can see that you're not okay. You want to talk about it?"

"I have work to do."

"Oh, I see how it is."

"I'm not shutting you out, Tanya. I mean it. Grier mentioned he spotted an email on your computer from the ME."

"Why, that sneaky—"

"What did it say?" she asked.

"See for yourself. It's in your inbox."

"Anything else?"

"I also emailed a link where you can view the footage you requested."

Autumn smiled, for probably the first time today. "You're a gem, you know that?"

The woman batted her naturally thick eyelashes as she left Autumn's office and closed the door.

Releasing a pent-up breath, Autumn tried to breathe slowly and naturally, letting the tension drain out of her. Not all of it, though—she needed to remain diligent, enough so that she could think clearly.

Grier had been fishing for information, and he'd made her uncomfortable. What was she doing trusting him so much, more than she trusted the officers working for her? Maybe it was like Birdy had said and she only needed to know someone's mettle. And Grier possessed a lot of it, at least his actions seemed to indicate he did. Maybe she'd turned to him because she felt like she'd been thrown under the proverbial bus, every decision she made questioned and labeled a mistake.

Grier's sudden appearance in her world had seemed like a lifeline and she'd held on. But if she knew what was good for her, she would rein in her interactions.

She couldn't afford any mistakes.

She'd left the council meeting hoping to convey that she didn't care as much about their decision as she did about doing her job. She needed to find out about the criminals who had shown up in Shadow Gap.

But she did care. She wanted to *keep* her job.

And right now, she had to push aside thoughts of Grier and

his good looks. His courage. Hero status. With his bearing, his skills, she pegged him for a Navy SEAL or someone of that caliber. One day, he might even willingly tell her the truth.

Blowing out a breath, she shook her head and focused on pulling up the email from the ME he'd referenced. She read it and learned some preliminary information about the body. Then grabbed her cell and texted Grier to meet her tonight at her house. She would use the info to negotiate.

She then began her own search into the dead man and his partner. "Okay, Alberto Acosta from Argentina and Oscar Evans from the UK, are these even your real names?"

An incredulous huff escaped.

When AST informed her of the men's identities, she learned they each had a Red Notice out for them. They were wanted by a country or an international tribunal. But she wanted to know why. Law enforcement agents from various countries worked on loan for Interpol, but Interpol wasn't a police agency in and of itself and had no authority to arrest or to compel countries to arrest someone who was wanted. They could work with law enforcement investigating, searching for, and arresting, but mostly they connected the police around the world. At least so far as countries chose to participate.

She skimmed the names of fugitives again, but in the case of these two, their crimes weren't recorded in the public information she'd pulled up. Autumn read more, learning there were almost seventy thousand such notices, but only eight thousand were made public. Still, she could search the nonpublic lists made available to law enforcement if she had time, which she didn't.

It was no secret that criminals fled to Alaska to hide, and Dad had often relied on Occam's razor—the simplest explanation was the best one. Meaning that Autumn shouldn't assume anything beyond the facts of the matter. Acosta was most likely in the hands of Homeland Security and possibly being extradited to his home country or to whatever country he had committed crimes against. Bottom line, like Craig said, it was out of her hands.

The man himself knocked lightly on the door and stepped in. "I'm heading out to look into the report of a stolen vehicle. Angie's finishing up with a domestic abuse call—Mr. Ainsley and his wife are at it again—but she's going to meet me there. Can I get anything for you? Anything else you need me to do?" Oddly, his expression appeared sincere.

This was the Craig she'd known all those years working by his side. "Thanks, Craig. Just keep me informed. I'm going to investigate a couple of things too."

He nodded, then stepped away.

"Craig," she called after him.

He appeared again. "Yes?"

"Thanks for all you do for the department, and for this town. I appreciate you, and I just wanted you to know that."

A frown flitted across his expression, then he nodded and gave her a tenuous smile. "Thanks, Chief."

Then he disappeared, leaving her door open.

Tanya stepped in. "Nice." She sat down in the chair Grier had occupied earlier.

"Honestly, I don't know where that came from."

"It came from your heart. You're a good person. A good cop, and the best chief since your father."

That elicited a chuckle, and Tanya joined her.

"What happened at the meeting?"

"It went as well as you might expect. Wally declared they would vote me out."

Tanya pursed her lips.

"Then I told them to go ahead and vote, but I had work to do, and then I left."

A broad smile spread across Tanya's lips. "I'm glad you stood up for yourself. Honestly, I would have lost respect if you had cowered before the great Wally Atkins."

Autumn waved her hand. Enough about that. Now it was time to do her job as she'd so boldly claimed she would do. She might not be able to investigate the international criminals, but she could look into the body she and Grier had found in the shipwreck, as well as follow up with Sarah.

"Did you happen to find contact information for Sarah?"

"You mean Sarah Frasier? The woman who lied about her boat?"

"That's not her real name, I'm guessing."

"The only Sarah Frasiers I could locate aren't in their mid-twenties and certainly don't fit her description."

Autumn sagged. "And she's gone."

"Not to worry, Chief. I'm sending you fake Sarah's cell number from a burner phone she used, per my cousin Jett. She chartered his boat to take her across to Haines." Tanya batted her lashes again.

Autumn never doubted that Tanya, her huge family, and their connections were an asset. "I love it when you work your magic and then flaunt your lashes." If Autumn had lashes like that, she might flaunt them too. She stood and grabbed her jacket. "I'll contact her on my way home."

"Say hello to your father for me."

"I will."

Autumn headed out of the office through the back door. Once inside the cab of her Interceptor, she called the cell number Tanya claimed belonged to Sarah but got no answer. She left a voice mail that she hoped sounded compelling and was filled with concern. But Sarah might simply toss the phone and get a new one.

Autumn was grateful for her family and friends, the local characters who made up the community of Shadow Gap and had been here for decades. Otherwise, her world might be filled with only murderous fugitives and those just passing through.

Her heart suddenly kicked up—was Grier just passing

through? She shouldn't care so much about a man she knew so little about.

But she cared. Oh, she cared.

Autumn sped home after she realized how late it already was. She wasn't sure how her father would react if Grier showed up before she got there.

Maybe she should have just turned up at his cabin and talked to him there, but she needed to check in on Dad as well—she had a feeling he thought she was neglecting him. Well, more than a feeling. She'd been busy. Did that count as an excuse?

It was dark by the time she got home with five minutes to spare. She opened the front door and stepped into a dark house.

Alarm kicked her heart rate into overdrive, and she removed her Staccato P from her holster and gripped it.

"Dad?"

She stared into the utter darkness and listened. Chills prickled her arms. Autumn took a step to reach the light switch and stumbled over something. She flipped on the lights, but the darkness remained.

Autumn radioed dispatch to request backup and ask for an ambulance, though she prayed one wasn't needed. Using her flashlight, she slowly crept through the house, clearing every room and searching for her father. Hoping she would find him and praying he was safe. But sensing something entirely different.

Fear gnawed her gut.

After clearing the house, she stepped through the back door, quietly. Her skin crawled—she felt it.

The sensation that she wasn't alone.

Leading with her pistol, she walked around the perimeter of the house and shined her flashlight into the woods to search for an assailant and her father, hoping those two were mutually exclusive—she'd find her father or the criminal, but not together.

God, I don't want to lose Dad too. Help me.

A hand covered her mouth at the same moment a voice whispered in her ear. "It's me. Turn off the flashlight."

Her heart jumped to her throat.

Grier? That he'd been able to get so close told her a lot—about herself and about Grier. He gently urged her into a crouch against the side of the house near some bushes.

In the shadows of the cool, wet night, she could barely make out his face, but she could see clearly enough that he pressed a finger against his lips. Before he gave her any explanation, he signaled for her to wait.

He started to leave, but she caught him. "I'm not sitting this out. What do you think you're doing?"

He leaned in so close, his warm breath tickled her ear when he said, "You're in danger. Stay here."

"No, Grier. I'm the law here. You stay." She started to move, but he held her in place. Her insides twisted. "Take your hands off me or I'm going to hurt you, and then I'll cuff you."

"I respect you, Chief, but I can't get to your dad until I take care of this. Stay here or you risk his life." He released her and was gone before she could move.

His words had stunned her and were the only thing he could have said to cement her in place. He knew where her dad was? And he was using that to his tactical advantage? How would she risk her dad's life if she moved?

She couldn't see much in the darkness but waited and listened. The seconds ticked by, and as the time increased, so did her heart rate. Her breaths came faster until she couldn't hear any sound over the pulse in her ears—not even the incessant rain.

Autumn slowly stood as her eyes adjusted to the darkness. No way was she going to cower in the bushes.

Grunts, groans, and punches resounded in the woods.

Then shouts.

Bursts of gunfire blasted the night.

No, no, no . . .

People she cared about were getting hurt. Autumn held her gun at the ready and maneuvered between the trees with stealth. She knew these woods next to her home and might be able to walk them blindfolded. An unsettling silence now met her ears. Silence except for the patter of raindrops.

She spotted a form emerging from the woods. Gripping his midsection, he stumbled forward.

Dad!

He was trying to make his way back to the house but collapsed. She rushed forward, panic swallowing her whole.

She crouched next to him. "Dad!"

More gunfire echoed, coupled with discharged flashes. She spotted the silhouette of someone shooting at Grier, then dashing behind a tree.

She aimed her gun at the shooter. "Police! Put your weapon down!"

The figure suddenly disappeared into the night. Autumn wouldn't give chase and put her gun away. Her heart lurched as she turned on her flashlight and saw the extensive blood coming from Dad's gut.

An image of Ross flashed in her mind.

She set the flashlight at an angle so it would give light, then decided against it and switched it off. She could do this without the light. She yanked off her jacket and pressed it against the wound to slow the bleeding. Holding back her panic, she steadied her voice to instill hope in her father.

Sometimes hope made the difference between life and death.

"Dad, you're going to be okay. Just hang on."

He made a resigned coughing/laughing sound as if he didn't believe he would make it, and that ripped her heart open.

No . . . Dad. "Help is on the way. I called as soon as I walked into the dark house."

As if confirming her statements, sirens echoed through the

night. If only the hospital and ambulance weren't on the other side of town, which was too far when seconds counted. Autumn was also a trained first responder, although she didn't lug a medical kit around on her person. But maybe she should. Maybe she should start carrying Celox gunshot wound granules in her pocket if this trend continued. Whatever. She couldn't leave him to grab the kit. For now, she would keep the pressure on Dad's gunshot wound and wait for help to arrive.

He gripped her wrist with his bloody hands. "You're in danger."

Grier had said the same thing.

"Why am I in any more danger than you?" Because, clearly, her father was in danger of losing his life, a thought she would try not to dwell on or she would fall apart.

"It's my fault," he said.

While pressing her jacket against his wound, she used her other hand to check his pulse. It was thready, growing weaker.

"Grier! Somebody! Help me!"

She radioed. "Tanya, someone, Dad needs help now!"

"They're on the way. I'm praying for you. Tell Miles to hang on. God isn't done with him yet!"

Sirens grew louder. "It won't be long now, Dad."

Her choice of words could be taken a different way than she meant. At the sound of a disturbance behind her, she reached for her gun while still maintaining pressure on the wound.

"It's me, it's me." Grier dropped to his knees next to her. "What can I do to help?"

"Can you get the medical kit for me?" She grabbed her keys and tossed them his way.

Catching the keys, Grier rushed off.

She waited. Prayed.

A mere thirty seconds ticked by. But thirty seconds felt like an eternity in this life-and-death situation.

What's taking him so long?

132

A minute, then two.

He appeared again, kneeled by her side, and opened the kit.

"You're going to make it." He directed the words to Dad. His voice sounded confident and reassuring, and even though he spoke to her father, she grabbed on to the words and held tight.

"Get the Celox for me." She wanted to keep the pressure on his wound.

He'd already found it and handed it off. Together they worked to doctor her father. In the dark, she couldn't see how much blood he'd lost. *God, please let him live.*

"If I can't do anything more, then I need to go." He scrambled to his feet.

"Where are you going?"

"I need to find the shooter. He's still out there."

"Grier, I can't allow you to do that. Stand down."

"I don't work for you." And then he was gone.

And really, Grier appeared skilled and trained—and she apparently couldn't stop him. Tonight she would find out once and for all who Grier Brenner was. With her luck, he was an FBI special agent gone rogue, and she would be seen as working with him.

Focus. Focus on Dad.

"I'm the police chief. Why does he have to be so—"

"That boy's got pluck."

She could barely make out Dad's words, but the fact that he'd spoken encouraged her.

Pluck.

Mettle. Courage. Whatever Grier had didn't lessen her frustration with him, but she couldn't chase after a crazy man—the shooter or Grier—with her father's life hanging in the balance.

# EIGHTEEN

Grier was tired of men with evil plots getting away, and he was done standing on the sidelines and watching. He raced after the assailant.

Sirens wailed in the distance, reassuring Grier that police support was on the way, though limited, and emergency services would get to her father. He prayed they got to him in time.

A dense fog rose, permeating the woods and making it difficult to follow his target. Grier walked as silently as possible. He had no way of knowing where the gunman had gone but suspected he hadn't headed for the road, where law enforcement and emergency vehicles traveled, or toward the water, where there was no escape. Unless, of course, he had a boat. Too bad the Alaska State Troopers' response team hadn't hung around longer after the manhunt so they could close in on yet another shooter. Grier would bet this was a record for Shadow Gap.

He watched, waited, and listened. Despite the cooler evening temperatures, sweat beaded on his back and brow.

A twig snapped—near or far, he couldn't tell with the eerie way sound echoed in the foggy woods. He pressed his back against a tree, slowed his breaths, and remained quiet. Angling his head, he caught a glimpse of a figure dashing away.

Grier pushed from the tree and followed, maintaining full awareness of his surroundings in case the guy hadn't been working alone—like they'd learned too late at the cabin a couple of days ago. As he headed for the edge of the forest, following the direction the man had run, he left the thickening fog behind. He stopped when the trees opened up. A sliver of moonlight that broke through the clouds shone on a half-acre meadow edged by more forest on the other side. A rocky outcropping at the base of a ridged mountain sprang up behind a swath of evergreens.

The gunman crossed the meadow and hopped over what must have been a creek or a gulley. After sliding down an incline on his backside, he bolted upright and raced out of the woods.

Memories that felt like they were from another life chased him. And here he was, running after danger again. For all the right reasons—again. He dashed across the meadow, then hopped over the creek before stopping behind a boulder to catch his breath.

He listened.

Pebbles slid. Rocks tumbled, echoing. Was the guy trying to climb? He peered around the boulder and, at this angle, could just make out a cave entrance. He caught the slightest movement inside the cave before all was still again. The shooter?

Grier scraped a hand over his mouth. The guy really had no better escape plan than to hide in a cave where he could get trapped? All authorities had to do was wait for him to come out. Grier blew out a breath. But the chief had only two officers, and the shooter might be skilled enough that those odds were still in his favor—he could overcome two officers with no problem.

Or . . . he knew another way out of the cave.

Grier made his way through more woods, heading toward the cave. Quiet footfalls sounded behind him. He slid down a trunk and crouched. Then he spotted her. He'd recognize the chief's silhouette anywhere. Her graceful movements were purposeful as she weaved between trees and pushed through underbrush as if she'd skillfully tracked him and in fact knew he was crouching at the base of this Sitka spruce.

He slid up the tree. "Chief," he whispered.

She startled and aimed her weapon, then he stepped out of the shadows.

"It's me."

She crept over to him. "When are you going to stop calling me Chief?"

She wanted to talk about that now? His heart kind of warmed at the implication.

"I—"

"Don't answer that now." She pressed a finger against her lips and gestured for them to hunker down.

She must have sensed they were no longer alone in the woods the same moment he had. Grier kept his gaze trained on the shadows while he sent up a prayer. He should have stayed with Autumn instead of going after this guy. He would have suggested she call in the state again—after all, another police officer had been shot. A retired officer.

A black-tailed deer—a buck—ran through the woods, and Grier slowly released his breath. "Your dad?"

"Ambulance is taking him in."

"You should be with him."

"No, Grier, I should be here. We need to apprehend yet another shooter. I appreciate what you're trying to do, but you're not the law in Shadow Gap. I'm going to need you to stand down. My officers are on the way, and we'll take it from here."

"Okay, Chief." This was no time to argue, and he imagined his response surprised her. He might be a jerk for smiling inside at the thought of surprising her, especially in the middle of this . . . situation. Her father's life was on the line.

"Having said that, did you see where he went?"

A few retorts scrambled through his head, and he pursed his lips, then said, "I thought he went into the cave. I don't know if he's hiding or if there's another way out. But we're definitely not going in there tonight. He'd have the advantage."

"You're right. *You're* not going in there."

The chief radioed for her officers, instructing them where to meet her.

That sensation crawled over him again. Someone was watching.

He lowered his voice. "Fine. I'm not sure he's in the cave. Either way, we're not alone in these woods."

"You feel it too, huh?" She slowly stood.

"Yes," he whispered as he stood too. "What about the state troopers? They could help catch him."

"They're gone, and we can handle this as long as it doesn't become a manhunt through the wilderness. Thank you for tracking him, Grier. Clearly you have skills, but you're still a civilian, and if you were to come to harm, well, I can't have that on my conscience."

Or record. He got it.

"Maybe we can draw him out. But I'll wait until backup arrives." The chief stepped to the edge of the woods, closer to the cave's entrance, her weapon drawn.

Grier didn't like it, not one bit, but she was the boss.

Had he made a mistake by believing the man went into the cave? He and the chief were focused on the cave when they should be—

He sensed the slightest change in the atmosphere behind him and squeezed the handgrip of his weapon.

He jerked around at the same moment the butt of a gun slammed into his head. Pain ignited in his skull and he stumbled, falling to his knees and dropping his pistol. A kick to his gut knocked him to his side, then he rolled onto his back.

He planned to keep rolling and then scramble to his feet, but the head wound slowed his reflexes. A bulky form stood over him, and Grier stared up into the barrel of a gun.

"Drop your gun now!" The chief's loud shout held no fear, only a lethal command.

Grier rolled as a gunshot blasted in his ears.

NINETEEN

F lashlight guiding her, Autumn rushed forward and aimed her weapon at the fallen man. She was surprised she'd hit him. In the dark, it had been risky, but she was able to make out the two silhouettes and knew Grier was about to die if she didn't take action.

She stood over the man—was he still alive and dangerous? Her eyes darted to Grier, who remained on the ground, unmoving. Panic swelled in her chest, suffocating her.

"Grier! Grier! Are you okay?" She gasped out the question.

Had he been shot? Had she been too late? The tightening in her chest eased when he stirred. Grier scrambled to his feet and leaned against a tree for support. Now she could breathe.

"Are you hurt?" she asked but kept her focus on the man still on the ground.

Grier didn't answer, so she radioed for help again, then knelt to confirm the man she'd shot had no pulse. She stood and turned her attention to Grier but kept her weapon ready in case someone else was lurking in the woods, waiting for the right moment to gun them down.

If only she could slow her pounding heart. Shining her flashlight, she looked Grier up and down.

"Please answer me. Are you shot? Are you hurt?"

He shook his head, then pushed off the tree. "That was a close call. I'm good."

He didn't sound all that good, but what did she expect? He'd almost been shot point-blank.

Grier took a couple of steps toward her. "Thank you for saving my life."

The emotion in his voice gripped her. Yes . . . he was shaken. As was she. She searched for the right response, her mind going a little numb. "Of course. It was all in a day's work."

That was all she could come up with?

Grier stepped closer, took the flashlight from her, and squeezed her empty hand. She felt the strength in his grip.

"Chief, have you ever killed anyone before?" he asked with compassion.

Was it that obvious? She shook her head, not wanting to risk that her voice might give away how disturbed she was. She needed to project strength and control over her emotions—and the situation. Being chief didn't mean killing someone would have no effect on her.

Then, finally, she asked, "Is he the same guy who shot Dad? Who fled to the cave?" She hoped Grier had gotten a good look at him since he'd engaged him.

"Looks like it, yes. He obviously found a way out and came back around to ambush us."

"Right," she said. "We can't know if he was the only one out there, though."

Grier found his pistol and picked it up. He held it, preparing to face off with another assailant.

Footfalls pounded the ground, coupled with shouts—a welcome sound when she recognized Craig's voice. "Over here! And watch your back."

She joined Grier in eyeing the woods as two sets of light beams bounced.

"Who's with Craig?" he asked.

"I'm guessing Angie." Who else would it be since Ross was still recovering?

Grier blew out a shaky breath. Yeah. He was working to compose himself too.

"What happens next in Alaska?" he asked.

"What do you mean?"

"In the lower forty-eight, an officer-involved shooting requires turning over your weapon and an investigation. You're chief here. Who are you going to turn it over to?"

Oh, right. She hadn't been thinking that far ahead, but maybe she should. "That will fall to the Alaska State Troopers."

"Shadow Gap can't afford to lose their police chief for even a day."

"No, no we can't, and we won't." This could be just one more proverbial nail in her coffin if Wally had a say in it.

Craig approached along with . . .

Her brother? "Nolan? What are you doing here?" Though she was more than relieved to see him.

Nolan stepped forward and gripped her arms. "Autumn, are you okay?"

"Of course." She took a step back, wishing he would keep his brotherly concern for later, when others weren't watching. Still, she was glad he was there because she could use the moral support. "Dad."

"I know." Apprehension edged his tone. "As soon as I heard about Ross, I got the okay to get to Shadow Gap. I'm so glad I did."

"Me too," she said. "Ross is recovering. He made it."

"Dad is going to live too. We have to believe that."

He sounded like Grier.

Nolan's gaze dropped to the man on the ground, then he glanced up at Grier. Accusation flared in his eyes.

"I shot him," she said. "He was going to kill Grier. We believe he's the man who shot Dad." Pain ignited in her chest. She wanted to be at the hospital. She wanted to radio Tanya and ask for an update. The sooner they got out of here, the sooner Autumn could go be with Dad.

"Why'd he shoot Dad?" Nolan crouched and searched for ID. As an Alaska State Trooper, he was within his authority, though they primarily focused on the areas outside city limits. Still, this section of the woods wasn't technically within Shadow Gap city limits.

"The chief is in danger," Grier said.

"He tried to kill *you*, Grier, not me."

"What are you talking about?" Nolan stood, his hands empty. The guy didn't have ID on him.

"Her father told her she was in danger. I'm relaying that information." He stared at Autumn, and she got the sense he wanted to add, "In case she doesn't tell you."

"He'd been shot," she said. "And was probably referring to the shooter. We were all in danger with a shooter out there." She glanced down at the dead man. "But he's gone and now we can't ask questions." Why had he shot Dad? Had it been intentional?

Plenty more questions swirled in her head. She lifted her gaze to Grier but didn't voice her thoughts. Not in front of Nolan. At least not yet, though she had no idea why she kept the question to herself.

Why had he tried to kill Grier?

 # TWENTY

Who was the shooter after? Miles Long or his daughter?

Was Grier simply in the way or was he a target?

Grier fisted and refisted his hand while tightening his grip on his gun. He took in the scene as well as the eerie woods as the fog caught up with them and puddled at the base of the mountain. He tried to ignore the questioning look on the chief's face. Yes, even in the foggy shadows cast by the flashlights, he could feel her eyes boring into him. She was probably wondering the same thing that had settled in Grier's mind. She hadn't voiced the question out loud in front of Craig or her state trooper brother, Nolan, for which he was grateful. And that led to another question—why had she remained silent?

Or was he imagining that she'd gone that far with her thoughts?

He watched her, barely listening to the conversation as she relayed to Nolan the details of what happened. Was he here as a concerned family member or in his official capacity?

Grier's imagination could be running away with him, but if she was in danger like her father said, then maybe the shooter's intention had been not to *kill* her but to *take* her, and he'd wanted Grier out of the way. He wanted to get to the bottom of this, but it wasn't his job, as she kept reminding him, even tonight—he wasn't law enforcement.

"We'll take care of the body," Nolan said.

"Good. I need to check on Dad."

"What about the shooting? You going to investigate that too? She's your sister, so you can't do that." Craig widened his stance.

"You can rest assured, Officer Atkins, that the Alaska State Troopers will look into it." Nolan's authoritative tone should shut Craig down.

Nolan hadn't asked for her weapon, but all the same, Autumn handed it off to her brother, failing to hide her indignance at Craig's attitude.

"You have your other gun with you?" Nolan asked.

She pointed to her SIG Sauer in her ankle holster.

"Good. Just wanted to make sure you're covered."

The chief said nothing in response but turned and hiked away. Grier took off after her, leaving Nolan with Craig. He wanted to say a few things about Craig, but nothing he could say would help the situation.

He caught up and hiked next to her. "We don't know if he was working alone, so you shouldn't go off by yourself."

"There's a lot we don't know, Grier. Let's keep our guards up, though I hope there's no one else. On the other hand, if there is someone else, we would have someone to question."

Oh, right. Guilt pressed in on his shoulders. "I shouldn't have let him surprise me like that, then you wouldn't have had to shoot."

She said nothing and they continued hiking through the woods, then hopped the creek and crossed the meadow while remaining alert to their surroundings. He could just make out Craig's and Nolan's voices echoing off the boulders at the base of the ridge and through the trees. The sound traveled surprisingly far. Sounded like Nolan was contacting someone on his radio.

"I used to love these woods. This meadow. Nolan and I used to carve boats out of fallen branches and float them down that creek. The only thing we had to fear was catching a momma bear with her cubs off guard." Her voice sounded weirdly muted in the cold fog. "But now, the body count is rising, and I don't know what's going on, but I'm going to find out."

Grier wanted to say he would be here to help. But he couldn't make that commitment, and she wouldn't accept it anyway. *God, what am I doing here in Shadow Gap?* He had the feeling it was time to come out of the shadows and stop hiding, even if it cost him everything.

The chief slowed as they approached the house she shared with her father. The fog settling near the water about twenty-five yards from the house cast an eerie glow. No one would ever guess there'd been a brutal battle filled with gunfire and fists. That a man had been shot.

The place looked quiet and normal.

The chief stopped at the edge of the groomed yard. "I told you not to go after him. To stand down."

"That, you did. But he'd still be out there if I hadn't gone after him. He'd remain a threat to you and your father."

And to me?

She sighed.

Using her radio, she contacted Craig. "As soon as possible, I need you to collect evidence at the house and surrounding woods. I really need to get to the hospital and check on my father."

Craig responded. "Sure, boss. Nolan says we'll get it. Go to the hospital."

She started for the front of the house.

Grier kept pace with her. "So what's with your officer? He sounded insolent back there in the woods."

"That's just Craig. You get used to it."

"Why get used to it?"

"His uncle is on the city council, that's why." She paused to look at him. Held his gaze. "Craig wanted to be chief."

Understanding dawned, and Grier nodded.

He followed her back to their vehicles. She stopped near the front porch and crossed her arms. "Tell me what happened—your side of the story."

"I got here on time," he said. "Well, okay, two minutes late. When I got here, the door was open, and it was dark, and I knew something was wrong. I searched for you and saw the shooter at the same moment I spotted you." The chief hadn't seen the shooter, and Grier's only thought was to protect her, so he grabbed her from behind, whispering quickly in her ear. That had been a risky move, but she was here and alive.

Her brow creased. "Who are you, Grier, that you think you can step into police business?" Her voice remained steady but still conveyed her anger.

"I'm just a guy who lives in Shadow Gap and likes to fish and eat at the Lively Moose." And needed to find a job if he was going to stay through the rest of the month.

"What did you do before you came to Shadow Gap?"

Before? None of that mattered at the moment. "You asked me to meet at your house tonight. What were you going to tell me?"

She reached for her vehicle door. "Let's make a deal. You tell me who you are, really, and I'll tell you what I know."

His throat tightened. He didn't need to know about the body, did he? Accepting her terms to learn more wasn't worth the risk. But he'd already made too many mistakes to have her asking these kinds of questions. He'd be surprised if she hadn't already tried to find out about his past, but she would come up empty.

Krueger had seen to that.

When Grier said nothing, she climbed into the Interceptor and started it, then lowered her window.

He understood that she was eager to get to the hospital to see her father.

"Ballistics isn't back yet, but the doctor told me about the entry and exit of the bullet that nearly cost Ross his life. You called it. I'm guessing you were some kind of law enforcement before you came to Shadow Gap—state or federal, it doesn't matter. Or military. Tell me, or else I have no choice except to think there's a seriously messed up reason why you won't."

Oh, she knew how to throw her verbal punches, he thought as the air rushed out of his lungs. But he would neither confirm nor deny her assessment. He didn't want to become a liability to her, especially if she was already in danger.

Maybe he could concede that, yes, he'd been military, but he doubted that would satisfy her. If he gave her one unredacted line from his past, she would ask for the whole page.

"I was nobody." He walked away and got into his truck.

She steered out of the drive, and he followed her. He needed to find out about the Red Notice fugitive. Usually, those answers could quickly be at his fingertips.

But now, using those resources would get him killed.

 # TWENTY-ONE

A t the small hospital in Shadow Gap, Autumn rushed down the hallway and ran headlong into a familiar nurse exiting the operating room.

Georgiana gave Autumn a compassionate look, then urged her toward the waiting room. "Why don't you have a seat."

"I don't want to sit. I want to know what's going on with my father."

"He's in surgery, Chief."

That news stunned her. "You're not sending him to Juneau?"

"Dr. Combs has got him. Remember, he worked in a level 2 trauma center in Anchorage. Your father needed immediate attention. Once he's stabilized, though, he could still be transferred. He's in good hands, don't worry."

Autumn nodded and decided to sit, after all. Nothing was worse than hanging around worrying, especially when she wanted only to pray while she waited for news about her father. But she had to figure out who shot him and why. And then tried to shoot Grier.

Oh, Dad . . .

Anguish twisted her heart. Working in law enforcement in Shadow Gap wasn't supposed to be like working in the big city—how many times had her father reiterated that fact? Now, here in Shadow Gap, he had been shot and was fighting for his life. He never suffered a potentially mortal wound when working in Topeka that she knew of. He often shared stories from his time there, and she was sure he would have told her about any serious incidents.

Regardless, this was her town, and she had to find the truth. Her father would want her to find answers rather than wait around for him to recover. She squeezed her eyes shut and tried to calm her palpitating heart.

The clock on the wall made the long wait much too brutal. She shifted in her seat. Got coffee. Paced the hall. Checked with Craig about their progress. And repeated it all over again.

A couple of hours later, she got up to pace. Again. Then sat in a different chair to look at a different stack of magazines.

Why is the surgery taking so long? What does it mean?

Rapid footsteps—a cadence she recognized—drew her attention. Nolan approached, his expression somber.

"He's in surgery," she said before he could ask.

He glanced around the small waiting room, noting a woman on her cell, then gestured for Autumn to follow. "We need to talk."

She remained sitting. "Not now."

"I'd prefer not to talk where others can hear."

"But what about Dad?"

"He isn't going anywhere," Nolan said. "Look, I'm here for a day, and then I'm back to my post." Nolan was in C Detachment, the Yukon-Kuskokwim Delta that encompassed an area larger than the state of Alabama—practically the other side of the mainland, as far as you could get from Southeast Alaska. She wondered if he had taken that post on purpose.

"I'm glad you're here, and I want to talk, but I just need to know he's going to be okay. I need to see him."

Nolan nodded toward the double doors. "Looks like we're going to learn his status."

Doors whooshed open and Dr. Combs walked toward them, drying his hands. "Your father has always been as healthy as a horse, and he came through the surgery fine."

"Can we see him?" she asked.

"He's in recovery now and sedated, but once we move him to a room, we'll let you know."

"Are you going to keep him here?" Nolan asked.

"Unless there are complications we can't handle, yes."

Relief filled Autumn. He'd lost so much blood, and she'd feared he wouldn't make it. She wanted to lean against the wall and catch her breath, let her heart settle.

"Thank you, Dr. Combs," she said. "Have someone call me when I can see him."

"Will do."

"Thank you, Dr. Combs," Nolan said. "We're glad you decided to make Shadow Gap your home."

Georgiana approached and showed Dr. Combs a file, drawing his attention away.

Nolan grabbed Autumn's arm and steadied her. "Ready for that talk now?"

"Sure." She walked with Nolan and was surprised when he exited the hospital. She followed him to the vehicle he'd parked next to hers. He'd borrowed Ross's Interceptor, probably thanks to Tanya.

An international fugitive had shot Ross. But what about Dad's shooter? Tension corded her neck.

"Someone shot our father, Nolan. I don't know who or why, and I'm worried he's still in danger. Can we secure a few troopers to watch him? I can't spare any officers."

"Grier said Dad mentioned *you're* in danger."

Everyone in Shadow Gap was in danger until she got a handle on things. "In the last several days—I've lost count already— we've had two dead shooters and taken one fugitive into custody. Judicial services quickly transported him from our jail, thank goodness. We've also recovered a body from the inlet—a man was murdered. This isn't what we see in Shadow Gap. I need to know what's going on. Anything the Alaska Bureau of Investigation can do to help would be appreciated. Did you and Craig find anything suspicious? Any evidence we could use to figure this out?"

"Not anything obvious. I took a lot of pictures, and you should go back and take a look and see if anything is missing at the house that could explain the attack. Craig and Angie will go back at first light to get a better look in the woods. But honestly, it doesn't seem to be a simple burglary that took a wrong turn."

"Agreed. A burglar would simply run off. He wouldn't hang around for a fist- or gunfight, or circle around to take out his pursuers."

"We'll get to the bottom of it," Nolan said.

"In the meantime, let's take this seriously and put a guard on Dad's door."

Nolan scraped a hand over his face. "In this case, it might be easier if we transfer Dad to Anchorage. Lots of Alaska State Troopers to watch and switch out with the Anchorage PD as well. I have a feeling your job just got more complicated, so I'll make those arrangements."

Exhaustion weighed on her. "Thanks, Nolan. I appreciate you helping with Dad. I was surprised to see you. What brought you here?"

"Can't a guy drop in to see his family now and then?"

"Sure, but you usually have more than one reason."

His lips flattened and his eyes grew dark. "I already told you. I heard about what happened to Ross, and I was worried . . . about you."

His brotherly concern warmed her. Autumn missed him but understood he enjoyed his job and couldn't necessarily control where they put him. He'd been the trooper here in the Shadow

Gap region until a year ago when they decided they didn't need a trooper, especially one they couldn't afford. Maybe this new criminal activity would bring him back.

"Angie and Craig have my back." She didn't mention that Grier had been the one to have her back more than once recently.

"That brings me to my question. What was Grier Brenner doing there with you? He said you saved his life."

Since Grier showed up, Nolan had come to Shadow Gap a few times to check in with her. The two had met, and Dad spoke highly of Grier.

Something in Nolan's tone made her bristle. "Is this part of the investigation into the shooting?"

"No, this is your brother wanting to understand what happened out there tonight."

She dragged her gaze over to the businesses along Main Street and then the police station. "I asked him to meet me at the house. When I came home, I found the place dark and went in search of Dad. Grier showed up and fought with the shooter. Dad was shot, and Grier went after the guy."

"And then you saved his life." Nolan crossed his arms. "Why did you need to meet him?"

"What is this? An inquisition?"

"Hardly."

"Then why ask about him? We have bigger concerns here, and you know it."

"The reason I brought up Brenner is because it seems to me there's something going on with the two of you."

"How did you get that out of the five minutes he was there?" And what did it matter to Nolan?

"That's not a denial."

"There's nothing to deny." She opened her vehicle door.

"I'm just worried about you, but you're right. There are more important things to be concerned about than whether Grier Brenner is someone you should get involved with."

Incredulity exploded in her chest. Why did he think he had any say in who she got involved with? But she held back her anger. Nolan was her older brother and probably thought that gave him a say. "His actions prove he's a good guy, but there's nothing going on between us. And if there was, why would that matter?"

"I don't want you to get hurt. You don't know anything about him. Where he's from or his background. He's a stranger. You shouldn't trust him."

And Grier doesn't know what I've been through. How messed up I am.

Autumn knew Nolan thought the same. He might even be as concerned for Grier as he was for his own sister.

"What do you know about it? Why bring him up at all? Oh . . ." She should have known. "Dad. He's been talking to you."

"Not much. Dad mentioned him a few times."

"I don't know what he said to you, Nolan, but Grier brought Dad home one night when he was too drunk to drive. I'm sure Dad failed to mention that part of whatever story he concocted."

"Relax. I . . . just don't want you to get hurt. You've been through enough already, and considering the last few days, well, let's just say that sometimes a person can look for help in the wrong places."

"You don't need to worry about me. I'm the chief of police, remember? I can take care of myself. As for Grier, he's just a guy who is willing and able to help at times." And she found herself trusting him, turning to him more than the people in her own department. Maybe if Craig wasn't Wally's nephew . . . "He came to Shadow Gap to fish and ended up staying. I can name a few people living in town right now who hadn't intended to stay but fell in love."

Oops. That was the wrong choice of words. She and Grier

were not in love. Nolan arched a brow. Was that what concerned him? Big brothers could be a real pain. She got into her vehicle and started it up, then lowered the window. "I'm staying at Birdy and Ike's until the house is no longer a crime scene. She has a couple of extra beds for stragglers if you need one."

"I know." He cracked a grin. "I wouldn't mind a bowl of her razor-clam soup, plus a chance to see them." He opened the door to the Interceptor he was driving and tossed her a wave. "Thanks, sis. I'll work on Dad's protection detail, get the investigation into the shooting tonight wrapped up, and catch up with you later."

She watched him sit in the vehicle—his mobile office—and put his cell to his ear. He could have worked out of her police department, but she suspected he wanted privacy. Right—he sure hadn't wanted to give *her* privacy. His grilling about Grier frustrated her. But at the same time, he cared about her, and that was important too.

Autumn whipped out of the parking lot and drove the short distance to park at the police station. She entered the building and ran into Angie, who was just leaving. Angie was an undercover DEA agent before she ended up in Shadow Gap and engaged to one of the locals, avalanche specialist Ridge Ledger.

"How's your father?" Angie asked.

"He's out of surgery and will recover."

Headset in place, Kelly looked up from the computer—she replaced Tanya on dispatch after hours. "Angie's heading out to answer a call regarding a drunk driver."

For a moment, Autumn's stomach took a dive. But it couldn't be Dad. He was in a hospital bed.

"Where's Craig?"

Angie stepped up to the counter. "Well, let's see, he finished up at your house, then I think he went home until the next call comes in. It's almost midnight."

"You need me to assist with the drunk driver?"

Angie hurried past her. "I got this. You look a mess. Get some rest. This will be my last call for tonight, then I'm heading home too."

She watched Angie leave. "Please be careful out there."

"Always." Angie disappeared through the door.

Kelly smiled at Autumn, then glanced down at her computer. If any calls came in after hours—and they always did—Kelly would route them to her cell and home.

Autumn headed into her office and closed the door, then glanced at the clock. She wanted to increase the number of officers and remain open 24/7, but it wasn't in the budget, so their main office hours were 8:00 a.m. to midnight. She couldn't sleep, so she might as well work, which would bring her closer to finding answers and take her mind off Dad's situation.

At her desk, she woke up her computer. Tanya had sent her emails containing the news footage she'd requested. She watched the video and replayed it several times. Grier ducked into Tex's boat at the beginning and she didn't see him again, but a few boat slips down, she spotted the suspicious man she'd seen in the alley. He was watching them unload the body. She stopped the video and zoomed in, wishing she had a much bigger department with computer techs and facial recognition software so she could get a good, clean look at his face. She could have her answers quickly.

She printed off an image of his face and would ask Angie and Craig to keep an eye out for him.

Nolan texted.

Dad's in his own room now. He's sleeping.
Come see him in the morning.

I'm on my way.

She wasn't waiting until morning. She locked up the office and got into her vehicle and drove the short distance back to the small hospital. Though it was well past midnight, no one would stop her from seeing that her father was okay.

She joined Nolan in Dad's room. While he slept, his face was creased and looked anything but peaceful. "He looks like he's in pain."

"He's on meds." Nolan spoke softly. "I doubt he's in physical pain."

"There are other kinds of pain." Autumn retrieved her cell and pulled up the image of the man from the video footage and showed it to Nolan.

He stared at her cell. "Who is he?"

"Don't know, but he's suspicious to me. If you see him around, find out what you can. Better yet, take this image and use the tools at your disposal to run it through the state system."

"I need more information. Why is he suspicious? Are you thinking he's connected to the shooting?"

She shook her head. "He showed up in town, and then there were two shootings. All within the same time period. I've seen him a few times, and he caught my attention. I can't put my finger on it, but he seems shady to me. Call it instinct."

Nolan pursed his lips. Would he agree? "Text me the image, and I'll do what I can. Now, get some rest. Tomorrow's another day, sis. You need sleep so you can think clearly for what comes next."

What comes next . . .

Nolan's words stayed with Autumn even as she lay in bed upstairs in Birdy and Ike's apartment over the Lively Moose. She tried to sleep, but images of the dubious stranger remained on her mind, floating in and out with the memory of her father's blood, then Ross bleeding out. Gunfire echoing in her head.

She tossed and turned until finally she fought, then failed, to escape her memories and dreams.

Autumn loved her swimsuit with pink flowers—the one-piece Mom had given to her as a surprise for their trip to the

Caribbean. She'd meant to give it to her for her eighth birthday only three days away, but with the trip, she needed the swimsuit. Dad bought a big, fancy boat, which they took to St. Thomas. It had a huge deck. Bigger than the Jessie Lynn, *which Dad kept at a lake near their home, and she had her own bedroom and everything. It was the best vacation ever—and would be the best birthday ever too. She stared up at her beautiful mother, with her long, dark hair. Mom wore a turquoise swimsuit underneath a pink T-shirt and white shorts.*

They'd go swimming as soon as Dad and Nolan got back from taking the skiff to shore to get forgotten supplies.

Men suddenly appeared behind Mom, who whirled around to face them. Where had they come from? Mom argued and shouted, pointed for them to get off the boat. Autumn was scared at what they might do, and she couldn't stop the sudden tears. Where were Daddy and Nolan to protect them?

Autumn bolted awake from her dream—a combination of memories and things that made no sense.

Like . . . her mother speaking another language.

And the suspicious man from the street in Shadow Gap was on the boat with her mother.

 # TWENTY-TWO

G rier might have been in a sour mood because he'd skipped his favorite breakfast at the Lively Moose and cooked up a plate of scrambled eggs at home instead. Hard to believe he couldn't even scramble a decent plate of eggs—but to be fair, he'd gotten distracted and burned the eggs. He would have gone into the Lively Moose, but he hadn't wanted to run into Autumn there. She must have stayed with her grandparents for the night since her house was still a crime scene.

But at least he'd made it to Main Street, where he had important work to do, breakfast or no breakfast. From his vehicle across the street, Grier watched Autumn walk into the hospital, presumably to check on her father. Elbow against the door, he rubbed his forehead as if that could work the confusion out of his mind.

Again, he had to ask himself—what was he doing? Why had he taken it upon himself to protect her under any circumstances? She was the police chief, after all. Still, those in law enforcement needed others to have their backs. And right now, Grier wasn't entirely sure anyone was watching Chief Long's back, at least at the required level. Not even her brother, an

Alaska State Trooper. But who was Grier to think he was the guy for the job?

Maybe playing the hero in this little town had gone to his head. Regardless, he sensed he needed to move on before it was too late.

The chief didn't need his help.

Just let her go.

Leaving this town behind might just take all his mental and emotional energy. But he could do it. He had to try.

Grier steered out of town and back to his cabin. He let Cap out and tossed sticks so the dog could retrieve them, and when Cap had had enough, Grier knelt and rubbed his head, behind his ears, and around his neck just the way he liked.

"I'm no good for you, you know?" Cap licked him as if to counter his statement. The reverse was true, and the dog had been good for Grier. "You'd be better off with someone else who could take you on long walks. Your kind loves to pull sleds, so you need to be with someone besides me."

Cap whined. Had the dog sensed Grier was saying his goodbyes? He allowed the beautiful husky with two different color eyes to lick his face once more. He couldn't just leave him here in the hopes that someone else would come along in the nick of time like Grier had, though Cap probably would have found a way to survive. Still, Grier would contact the property manager and let her know his plans to leave, cutting his lease short. But more importantly, Cap needed someone to watch out for him. If she offered him no reassurances, he could always ask Hank to take him.

Inside the cabin, Grier had just started packing up his gear when he heard tires crunching across the gravel. No one ever came out to see him. The people he expected to show up were not the kind to knock on the front door. He gripped his weapon, then peered out the window.

A Shadow Gap Police Department Interceptor. His pulse kicked up. What was this about?

Cap barked before the knock came. Grier opened the door and stared into Autumn's striking-colored eyes, then ran his gaze over the crazy, curly hair she'd tried to tame. Why did his heart have to knock around inside at the sight of her, skipping a beat or two or three?

And yeah . . . he should go ahead and admit to himself that this woman was the reason he hadn't left sooner.

"Chief"—he cleared his throat—"what are you doing here?"

He grinned at the fact that it was finally his turn to say those words to her.

Without an invitation, she walked right by him and into the cabin. He shut the door and crossed his arms as she glanced around the small space.

She turned to face him. "You were surveilling me. Why'd you stop?"

Wow. Her question startled him. She didn't mince words. But how did he answer? He moved to the already burning woodstove. *"Why'd you stop?"* He couldn't help the smile that formed, but he needed time to figure out his response. He grabbed a couple of mugs from the cupboard to the right of the stove. "You want coffee?"

Uh-oh. She was eyeing his gear. "What is this? Why are you packing up?"

"Too many questions." He poured her a cup to go with his, then turned and offered it to her. "Careful, now, it's hot."

"No thank you." She rubbed her hands, then crossed her arms. Why was she so agitated?

"Suit yourself." He set the extra cup on the round kitchen table.

Whining, Cap sat next to the chief and looked up at her. The dog was instantly in love. How Grier understood.

"Answer my questions."

"You're awfully demanding today." Actually, she'd been demanding last night, but he hadn't struck the deal she'd wanted

160

and answered her question about who he really was. That information wasn't worth the risk to *her*.

She took a step closer. "Nolan told me not to trust you. That you were a stranger." She gave him a soul-searching look as if wanting him to say she should trust him.

"Good advice." *What am I doing?*

"I tend to look at actions rather than words. You've done nothing but good since you've been here. In a short time, you've won the town's trust. People look up to you."

Exactly why he needed to disappear. Try again somewhere else. "Why are you here, really, Chief?"

"Why don't you call me Autumn?"

Why did she care? This wasn't the first time she'd asked. He felt it then . . . the strong connection between them, growing stronger every day and, here, in this small cabin, every second. Every breath.

Drawn to her, he stepped closer. He wanted to touch her hair, press his palm against her soft cheek. Kiss her lips. Something entirely too warm stirred in his belly. She had come here for him. What had he gotten himself into? He was no good for her.

He had to break the spell—for them both—but instead, he set his mug on the table and took a step closer.

"Why don't you call me Autumn?"

Why, indeed. How did he tell her that calling her Chief kept her at a safe distance when he couldn't even explain that to himself? What was she thinking at this moment when she stared at him, searching, grasping for answers she desperately wanted and he refused to give? She wouldn't like what he told her, and that was only one reason why he couldn't share.

Hurt flashed in her eyes. He was at a loss and had no clue how to respond.

"Forget it." The chief turned around to walk out.

She opened the door and Grier remained in the cabin, watching her stomp back to her vehicle.

He'd pushed her away, but he'd had no choice. And so much more was going on here. She was in need of help—the city council was out to get her and some criminal element had arrived in town, putting her in danger. He suspected it was someone out to get her father for some bad dealings while he was in charge. Someone he'd put away in the past. But his suspicious mind was getting away from him.

God's purpose for you . . .

If God had a purpose for him, Grier had no idea what it was.

Cap barked and stared up at him, his blue and brown eyes seeming to tell Grier to go get the girl and bring her back. Or at least Grier imagined the dog wanted the chief to stay and warm up his cabin as much as Grier wanted that. Grier growled through clenched teeth and started out the door, chasing down her Interceptor, which was already bumping along the double tire tracks someone called a road.

Suddenly the vehicle stopped, sliding forward in the mud, as a figure emerged from the woods.

Grier tensed and glanced behind him, wishing he'd brought his gun.

Barking, Cap raced by. Grier called the dog, but Cap kept running toward the vehicle. Grier followed. The chief got out as Grier rounded the grill. Hank stood in front of the Interceptor.

She directed her words at Hank. "Why'd you step out in front of me like that? I could have hit you."

"Bear found something you should see."

Grier could almost hear her groan inwardly, but she kept a straight face so she wouldn't disrespect a decent guy—though others treated him poorly. And Grier admired her for the effort.

"I'm afraid I need more than that, Hank. I have a full day ahead of me already. And how did you know to find me here?"

"Bear and I were on the hill when I spotted your vehicle on the road." Hank glanced between the chief and Grier. "I saw you heading to this cabin, so I took a shortcut and came this way. Almost missed you."

She nodded. "Hank, if this is about a Bigfoot sighting, I'd prefer it wait."

Disappointment registered on his face, and for some reason he looked to Grier for reassurance. Grier subtly nodded. *Please don't let it be about Bigfoot . . .*

"Bear found remains. I don't think they belong to Bigfoot. They're human."

 # TWENTY-THREE

Autumn had changed into hiking boots and donned a heavier jacket that she kept in her vehicle. The rain made the temps in the sixties feel cold, but the higher elevations would be even colder—and it could snow.

Hank and Bear led the small motley crew up the mountain and through the trees, the leaves and needles dripping with a steady stream of cold rain. At least they weren't hiking through several inches of snow. Grier insisted on coming along and bringing his husky, Cap, even though by the look of things in his cabin he was packing up for a trip, if not leaving the area for good. She wasn't sure why the idea had sent a spike through her heart.

He owed her no explanation.

Anger at herself—replacing the misplaced hurt—burned in her chest for going to his cabin to begin with. She shouldn't need anyone's help, but with the escalation in criminal activity and nearly losing her father, Autumn had wanted to reach out to the one person who seemed to have her back at every turn. The one person she connected with—though she hadn't been ready to admit that to herself. She'd been drawn to Grier for a thousand reasons she didn't understand and plenty of reasons she did.

He had a presence about him that caught her attention the first time she saw him in town. Good looks to go with what she believed was a good heart, and the mettle Birdy had brought up. Everyone saw it. And Grier . . . when he looked at her, he seemed to reach into her soul and touch the deepest part of her.

But she had no business thinking about that now, or ever, especially since he intended to leave. Her fear that he was a transient like so many others was coming true. She shouldn't be so hurt by it since nothing tangible had transpired between them, and it was obviously all in her head. He had never even called her by her first name. Maybe she'd imagined their connection, but she didn't think so.

And now, he should be on his way to wherever he was planning to go but instead was hiking up a mountain with her. Maybe he was here for Hank and not her. The two had a camaraderie, and Hank felt indebted to Grier for helping him find Bear.

As they continued up the mountain, Hank talked about spotting Bigfoot, and Grier responded as if he believed Hank, reassuring him. Though he wasn't obvious about it, Grier had the bearing of a man who was well aware of his surroundings. She had no doubt he was one of the good guys and had exceptional training and skills. Why was he even here in this isolated fjord instead of out in the world serving the greater good?

His secrets bothered her, but she had enough to worry about without thoughts of Grier occupying her mind.

After hiking at least twenty minutes, she wished she'd assigned this task to someone else, but Hank often requested her specifically and seemed to trust her, so she would take that to heart as his vote of confidence. At least she had a few of those around town, but in the cryptozoologist's case, she wasn't sure what that said about her. Truth be told, there was no telling what Hank had found, and this could be a colossal waste of time.

Still, given the last few days, Bear very well could have found human remains.

"How much farther, Hank?" Autumn was growing breathless, and they were fast approaching the tree line.

Bear barked and ran toward a boulder. Cap joined him. The two dogs sniffed around.

"We're here." Hank walked toward the dogs. "Get back, Bear, Cap."

Bear left the lump he'd been pushing around with his nose and sat at Hank's side, but Cap wasn't so willing to give up the find. Autumn approached the pile of clothes and remains. Using the satellite messenger, she texted Tanya that she needed assistance gathering evidence and supplies for transporting human remains, then shared their location.

Grier called to Cap, but the dog had no true master. Finally, Grier moved in and picked up the husky.

While she waited for her officers, Autumn donned gloves and pulled her camera from her pocket. She took pictures of the body and the surrounding area, then searched the jacket and pants, finding a waterproof wallet. She flipped it open.

"Who is it?" Hank asked. "I wanted to find you as quick as I could and didn't bother to search for ID."

"You did well, Hank." She stared at the Michigan driver's license and the name. Her stomach lurched.

"Well?"

"I should contact the next of kin to let them know first, Hank." Except . . . she blinked up at him. Could it be coincidence? She hoped so. She looked into Hank's brown eyes. "His name is Kenneth Duncan. Any relation?"

Hank's jaw dropped, and he stared at her. "Kenny? No . . . no, no, no. It can't be Kenny." Hank rushed forward. "Let me see the driver's license."

She handed over the ID. Hank stared at the image, then dropped to his knees as a deep, gut-wrenching sob burst from him, as though his chest had split open. The sound echoed against the mountain.

Autumn comforted Hank as best she could, then rose to her feet and joined Grier. His pain-filled eyes remained on his friend.

"I need to gather evidence," she said in a low tone so Hank wouldn't hear, though she doubted he could hear over his grief.

"What do you think happened?" Grier asked.

"The way the body is tangled in the trees, one would initially think an avalanche got him, but I can't know when. The ME will have to determine that. Avalanche season typically ends in mid-May but can go through June."

Grier nodded. "Coming in, I spotted a snowmobile a quarter of a mile down that looked like it had been abandoned months ago."

"Could belong to him. If he rented it, then the company should have reported it missing, so we would have known to look into this. We'll check it out." She eyed the cornice of the still-snowcapped mountain. "I need to find out more. When did he leave Michigan, and did Hank know he was missing? Can you help me get Hank away from the remains?"

Grier nodded and got closer, dropping to his knees next to Hank. He put his arm around the man, hugging him like he was sharing the pain with a brother. He spoke softly to Hank, who nodded and then finally stood and stepped away from the body.

Hank drew closer to Autumn, and when he spoke, his words came out raspy and broken. "He's my youngest sister's son. My nephew. I wanted him to come and see me. We talked about it a lot, but he didn't tell me he was coming. Or that he was here. My sister thought he was in Oregon with friends. This is going to break her."

"And your sister didn't become concerned when she hadn't heard from him?" Autumn asked.

He subtly shook his head. "He'd go off here and there, and she wouldn't hear from him for months. It wasn't unusual. I invited him to come see me, hoping I could give him focus and a reason to settle somewhere. I just can't believe . . ."

Hank sobbed again. He crouched to nuzzle Bear and let the dog lick his face. Cap joined in comforting Hank.

Autumn approached Grier, who remained near the body. "Can you escort Hank back down? I'll wait here for my officers. This is a crime scene now."

Grier climbed to his feet and stood next to her, speaking quietly. "You said one would initially think it was an avalanche that got him. I still think an avalanche moved him, but what you meant was that he was already dead—gunshot to the head."

She nodded. "Yes."

"You got the bullet?"

"No. It's . . . I need better tools. We'll deliver the remains and the ME can get it." She stared up at the mountain and thought of the body in the shipwreck, then caught Grier looking at her.

He held her gaze, and she knew his mind had gone to the same place.

"Ballistics can tell us if the same gun was used." And if the same gun wasn't used, that didn't mean the same person didn't shoot both men. Though the incidents appeared to have taken place months apart, the medical examiner would be able to tell her more about when they died. The Alaska Bureau of Investigation was investigating the first body recovered and would want this one too. But she wouldn't be cut out of the inquiry into what had happened near Shadow Gap, especially when she doubted these murders were a priority for the AST in a state the size of Alaska.

In addition to the investigations into these two murders, she also needed to question her father before he was transported to Anchorage. But first things first. "I know this sounds like a strange question, given that we're standing next to the remains of Hank's nephew, but you're packed. Are you leaving town, Grier?"

She studied him.

"Not anymore."

Really. What had changed his mind? Why had he planned to leave in the first place?

"Why do you want to know?" He crossed his arms.

"I thought at the very least we were friends. That's something you tell your friend."

He shrugged. "I haven't gone anywhere, Chief. Looks like I'm staying for a while longer."

Hank's face remained stricken as he looked at his nephew's remains. This conversation with Grier was not appropriate, but then there was no time like the present—she should have done this days ago.

"You're obviously not going to tell me, but before you came here, you were clearly working in a capacity to serve others. You still retain that training and those skills. Grier, I want to hire you."

"I'm not a cop."

He'd told her that the day of the dive. *But maybe you should be.*

"As a consultant." She needed his help. Her department wasn't prepared to handle this level of crime. She could still work with the state bureau of investigation, but Grier was here, and time was wasting. Hiring him would mean she'd need to run a background check to appease the city council, and that would give her a few answers too. Although, she'd hire him without the background check if she could.

"Sometimes you only need to know what a person is made of. Their mettle."

"You don't want to hire me. That's me, giving you *free* consulting advice."

Autumn pushed her way through the hospital doors. Dad's transportation had arrived, and they were preparing to move him to the hospital in Anchorage, though he would likely be released in a day or two. Nolan had taken care of the paperwork and arranged for security for Dad. She wasn't sure if he was truly in danger, but she wouldn't take any chances and appreciated that Nolan agreed.

She entered the hospital room and found Dad awake. Good. Earlier he was asleep, she had headed to Grier's cabin and got sidetracked.

He blinked at her and smiled, but it quickly turned to a frown. "Autumn . . ." His voice sounded strained.

She approached the bed and reached for his hand. Squeezed. "Dad, I'm so glad you're okay. I've been worried."

How did she broach the topic? She had so many questions she wished she'd asked sooner. But there was never a good time.

She sat on the edge of the bed. "I'm sure you've been informed you're being transferred and why."

He shook his head, and fear welled in his eyes. "Not me, Autumn. You . . . you're the one."

"I'm the one what?"

"You're in danger."

"A man shot *you*, Dad. But I'm listening. Tell me what you know."

"It's all my fault."

Her breath built up in her chest, growing with her impatience. "Please, Dad. I need to know everything so I can close this down. Find out why you were shot." The man still hadn't been ID'd, at least that she'd been informed of.

"No. Don't go after him."

She leaned closer. "Go after who? The guy who shot you is dead. Is there someone else? Who's behind this?"

The beeping on his heart rate monitor increased. She'd upset him. How did she make him tell her?

"He wants to take you from me." He croaked out each word.

She moved off the bed and a nurse rushed in but didn't look at Autumn.

"What pain med is he on?" Autumn asked.

"He's on a variety of medications."

That didn't help. Autumn had to assume the medications and his recent gunshot wound were unfortunately interfering with his mind and responses, which wasn't unusual.

"I promise I'll be careful, Dad. Just calm down. You want to help me, then calm down and talk to me."

He closed his eyes and took in a few breaths. The nurse injected something into his IV, then glanced at Autumn. "This will help him calm down."

"I need him to answer questions."

The nurse smiled at her father, ignoring Autumn's comment.

"They'll be in soon to move you, Mr. Long." The nurse patted his arm and then exited the room.

Angie quietly knocked against the doorjamb and glanced at Autumn, who waved her in. "How's he doing?"

"He's holding on. Strong as a horse, Dr. Combs said."

"I'm glad to hear it." Angie chewed her lip, looking like she wasn't convinced.

Neither was Autumn. Nor was she sure that her father would be willing to share what he knew with someone else present, but she needed answers. Pulling out her iPad, she retrieved the images she'd created—a virtual lineup—then turned the iPad to him.

"Do you recognize anyone?" The lineup included five men and two women.

Dad finally opened his eyes and took the iPad from her to glance at the images. This wasn't ideal, but she didn't have the luxury of time. She watched his eyes for a reaction, but he didn't respond. Didn't react.

Disappointment filled her.

She pointed at the man who had followed her. "Dad, he was on the boat with Mom the day she died. Who is he? I need to know everything *right now.*"

The nurse came back in and flashed an apologetic look Autumn's way. Behind her, hospital staff rolled a bed for transport into the room.

Dad closed his eyes, his words garbled. She would get no answers today. Angie indicated she needed to talk to Autumn. After she said her goodbyes and watched them wheel her father out of the hospital and load him into a helicopter, she gave Angie her full attention.

Angie's expression was unreadable, but Autumn knew it must be important.

"What is it?"

"We found Monica Nobel."

The woman had gone missing a few months back—May, in fact. Finding a missing person was the end goal, but sometimes the outcome wasn't as good as they'd hoped.

"And?"

"Ridge and Thunder found remains not far from the Duncan body—Hank's nephew."

Thunder was Ridge's SAR avalanche dog.

Autumn's gut clenched. "Walk me out and give me the details."

"We wanted to make sure we found *all* of Duncan's . . ."

Angie didn't need to finish the sentence. "Right." Autumn nodded. "In case wildlife carried some of the remains away."

"Thunder found her in the same area. Both sets of remains"—Angie cleared her throat—"are headed to the ME now."

"What aren't you telling me?"

"Same wound to the head." Angie's frown deepened. "What's going on, Chief? This is disturbing. I haven't been here that long, but I know this isn't what we normally see around here in this quiet fjord. Not who we are."

172

"You're right, it's not. We'll find who's responsible, Angie. Stay vigilant."

Angie crossed the parking lot—she'd walked to the hospital from the police station—while Autumn watched the helicopter fly away in the pouring rain.

Be safe, Dad.

At least she didn't have to worry so much about him now, and she could focus her attention on the rising danger.

 # TWENTY-FOUR

With Dad in Anchorage and Nolan back to his trooper post on the far side of the state, Autumn felt oddly alone, when she wasn't. She had Birdy and Grandpa Ike across the street. Tanya and the rest of her PD team. Maybe she missed Dad. That was all.

If only she could stop thinking about Grier. He was the one she wanted in this with her, yet he refused to officially help. Nolan was right—she never should have relied on or trusted him.

Angie and Craig were both out responding to calls and patrolling the small town, keeping their citizens safe and looking for the stranger Autumn suspected was connected to her past. By being seen in town, the two brought a much-needed sense of security to the residents of Shadow Gap.

Meanwhile, Autumn focused on learning more about the Interpol fugitives to see if there was any connection to Dad's shooter. She'd let that investigation go, but that was before someone shot Dad and they found the remains of Kenny Duncan and Monica Nobel. Had someone been lurking in the shadows for months now?

She'd tasked Tanya with entering the murders and shoot-

ing crimes into every possible database that collected and ana-
lyzed crimes of violence to search for similarities and possible
matches. Nolan was supposed to look into the image she'd sent
him to see if the AST could identify the man through facial recognition software or some other means. She'd contacted various
agencies, including Interpol and the US Marshals. Autumn had
used every resource available to get information and had come
up empty so far—but all she had was a picture.

If the suspicious man was still in town, she needed to find
him—that would be easiest, wouldn't it? He had to stay somewhere. She'd stopped by the Eagle Bluff Motel and talked to
Clair, but she hadn't seen him.

Autumn was stumped.

She told Nolan she thought the man could have been on the
boat the day of their mother's death but left out the part about
him showing up in her dream.

Maybe the fact that he'd been in her dream convinced her
that he'd been on that boat, and he was a criminal. Seeing him
in a dream wasn't enough to prove he'd been there that day with
her mother, but she knew she'd seen him before. *Somewhere.*
He struck an inexplicable chord of fear in her heart, and there
had to be a reason why. What better reason than that he was
on that boat?

A knock came at the door. Mayor White stuck her head in
and smiled.

"Mayor White, what a surprise." Dread settled in Autumn's
chest.

"Have you got a minute?"

"Always." What was she going to say? It was the mayor.
"Come in and have a seat."

Holding a paper sack, the mayor closed the door behind her
and sat in the chair across from Autumn's desk. She placed the
sack next to the chair. "And please, you know you can call me
Cindy."

Autumn smiled. She'd always liked Mayor Cindy White. "Yes."

Cindy's smile shifted, and her expression became pinched. *Uh. Oh.* The mayor always favored Autumn's father while he was in charge, and even after—at least before he started drinking. Cindy had pursued him, but everything had crumbled, understandably. So maybe that's why Cindy liked Autumn and extended her grace. Still, that could have gone either way.

"Autumn, you know I respected your father, and you were the only one for the job when he stepped down. No one disputes that."

But . . .

"No one is blaming you for the uptick in crime lately, but, well, the city council has been talking, and a few made a good point that you're distracted."

Autumn didn't have to think too hard to know who had made the point. She held back her retort and pushed down the growing anger. "And right now, you're distracting me from my laser focus on finding answers." Autumn revealed the list of entities that she'd contacted. "So you can't pin dereliction of duty on me. The Shadow Gap PD will do our best, but we've never had enough officers to truly protect the citizens. And we need to bring back a trooper to the area."

Cindy's eyes widened. "Let's hope this crime wave isn't here to stay. And if not, then we don't need a trooper we can't afford. We have a police department, and that's all we need."

Autumn couldn't exactly counter with the hope that the crime wave would continue. "Why are you here?"

Cindy stared at her hands before looking up. "I can't say you're not doing your best. Just make sure that your best is good enough, Autumn, and I'll back you every step of the way."

Without waiting for Autumn's reply—which was good, because she didn't have one—Cindy reached down and lifted the sack. She pulled out a plastic container and handed it over. "I brought some Tongass Forest Cookies."

"Oh, yum. The family recipe. I love these. Thank you, Cindy." Autumn opened the container and reached for one. She bit into the oatmeal coconut cookie.

"I know you do, and that's why I made them."

To soften the blow.

Cindy stood. "Well, thanks for your time, Autumn. Let me know if you need anything at all."

With a nod and a smile, she left, closing the door behind her.

Autumn stared after her and finished off the cookie.

Every officer wanted to do their best, protect their community, and of course, keep their job. But so much more was on the line—like lives.

Pushing the mayor's visit out of her mind, she spent the next several hours searching the fugitive databases to see if she could find the suspicious man, as well as the unidentified man, now deceased, who had shot her father. She had no guarantee the ME would be able to identify his body, even with DNA.

After all, at least two of the criminals in town had a Red Notice out for them. Maybe the other two were on the list too. But there were other international fugitive notices—yellow, blue, black, green, orange, and purple.

Tanya had gone home long ago, and at around midnight, Kelly peeked into Autumn's office.

"You're working awfully late these days. You should go home, Chief."

"I will. I won't be long."

A half hour later, Autumn rubbed her eyes. Kelly was right. She needed rest. She locked the door and hurried across the street, where Grandpa Ike was waiting at the door with his shotgun. She couldn't help but smile. She had family here who loved her and Nolan, and yes, her father too, regardless of his struggles. She couldn't ask for more.

With another yawn, she stepped inside the dimly lit Lively Moose.

"I was about to come over and get you," Grandpa Ike said. "Too many strangers around town lately."

"I know you have to get up in a few short hours, but I need to talk to you."

"I expected you would." The way he said the words sounded as if he meant this specific conversation. "Have a seat, and I'll be right back."

She settled into his favorite booth, and he returned with a plate piled with a burger and sweet potato fries.

She smiled. Her stomach growled at the sight of the food.

"You're not eating, gal. You need to keep up your strength."

She bit into a fry. "How do you know I'm not eating?"

"You don't cook. You get your food from me."

"That's fair." One bite of the fry, and she was ravenous. She bit into the burger.

"How's your father?"

He *would* have to ask her while she was chewing. She finished off the bite. "I heard he has safely been transferred to the hospital in Anchorage." Autumn took another bite, and Grandpa Ike talked about the delay in getting their shipment of potatoes and that she was eating the last of the sweet potato fries. She didn't interrupt him because she was busy stuffing her mouth.

Finally, she slid the last fry through the ketchup on her plate.

Quiet filled the restaurant. Even the rain outside had stopped. Her turn to talk.

She lifted her gaze to find her grandfather studying her.

"What do you know about what happened to my mother?"

He broke off a piece of homemade bread and chewed on it while he considered his answer. Finally, he said, "I don't think it's my story to tell."

"You took your time responding, and that's all you can say? I have to wonder if Dad's shooting is related to the past. While he was bleeding, he told me I was in danger. Later in the hospital, he said it was all his fault and not to go after him—whoever that is. There's a stranger around town. Perhaps you've seen him, but I think he was on the boat the day Mom died. So, please, Grandpa Ike, if you know something, now would be the time to tell me everything."

Her grandfather's expression had turned grim while she spoke, and he hung his head.

Oh. "You're not . . ." *Is he crying?* "Please, I'm sorry. It's a lot to lay on you. But I simply want to know what happened back then. What's happening now, and is it connected?"

"I can only tell you what your father told us, warning us in case this day ever came." Her grandfather's words were barely audible as he shared the truth about that day.

Her throat grew thick with emotion, and tears surged behind her eyes as she listened. Disbelief gripped her. *No . . . it can't be.*

This news . . . changed everything.

Grandpa Ike's words left her gutted.

 # TWENTY-FIVE

An eerie feeling crept over Grier as he remained parked in the shadows across from the Lively Moose, now well after midnight. The clouds had broken up, giving way to moonlight, but he wasn't sure for how long. As a precaution, he sank down in the seat. The chief needed him, and he could kick himself for shutting her down. But he couldn't work for her in any official capacity—and he couldn't explain that he'd been assigned to a classified program that didn't officially exist.

After too many hours sitting in his parked truck, the chilly night started creeping into his bones. Maybe his efforts were overkill. He could be sleeping in his warm bed, Cap curled next to the woodstove fire, instead of on this fool's errand.

Then movement drew Grier's attention to the alley next to the restaurant, and all his senses became fully alert.

Could be nothing at all. A bear trying to break into the bear-safe garbage cans? August meant increased bear activity—at least Otis and Sandford had warned him. But a bear would make more noise.

Could just be someone out and about at a strange hour—no crime in that. Shadow Gap had no curfew. Except the stealthy movement raised suspicions. He grabbed his Glock 9mm and quietly slipped from his vehicle. A normal person would call the police. He wasn't normal, and these weren't normal times.

Grier crept across the street, edging his way in front of the Lively Moose until he was under the awning. He peered around the corner into the alley between the restaurant and an office building. No one was in the alley, but for a few seconds, a man's shadow was visible behind the building. His heart rate kicked up. Was someone trying to break into the back of the Lively Moose? If so, then Pearl and Ike Lively could be in danger, along with Autumn.

Grier quietly but quickly maneuvered through the alley. A noise from behind drew his attention, and he pressed back against the wall and remained still.

He startled when he spotted Autumn creeping toward him, and she had already made it to within arm's length. He was getting rusty.

"You stay this course, come in from this side," he said, "and I'll approach from the other. We'll trap him."

She nodded.

He rushed back up the passage, cut across the front of the building, and then ran around to the back. Pressing his back against the cold wall, he waited and listened. He didn't see the man's shadow this time. Carefully, he peered around the corner of the building.

No one was there.

Where did he go?

Holding his gun up and ready to fire, Grier crept forward and studied the back door. Had the man gone inside already? Heart pounding, he crept up the steps and tried the door.

Locked.

Quietly bounding down the steps, he hurried toward the other corner, then paused.

Autumn was waiting in that alley. Had she already apprehended the guy? If so, he would know that by now. Maybe she'd had trouble. His breaths quickened.

Please, God, let her be okay.

He peered around the corner again into the dark—*empty*—alley.

Huh?

Had she circled back around? What? Grier tracked down the back alley behind the buildings and surveyed the area until he reached the end of the block.

Nothing.

Not. Good.

Gripping his pistol much too tightly, he raced toward the front, then stopped. No sense in rushing out into the open and getting shot. After making sure it was safe, he stepped around to the front of the Lively Moose. He glanced up and down the street. No Autumn.

No bad guy.

A knot twisted in his gut.

Where are you?

How could he have lost her? Fear squeezed his chest. Something was wrong.

He waited and listened, sending up a silent prayer that he would find her safe and sound. All he heard was his pulse pounding in his ears.

Until . . . A vehicle started up. He sprinted toward the sound coming from a block away. Grier watched in horror as a man tossed a body into the back of an SUV.

"Hey!" Grier sprinted toward the SUV, anguish squeezing his chest.

This couldn't be happening.

The man climbed into the vehicle and sped away and out of Grier's reach. He raced back to his truck, fumbled with his keys, then peeled away from the curb, accelerating down the street. He called 911 to ask for backup, stating someone had abducted the chief.

At least he hoped she was still alive. She wasn't someone who could easily be taken, and he had no idea what had happened. He could have misread the situation.

But . . . he hadn't. She was in the back of the fleeing SUV. The rear lights grew dim—he was getting away.

No, no, no. *God, please let me catch him. Please keep her safe!*

Gripping the wheel, he floored the pedal and focused on the road. Soon the town lights faded to a memory, and he could see only the road and those red lights ahead.

Come on, come on, come on . . .

The rear lights grew brighter, closer, but Grier didn't slow until he'd caught up with the SUV. It suddenly lurched forward, speeding away again.

Where exactly did this thug plan to take her? This two-lane road branched off to various cabins and homes, and one of those could be the man's destination. Otherwise, it ended at the small airstrip. The thought terrified Grier. Did the man have a bush plane or helicopter waiting?

Up ahead the road twisted around a mountain, then turned onto a bridge over the Goldrock River. The SUV raced around the corner much too fast for comfort. Even Grier slowed to make the turn as he rounded the switchback and approached the bridge. He followed at a distance now so he wouldn't force the man to take too many risks.

Not with the chief in the SUV too.

The vehicle drove across the bridge, then suddenly fishtailed. Gripping the steering wheel, Grier's gut clenched and he held his breath while a litany of silent prayers poured from his heart.

The vehicle plunged through the guardrail and disappeared into the blackness of the ravine.

Horror twisted Grier's insides as he sped forward, then

slammed on the brakes where the vehicle had gone over the bridge.

Shock and fear strangled him. Paralyzed him.

He couldn't believe it.

God . . . please help!

This wasn't the moment to let fear control him.

Move. Move. Move. He forced his numb limbs to work. Grabbed his flashlight from his pocket. Jumped from his SUV and shined the light down into the water.

No way could he see into that black, rushing water. But the vehicle . . . it hadn't sunk completely. Not yet. The back end had caught on a rocky outcropping near the bank—that could be a good thing. But on the other hand, it could have meant instant death.

Sliding the flashlight back into his pocket, Grier ran to the end of the bridge and maneuvered down the slope along the rocks. This could be a one-way ticket, but he wouldn't stand on the side and let her die.

He took a few quick breaths, then slid into the rain-swollen Goldrock River, the cold water shocking through him. With only the moonlight to guide him, he swam toward the silhouette of the rocks, using the current to his advantage until he slammed into them. Grabbing on, he dug his fingertips into the slippery surface and maneuvered around to the vehicle. The arctic water roared in his ears, disorienting him, and the cold threatened to render his limbs useless.

The back end of the SUV remained above water. Grier got into position and kicked the back window repeatedly to no avail, then remembered the flashlight. He slammed the glass with it until the window finally broke.

"Chief! Chief!" *Please answer.*

"I'm here."

Overwhelming relief surged through him, but she wasn't out of danger yet.

"Can you climb up?"

"Yes." She coughed. "I'm coming. Climbing up. The water's getting deeper."

He couldn't see her, but the water was quickly pulling the SUV down.

"Hurry." He thrust his arm through the broken window. "Grab my hand."

He felt her cold but strong grip, then pulled her up and out. The SUV slipped from under them, and they tumbled into the water.

"Grier!"

"I got you!"

She gripped his arm and the rock. "Thank you." She coughed and choked, then said, "Now, what's the best way to get out of here?"

"Together. We'll swim together. Don't let go of me. Let the current carry us and we'll try to aim for the bank. It's steep here, but we can make our way up. Okay?"

"Okay."

Together they worked their way to the riverbank. He'd been fortunate to make a quick in and out of the river, and his limbs still functioned, but the cold was getting to him. The chief had been in the water much longer. Every time the current tried to pull them apart, he gripped her tighter and pulled her closer. His feet finally touched the bottom, but suddenly he slipped on a slick stone and, flailing, lost his grip on her as he went under. But she reached for him, caught his hand, and hauled him up and out. He choked and coughed up river water as they crawled up the bank.

Shivering.

He'd almost lost her, and the close call overwhelmed him. Grier pulled her to him, surprised she didn't resist. He held her. No words could convey the emotion surging through him, the relief.

Sirens rang out, growing louder.

Took them long enough. "Let's get up the hill and to my vehicle. We can get blankets and warm you up."

He got to his feet and started forward, but the chief collapsed.

"Are you okay?"

"Yes. I'm fine." She climbed to her feet but appeared unsteady.

He lifted her into his arms and carried her.

"No, please, put me down."

"You're not okay." Adrenaline still coursing through his veins, Grier carried her up the incline. "What happened back there anyway?"

"I think he drugged me, so I'm feeling a little woozy, that's all. I got the drop on him and was about to cuff him but felt a prick in my hand, then nothing. Then I woke up in the back of his SUV."

"So that explains it. You're the reason it went into the river."

She gave a strained chuckle. "I tried to escape the vehicle, then things got out of control."

He reached the top of the embankment and could have put her down, but he kept her close and tucked against him all the way to his truck, still parked on the bridge. Then she slid out of his arms. He opened up the truck, grabbed some blankets, then wrapped her up and held the blanket near her neck. Her face remained inches from him.

Her lips were blue, and he wanted to kiss her and warm them up. The night sky offered them a reprieve from the clouds and rain, and when she looked up at him, he caught a shimmer in her crazy-colored eyes. It took his breath away. *She* took his breath away.

"Grier," she whispered.

He didn't think he'd imagined the need, the longing in the

way she said his name, and he wanted to pull her close and let her melt into him.

"You risked your life coming after me. Thank you. I owe you—"

"Nothing. You owe me nothing."

He leaned a few millimeters closer until his lips almost touched hers. He closed his eyes . . . just a little closer, but . . . he hesitated, denying himself the feel of her lips against his, the feel of Autumn Long against him. She could have died. He could have died trying to save her. Taking advantage of their raw emotions was the wrong thing to do. Wasn't it?

It might have been the hardest thing he'd ever done, but he stepped back, putting distance between them. When he looked at her, he forced an indifference he didn't feel into his heart and mind. He hoped he hadn't hurt her.

Exhausted, she turned and got into his truck. He ran around to the driver's side. Once inside, he turned on the vehicle and cranked up the heat.

"Do you think he's dead?" he asked. "Drowned in the SUV?"

"We can't know until someone goes down to check."

Grier groaned inside. That someone might be him. "Make sure to get a blood test to see if he drugged you."

"I know how to do my job."

Lights flashing, an Interceptor parked behind them. One of her officers had finally arrived. An ambulance and two other emergency vehicles parked along the road near the bridge entrance. "Time to go to work." She started opening the door but glanced back at him. "Tomorrow, we need to talk."

The next day, Grier sat in his truck and waited.

He'd learned from the chief that instead of utilizing their recently cobbled together local recovery team, she'd requested assistance from the AK Dive Search, Rescue and Recovery team out of Anchorage. She hadn't wanted Grier to be involved, she'd claimed, after their close call last night. Her way of protecting *him*, he guessed.

The AK team had swooped into town early this morning. Dove into the dangerous, swollen waters of the Goldrock River to recover the body of the chief's abductor. But they found the driver's-side door open and no body. The driver could have escaped, or the river might have taken him. They recovered the SUV's information, which revealed it had been stolen from Amelia Whitson, who was away from home visiting family in the lower forty-eight and hadn't called it in as stolen. The chief was still waiting on the toxicology report, but she believed she was drugged.

She'd called to give him the information and asked him to meet her, or rather, wait in his vehicle and she would meet him. He didn't have to wait long. The chief exited the police station and was the epitome of someone on a mission. She marched to the curb of the street, then glanced around before making a beeline for his truck.

That she sought him out shouldn't warm his insides, but it did. In the end, it only meant she was desperate for help. And he would eagerly give it, but he feared she would eventually discover the truth he fought to hide.

She opened the passenger-side door and slid into his truck, instantly filling the cab with her scent and presence, and his heart rate kicked up.

Her gaze caught his and held on. "Thanks for meeting me."

Get a grip. Don't stare at her eyes. He looked straight ahead and tried to calm his breathing. "It sounded important." Who was he fooling? He would have been here anyway, keeping an eye out. Someone had almost succeeded last night. In what— abducting her? Killing her? Where was that state trooper brother of hers?

"Well, I owe you."

"You don't owe me anything."

"You came to my office the other day, and I sent you away. I thought you might agree to tell me who you really are if I offered the information you wanted. You saved my life last night, Grier, so I owe you this much. The ME emailed me the ID of the guy we pulled from the shipwreck. I suppose if I were in your shoes, I'd want to know who I recovered."

"Don't forget, he was shot in the head, same as Hank's nephew." Grier's chest tightened. "I'm concerned about you. Concerned that whoever is responsible is still walking the streets."

"Or floating in the river—maybe it was the man who took me last night all along."

"But we don't know that he didn't escape, so let's act like he's still alive until we confirm otherwise." Next to him, she tensed. Grier added, "Sorry. You're the boss. I didn't mean to overstep."

"I might be dead if it wasn't for you, so—I can't believe I'm saying this—go ahead and overstep." She grinned.

How could she smile in this morbid context? But he adored her smile and wanted to draw her closer and kiss those lips he'd almost kissed last night when they were blue. Now they were a warm pink.

He was losing it. Really losing it. Grier scraped a hand over his face. Time to focus. "So who was the guy in the shipwreck?"

"Let me pull up the email." She found the information on her iPad. "His name is . . . Martin Krueger."

TWENTY-SIX

G rier stared straight ahead, his knuckles turning white as he squeezed the steering wheel. His tanned, healthy complexion had paled. He must be remembering the dive to recover the body. She understood—she had tried to push away the memory of finding it.

"Grier, are you all right?"

He didn't respond. Had he even heard her?

"Grier?" Concern rippling through her, she put her hand on his arm. A warm current surged, bringing with it flashes of memories—her in his arms as he carried her up the hill. Holding her against him. Nearly kissing her. She closed her eyes and forced her pounding heart to slow.

"I'm fine."

She opened her eyes to find him staring at her.

"What else can you tell me?" His emotions were shuttered away.

She couldn't read him. Unease crawled over her. "You're not consulting for me, remember?"

"Aren't I?"

His reaction to her news sent a sliver of fear shuddering through her. She glanced at Main Street, taking in the daily bustle, everyone going about their business as if danger hadn't invaded their town.

"You're in danger."

What was she even doing here, talking to this man—who remained an enigma to her—about police business? Had she made a mistake by involving him? But she reminded herself he had the kind of grit she needed. Her throat tightened, and she swallowed. She had to admit there was so much more to Grier than his ability to assist her, so much more about him, and she wanted that in her life. Him in her life.

"Chief, time is short. What else can you tell me?"

"We're waiting for ballistics to tell us if the bullet we found in Kenneth Duncan is the same as the bullet found in Monica Nobel and Martin Krueger, but we've confirmed that Kenny died months ago. And looks like Monica was within the same time frame. Martin, however, died recently, which seems obvious. Though I don't know how they could be linked, the similar method used in all three murders tells me I need to connect them. What I know for certain is that we have strangers among us, and not the usual tourists."

"And what about Sarah?"

"Good question. I would have liked to talk to her to ask why she lied. I don't know how or if she's connected to any of it, but her scenario is suspicious."

"And why can't you talk to her?"

"She left. I have a burner phone number that I've called several times."

"Give me her number, and I'll try."

Autumn narrowed her gaze. "Why would she . . . Oh. You pulled her from the water and saved her. You're banking on that."

"Worth a try."

"That, it is." Autumn found Sarah in her contacts and sent the number to Grier. "Listen. Me sitting in this truck with you talking about an investigation, especially since you won't allow me to officially hire you, is risky. People are watching. I should say, certain city council members."

"Then why are you here?"

"You know why. With my career hanging in the balance and not being able to trust at least one person in my own department, I need to use the resources available to me." *That would be you.* It was like God had brought him into her life at just the right moment. Would she even be friends with Grier, know him or trust him, if he hadn't brought her inebriated father home? "I'll ask you one more time, can we make it official?"

She risked a look at him, and he flashed her a rakish grin as he took in her face. Her eyes, then her lips. Her heart pounded, and she was sure he could hear it. What was she doing falling for a guy she barely knew in the middle of a veritable crime wave with her career on the line? Why couldn't she and Grier have grown close when her career wasn't turning into a dumpster fire and she didn't have a rising body count?

He ripped his eyes away and shook his head as if torn over a serious decision, then finally said, "I can help you, but not on the books. What do you need me to do?"

She figured as much.

"I questioned my father about the shooting at our house, and he told me again that I was in danger. At the time, he was on pain medication and simply could have been in a drug-induced delirium, especially since he said it was his fault."

"He didn't dream up the shooter. Nor did you dream up the man you shot or the abduction last night."

"Don't you think I know that? I showed him these images." She brought them up on her iPad. "See if you recognize anyone in this digital lineup."

He shook his head. "Can't say that I do. What about you?"

"I believe this man is the man we prevented from breaking into the Lively Moose last night. I believe it's the same man who has been following me. I didn't get a good look at his face, but I got the eyes."

Autumn brought up the image of the man.

"Did your father recognize him?"

She pursed her lips. "I think he might have, but he didn't commit."

Grier stared at the image, tension rolling off him as he lifted his shoulders and released a heavy exhale.

"I've asked for Nolan's help to identify him, and I've made all the appropriate communications to the many agencies in search of answers. I'm getting nowhere fast."

"Tell Nolan this takes priority. This is a very real and present danger. Don't stay at your house. Stay with your family in town."

"After last night, I think we can safely say this person is after me like my father believes. I would bring danger to their door. I can't stay with them again. That man was going to come into the restaurant, head upstairs, and then who knows what would have happened."

"There's a strong possibility he's connected to the man who shot your father."

"I agree. We need to identify him, then we'll know more. I'm looking at the possibility that all the shootings are connected. Though, given the time period, it seems unlikely, but I'll leave no stone unturned." An ache shot through her head, and she rubbed her temple. "I trust Tanya and Kelly, and my officers too, but Craig has been twitchy lately, influenced by his uncle Wally. I don't think Craig would intentionally sabotage my efforts, but I'm not sure—and it's too risky. So I'm treading a thin line here, talking to you. I hope you know that."

She also hoped he would share his own deep, dark secrets that he was holding back from her. She tried not to feel slighted or hurt on a personal level. And professionally? She'd made the decision to talk to Grier and work through this with him.

He had her back.

"I do. Tell me the rest."

She shrugged. "I'm only hypothesizing, but it appears my father brought trouble to this town when he moved us from Topeka, Kansas. My guess is that the criminal in question recently got out of prison, or else why wait all these years?"

Grier stared straight ahead again as if lost in thought. "Relocating a family from Topeka to Alaska is a big move. Why'd he do it?"

"After my mother died, he needed a change of scenery and wanted us to know her parents. To have a support system. Family. That, and since he was the police chief, he didn't have the time to devote to us in Topeka like he believed that he would in this small town."

Grier started up the vehicle and steered onto the street.

"Wait. Where are you going?"

"I feel like we're a sitting target, either for the man who survived the river or for the gossips watching you." Apprehension that hadn't been there moments ago edged his tone. "Tell me the rest while I'm driving. What happened to your mother?"

Where do I start?

What Grandpa Ike had told her still left her feeling shell-shocked. A wave of nausea hit her at his revelation, but she put it aside. She tried to calm her emotions so she could share with Grier what she was willing to share, but her voice shook, even so.

"I was only eight. Dad had arranged for us to have a special vacation in the Caribbean. He always said, 'Memories made on the water last forever.' I think Mom and Dad had been fighting a lot, and he wanted to do something special. He and Nolan went to shore to get supplies. Mom and I were on the boat. Men showed up, and they argued . . . I don't remember a lot. What happened next, well, Mom didn't make it out of that."

"I'm so sorry," Grier said.

Me too. She squeezed her eyes shut for a moment. Sucked in a breath, then opened her eyes again.

"Recently I dreamed that she had talked to them in a different language, but now I think that was an actual memory. Plus one of the men in my dream is the same man in this picture. I'd seen him before in town, following me, and I knew he seemed familiar. Now I think I know why. He wasn't just from my dream. He was actually on the boat. And he's the one who abducted me last night."

She risked a glance in his direction to gauge his reaction. He appeared rigid, working his jaw. She'd give him time to digest her words as he steered them out of town.

"I know it's a lot to take in," she added.

Grier released a heavy exhale. "It sounds like your suspicions are right and your father got involved with some seriously bad people while he was a police chief in Topeka. Your family paid the price, your mother with her life. So your father has the answers you need."

"Too bad he couldn't tell me more. As for the man who shot Dad, his fingerprints aren't showing up on any criminal or military lists that we know about yet. And Nolan hasn't learned anything from the Alaska Bureau of Investigation that he could share. He's working all angles on the side, in addition to his job, using his connections."

"And Nolan hasn't learned the identity of this guy who was on the boat how long ago?"

"Twenty-two years."

"If he's a notorious criminal with a past, then you should know something soon."

She nodded. "I'll give Nolan a call. Tanya and I have been searching databases, but with the number of criminals listed, it's overwhelming."

Grier drove up a muddied trail, then parked in a thicket. He shifted toward her, his expression somber.

"Let me take you somewhere safe. From there we can find out who this guy is and wait for the authorities with more resources to apprehend him."

His words stunned her. "Are you out of your mind? I'm the head of the police department here. Shadow Gap might not be much, but it's my town, Grier."

"Well, it was worth a shot to ask, though I didn't think you would go for it, even though it's exactly what you did for your father. You sent him somewhere safe. After last night, you need to do the same."

"That's different."

"I don't agree, but it's your call." Grier climbed out of his truck but apparently had more to say since he leaned back in. "Stay here until I get back."

This is what she got for asking for help. She had to crawl out on his side because he'd parked next to a tree and she couldn't open the door.

She rushed through the underbrush until she caught up to him standing behind a thick spruce. "Grier." She hoped he heard the growl in her tone. "What's going on?"

"I need to get something from my cabin."

Confusion rocked through her. Why not drive there? She suspected she knew why he wouldn't tell her about his background. Still, she would ask again. "What aren't you telling me?"

His clandestine actions must have everything to do with his life before Shadow Gap.

He turned to her and gripped her arms. His expression had shifted.

Autumn tensed and moved her hand toward her gun. Reflex. Training. Whatever. But Grier had kind of morphed right in front of her eyes, and doubt rushed through her.

That infuriating, rakish grin erupted.

"How can you smile?"

"Anyone else might be scared right now. But not you. You

face your fears head-on, Chief. It's what I admire about you."
And just like last night after the swim in the cold, dark river, he
leaned in close enough she could smell that woodsy, masculine
scent on him. Before she could catch her breath, he planted his
lips against hers—gentle, testing at first, then harder and eager,
promising more.

Then he suddenly stepped back, leaving her bewildered and
wanting more.

"I'm hiking in, using stealth, because I can't be sure my
cabin is safe."

No apology. No nothing. Stunned, Autumn didn't move.
What just happened? She'd kissed him back, that's what. She
couldn't blame him for acting on something they both wanted.
Seconds ticked by before she could clear her mind and focus—
apparently, he didn't have that issue. He'd already started off
into the woods, so she caught up and hiked behind him, pulling
her jacket tighter.

She could try another angle to get the truth out of him. "Why
would anyone mess with your cabin? You aren't the target."

"That's where you're wrong."

Moving between two trees, she jogged and hopped over a
log to sidle up next to him. "I need to know what's going on,
Grier. Or I'll hike down this mountain back to town. This isn't
how I work or roll. I need to know what you're thinking. What
you're planning." She glanced through the woods, taking in her
surroundings. Was her would-be abductor out there, tracking
her now?

She hoped so, because he wouldn't best her again. She was
done with his games.

Done with Grier's games too. Because if his secrets held a
dark side, maybe he didn't possess the heroism she was looking for, after all.

"I never should have gotten into your truck." She turned away
from him and headed toward the road, carving out her own

path. She'd radio for a ride, and that would go over so well if Craig was the one to respond.

Grier followed. Catching her arm, he turned her to face him.

Idiot that she was, she let him. She wasn't in control of her faculties when she was near Grier, and that's what it all came down to. She should keep her distance. The sooner she accepted that, the better. She'd have to take her chances with Craig and Wally. At least she *knew* them. Who they were, where they came from, and the trouble they were up to.

She'd known Grier was trouble, and she'd kept him close. The problem was, she didn't know what *kind* of trouble he was—other than to her heart. But he was also much more, she had realized too late.

Grier stared down at her, his deep forest-green eyes pushing back the protective layers to get to the heart of the matter. "I realize I've asked too much. You're right—you never should have gotten in my truck. I never should have made myself available to assist. But here we are. This will go much better if I tell you who I am."

Her throat constricted. She'd wanted the truth, hadn't she?

He released a pain-filled sigh. "Chief Long . . ."

Her heart pounded at the way he looked into her eyes, and she was a coward all over again. How many times had she thought she wanted to know about her mother's death—the day on the boat that she couldn't remember. And then she'd ended the conversation with her father before it truly began.

And now here she was, wanting to know the truth about Grier. Or did she prefer to run from what he might say?

Anguish twisted his features. "I'm a fugitive."

 # TWENTY-SEVEN

T here. He'd told her what he'd been keeping from her.

The rain started again.

Great timing.

Autumn's face scrunched up. Panic surfaced in her eyes as she stepped out of his grip. He'd expected this reaction from her, but he hadn't anticipated the hurt that pinged around inside his own chest. Still, he could appreciate the disbelief projecting from her face, and the fact she hadn't reached for her gun or her handcuffs.

"What do you mean . . . *a fugitive*? That could mean anything you want it to mean. You're running from someone. So what?"

He could have grinned at that—her grasping for a way to make this positive, searching for a way out of the truth. He could have grinned and picked her up, hugged her to him and maybe even whirled her around. Except the chief wouldn't go for that and, in light of the news he still had to share, neither could he.

He hung his head, took a breath, then lifted his face again. He'd opened this door, now it was time to walk through it. "I'm a *wanted* fugitive."

He expected her to gasp, but she just stared at him. Her eyes narrowed.

He knew she was making a concerted effort to push past her disbelief and absorb his words. Sift through them to find the truth. And actually, he should feel flattered that she thought so highly of him when she knew nothing at all about him. Instead, her belief in him touched his soul and gave him hope that he had a way out of this.

Hands on her hips, she stood taller and lifted her chin. "You can't be a wanted fugitive. I would know about that. My police department would know. I've spent countless hours combing through wanted lists, and your picture, your name, wasn't on any list. You can't be a wanted fugitive, Grier, without anyone knowing. Quit messing with me."

That she didn't know about him even though she was in law enforcement did little to comfort him.

You wouldn't know because . . . "It's complicated." The less she knew, the better. But he'd taken this big leap, this big risk, and told her at least that much. In the span of a few months, she'd gotten deep under his skin—or else he wouldn't be with her now, telling her anything at all.

"I'm all ears. Who wants you? The FBI? ATF? DEA? US Marshals? What crime did you commit?"

"That's just it . . . I didn't commit a crime."

Would he ever be able to put this behind him and live a normal life? Doubtful, even if Krueger hadn't been found with a bullet in his head. The news of Krueger's murder had crushed Grier. He'd struggled to control his anger. The fact that he hadn't recognized the body of the man he'd known so well and trusted with his life burned a hole through his heart. Krueger had been beaten until he was unrecognizable, and the underwater life had done the rest. Anguish surged in Grier's chest again, but he pushed it down. He'd have time to grieve later, after he caught those behind his friend's death.

Grier started toward his cabin again. Autumn followed, and he wasn't sure if he should be happy about that, but he was relieved all the same.

"We should keep our voices down," he said.

"You're going to have to explain, Grier. Why put it off?"

He paused long enough to watch her reaction to his next words. Would she believe him?

"I didn't commit a crime. I witnessed one. But I was framed. Martin Krueger was working to clear my name. He was my only contact with the outside world, with my old life. He knew the truth and was in a position to collect the evidence needed to prove my innocence." And the person behind situating Grier here in Shadow Gap, of all places.

Unblinking, her multicolor eyes stared up at him as she processed the information. She chewed on her lip. He'd never seen her do that. There was so much more he wanted to know about this woman, but they'd met at the wrong place.

The wrong time.

"If he was found here in the inlet," she said, "then that means—"

"Someone knows I'm here. Maybe they tortured him to find out more, then killed him and stuffed him in that boat. Or maybe it was a warning. Someone would find the body—because divers visit that shipwreck—and then I would know and come out of hiding."

"And there is no one else you can go to? Police? FBI? Turn yourself in while they investigate?"

He slowly shook his head. "I would be dead before my name is cleared."

"Who are these people that can get to you, kill you even while you're in custody?"

"Dangerous people."

"And I thought *I* had problems."

"You do. You have problems. And me staying here—now

that I know my location has been exposed—only puts you in more danger. Brings more trouble to your town."

"So that's it? You're going to leave?"

He turned and started hiking toward the cabin, because he could no longer look at the complete shock and maybe even a little disdain in her eyes. How did he make her understand? She followed, and this time he wished she hadn't.

"I can protect you, Grier," she said. "Let me help you."

"Just like that? You don't even know my story. I just told you I'm a fugitive, as in from the law."

"And I told you I know nothing about it, and I *am* the law here. I want to know the story. Tell me what crime you witnessed."

This woman. She was feisty and determined. A force to be reckoned with.

A knot lodged in his throat. The day was getting away from him, his life was getting away, and with it, the chief—because he couldn't stay here. How would he protect her? "Look. I . . . I need to leave." Indecision gripped him. "Just come with me." Before she could argue, he added, "Tell your department you're in protective custody at a safe house. They'll understand."

She crossed her arms. "I don't think that's warranted. At least not yet. You know my job hangs in the balance."

"And what about your life?"

"Look. I get it. You've had my back several times the last few days. We . . . we work well together." She fought a smile. "Now I understand why you won't work for me. But we could still work together and solve both our problems. I have an idea."

"What do you have in mind?"

"I need to track down Sarah and question her. Wouldn't you like to know her story? She was out there in the water, and you saving her led to you finding Krueger's body. There's obviously more to her story. You need answers, and so do I. We'll have to travel to find her. So that gets us both out of town while I'm waiting to learn more about the guy who got to me last night. And Grier . . . I *can* help you clear your name." She crossed her arms. "But I need to hear the whole story."

If only it were that easy. "You saw what happened to the last person who tried to help me." A trained officer. If only Grier hadn't landed in Shadow Gap and gotten involved with her. "We could both die, and no one would ever know the truth."

And the worst-case scenario? Her town would think she was a dirty cop who helped a wanted fugitive.

He slowed as they approached his cabin, which rested about fifteen yards ahead, and lifted a finger to his lips. Sounds traveled here. He motioned for her to wait, and she crouched near the base of a cottonwood, gripping her gun. He watched the cabin for movement and saw nothing.

If the person after him had gotten inside, he could have let Cap out, in which case the dog would have run right up to Grier. So either Cap was still inside or they'd taken or hurt him. He released a low whistle that Cap would recognize.

Barking resounded inside, and relief whooshed through him. He drew in a breath. But before hiking out into the open, he studied the trees, searching for a sniper. Someone waiting to ambush him. Cap continued to bark.

Should he trust his gut that no one was already here or watching him?

He scrambled down the incline and jogged over to the cabin. His gun ready, he unlocked the door and headed inside. Cap dashed out to play, and Grier quickly cleared the small space.

If someone was out there, the dog would let him know—he hoped. Cap found someone, all right—the chief emerging from the edge of the woods. He motioned for her to join him in the cabin.

"I should check in with Tanya," she said as she stepped inside and closed the door behind her. She pulled out her cell and contacted dispatch.

He let her do her thing while he finished packing everything up.

While Grier was supposed to be hiding here in this isolated corner of the world and waiting for Krueger to help—the only way they figured their plan could work—Grier had put himself out there, maybe too much, to help the chief. His focus had been on her and not so much on what Krueger was doing.

But now two nefarious forces were bearing down on this town, and on the chief. One of them Grier brought with him. He thought the news footage would have given away his location, but Krueger had to have given him up. He imagined the amount of torture it would have taken to cause Krueger—a highly trained officer—to talk.

Grier squeezed his eyes shut and let the thought of his friend suffering rock through him for just a moment.

Unease settled deep in his bones.

Why hadn't those who wanted Grier silenced already come for him? What were they waiting for?

Maybe they had learned from Krueger that he was *somewhere* in the Shadow Gap area, but they didn't want to be seen in the small town looking for him or asking questions about where he lived.

They were biding their time for him to find their warning and then, once he tried to flee the area, they would follow and make sure he disappeared forever in Alaska.

But only after they retrieved the information they wanted from him.

The pressure was increasing, closing in around him—around them both—and he paced the small space, trying to figure out what to do next. If he hadn't gotten entangled in Chief Long's life, he could just walk away and disappear on his own.

Get lost like so many others in Alaska. He could go to the Alaska Triangle—disappear there. But that wasn't happening, so he wouldn't waste another thought on it.

God, where do we go? What do we do?

"Earth to Grier." The chief had ended her call and now pulled him back to the moment. To the here and now.

Her brows furrowed, and she stepped closer. "So what do you say? Let's go find Sarah. I informed Tanya I would be following up on that lead while we wait to learn more about my stalker. Are you with me?"

"Where is she?" he asked. "You said you didn't know."

"And you said you would contact her—so do it. See if she responds."

He dug his cell from his pocket. After he found the number the chief had given him, he texted a message identifying himself and asking Sarah to meet. On his cell, he noticed he had a new email.

"How is that possible?"

"What is it?" She peered over his shoulder.

"The only contact I had with Krueger was through an anonymous and untraceable email account. But he sent me an email this morning."

She peered at him. "He's dead."

"Right."

"Someone obviously got access to the email account," she said. "Maybe it contains a threat or a warning, or if you open it, you'll download tracking software or an app that will allow them to hear you and watch you. I wouldn't open it."

He looked at her, took in her amazing, one-of-a-kind eyes filled with determination. "You need to go. Get as far away from me as you can. That's for the best."

"I'm staying."

Fine. "And I'm opening the email."

She pursed her lips. "Then we'll read the email together. You're going to help me find Sarah and learn the truth. I'm going to help clear your name."

Why would she go so far out on a limb for him? "How do you know I'm telling the truth?"

"Granted, I've only known you for a few months, but in that time I've seen you step up and sacrifice for others repeatedly. Actions speak louder than words. As Birdy pointed out, you've got mettle, and I know what I need to know about you, Grier."

That surprised him. "She said that. About me?"

"Yep."

"I could be a criminal who's lying to you right now."

"You could be, but I don't believe that's the case. Now, are you going to open that email or not?"

Grier clicked on the email from a dead man.

# TWENTY-EIGHT

I n the passenger seat of the cockpit in Carrie's Helio, Autumn stared out at the stunning snowcapped mountains and the glaciers spilling into the waterways. The Juneau Icefield especially captivated her.

Grier sat quietly in the seat behind her, probably thinking through their next steps. Carrie hadn't asked any questions—wasn't good for business, she'd claimed—as she flew them to Juneau, where they would catch the next Alaska Airlines flight to Anchorage. In total, flying from Shadow Gap to Juneau and then over to Anchorage took three and a half to four hours—and by plane was the fastest route, versus bus or car from Haines (after they took a boat to Haines), which took from one to two days.

As the plane hit a rough patch, Autumn squeezed her eyes shut, trying to ignore the queasiness building inside that had nothing to do with the turbulence and everything to do with the man sitting behind her—he still hadn't told her what or who he was running from.

And her father, who remained hospitalized in Anchorage, wasn't faring well. At first, the transfer had been for his protection, but he'd since developed an infection, so moving him had turned out to be fortuitous. Providence Alaska Medical Center in Anchorage was better equipped to deal with the hard stuff.

Autumn had worked as a police officer under her father for seven years, and now as chief, she had to ask herself if *she* was equipped to deal with the hard stuff. She'd gone through trauma at eight but had gotten over it, and the incident had only solidified her desire to work in law enforcement. But she had no experience with major crimes, only small-town ones, for which she was grateful. Shadow Gap had felt like the perfect place.

Hiding in the shadows of the fjord, the town had felt like a refuge from the world. But what did Autumn know? Now that the outside had crept into her town, she had to fight the waves of nausea and force a calm she didn't feel. But resolve flooded her—she would beat this new criminal element that had entered her world.

As for Dad? She saw now that he hadn't prepared her for what she might face in the future. Come to think of it, neither had Grandpa Ike. He'd only shared the shocking truth when it became necessary, which to Autumn's way of thinking was entirely too late. She hadn't had enough time to process what he revealed, but the night he told her the news, she wasn't able to sleep and that's how she ended up spotting the man skulking around the Lively Moose—and Grier closing in on him.

Too much blood and death had rained down on Shadow Gap in the span of a few short days, and she wanted to know why now. Why ever? She had two investigations to solve before someone else was hurt or killed, and that was two too many.

But she refused to let self-doubt creep in and paralyze her or knock her off her game.

With God's help, I can do this.

And admittedly, maybe she'd been a little impulsive when she told Grier she would help him. She had no idea what she was getting into.

Whatever was going on with Grier, she knew in her heart that he was innocent, and apparently all alone. But not anymore. Autumn was with him in this. When he first showed up, she'd sensed that he was trouble—but that wasn't quite true. Trouble simply followed him, and apparently she'd joined him in being a trouble magnet.

He needed her help.

And, he insisted, she needed his.

So be it.

Now, together, they had set out to protect each other and find answers. To get those answers, Autumn would question her father and one other person. Yesterday via the account that Martin Krueger had used to communicate with Grier, they discovered an email from Sarah with instructions for Grier to meet her alone in two days in Skagway. She hadn't received Autumn's or Grier's texts. She'd gotten a burner phone because she thought she was being followed.

Sarah—if it was actually Sarah who emailed Grier—said she would find him in Skagway, after she confirmed that he hadn't been followed. Autumn wasn't in a position to argue the best place to meet, so they planned to head to Skagway after talking to her father. But they had time to figure out the details while they traveled to Anchorage to see Autumn's father.

At least by following this lead, Autumn was working on an investigation tied to Shadow Gap instead of hiding in some off-grid safe house. Staying on the move and being unpredictable in her activities with Grier at her side was a win-win. She'd informed Tanya she was investigating, and Tanya would know how to hold the proverbial wolves at bay until she got back. Craig and Angie could handle Shadow Gap while she was gone. Everyone would keep their eyes open for her still unidentified abductor.

Or . . . would he follow her?

If so, all the better. She wanted another chance to take him down.

Four hours later, they finally entered the hospital in Anchorage. Autumn pulled her Shadow Gap police jacket tighter as they maneuvered the hallways.

They stepped into an elevator alone. "Nolan is supposed to meet us here."

Jaw tight, Grier's expression remained drawn.

She wouldn't bother asking if he was okay. Neither of them would be okay until they untangled this mess.

"Maybe he's learned who's behind your abduction," he said. "Who's after you."

The elevator doors dinged open, and she stepped out into the sterile hallway, followed by Grier. They passed a small chapel, and she had the sudden urge to run inside and fall to her knees and pray.

God, why is my quiet town suddenly filled with terror?

But one step at a time. She'd question Dad, and after she had those answers, she would focus on finding out what specific crime Grier hadn't committed.

But first, Nolan had some explaining to do. After what Grandpa Ike told her, she could better understand Dad's awful spiral into depression and alcoholism, at least to a point. He hadn't been able to bring himself to tell Autumn the truth. But Nolan?

Why hadn't he ever told her that their mother was still alive?

# TWENTY-NINE

Autumn walked the hospital halls, heading to her father's secured room with Grier at her side. She tried to ignore the tension spilling off him. He'd been forced from his self-imposed hiding place in Shadow Gap and probably felt exposed on all sides.

She certainly did. She would help him, but once the news got out, it would appear to others like she was working with a *wanted* fugitive. She'd received the ballistics report and now knew that Monica and Kenny were shot with the same gun. Not unexpected. But Martin Krueger had been shot with a different gun. That didn't negate the possibility they were all murdered by the same person. So in the meantime, she still didn't know if Monica's and Kenny's deaths were related to Grier and his fugitive status. Although, clearly, this fugitive had already been found—but by the wrong sort of people.

And it made her wonder—what were they waiting for?

Why wasn't someone pulling Grier out of a sunken boat with a bullet in his head? She shuddered at the thought. Maybe Grier held information they needed. Anxiety pressed in on her and she wanted to glance his way, but instead she concentrated

211

on the Anchorage PD officer standing in the hallway focused on his task three doors down.

Together Grier and Autumn passed the nurses' station and finally came to Dad's door. Her palms grew moist.

She showed the officer her credentials, and he grinned. "I've been expecting you. Nolan told me to tell you to wait for him. He'll be back."

Great. Nolan was supposed to be here. She wanted answers from him before she faced Dad. "Did he say when?"

"I'm afraid not."

No matter. She sent Nolan a quick text to get back ASAP, then nodded at the officer. "Thanks for watching over Dad for us." She gestured to Grier behind her. "And he's with me."

Autumn fisted her hands rather than wipe the moisture on her khaki pants, then opened the door. She tried to project confidence she didn't feel as she entered Dad's private room. He was paler than he'd been after the gunshot wound and blood loss. Multiple IV tubes connected to one main tube in his arm.

His eyes were closed. Now might not be the best time to ask him, but if not now, then when? What if he died and she never got those answers? Unfortunately, she'd avoided learning the truth for far too long. That was on her.

"Chief." Grier's gentle nudge from behind encouraged her to enter all the way into Dad's room.

And . . . Dad opened his eyes and was looking at her. She forced a smile as she moved to stand next to his bed. "How are you feeling?"

Sweat beaded on his forehead and temples. "Water."

She reached for the pitcher and poured him a cup, then handed it over. His hands trembled, and she assisted him in drinking. Her heart stumbled. Was she going to lose him? She blinked back the sudden ache of tears.

"Dad, you're burning up."

"No, the fever is breaking. I'm doing better. The doctor says the infection is under control."

She wasn't so sure, but she held on to that hope.

Grier eased into a chair in the corner while Autumn pulled a recliner close and sat on the edge. "I'm so sorry this happened." She grabbed his hand.

"I'm the one who's sorry," he said.

"I know this is probably not the best time to talk."

He nodded. "But you want to know about that day."

"I do."

"Now's the time," he said. "I had hoped this day would never come, honestly. We were doing well in Shadow Gap, weren't we?"

"I think so, yes. It's been a nice long run of peace and quiet. But now I need to know the truth behind what's been eating you. I need to know everything about what happened the night Mom drowned and what it has to do with the shooting and the danger you're in."

"You're the one in danger."

She hadn't told him about her abduction, but he'd warned her. "Clearly he wanted you too. Though we got your shooter, someone is still out there, Dad. Do you remember the picture I showed you?"

Dad closed his eyes and nodded.

"You said you didn't recognize anyone. But I recognized the man. I'll show you those pictures again, but in the meantime, I want the story. I want to know what happened that day—behind the scenes. I only know parts of the story." Autumn glanced at the door. *Come on, Nolan . . .*

"Does he have to be here?" Dad stared at Grier.

"He's here at my request. So, he stays."

Dad's painful sigh pinged through her heart, and she was glad she was sitting for this return to the trauma of her past. Would Dad tell the same story as Grandpa Ike?

"Your mother and I had been having a lot of issues, and she decided to leave me for another man."

Autumn's insides tightened. She'd already heard as much from her grandfather, but that didn't make it any easier to hear again.

"He was . . . a bad man. As a defense attorney, she somehow connected with him while representing one of his associates. I don't think she knew how bad he was, so I did a lot of digging and tried to show her that she was making a mistake. The man was the head of a transnational organized crime group. You can't get any worse than that. If she went with him, I wasn't going to let her take you from me or even have visitation rights."

Autumn still struggled to believe her mother would have gotten involved with the person Dad described. He closed his eyes and released a ragged sigh. Autumn felt his pain slice through her too.

"She chose to give us another chance—for you and Nolan. I was desperate to fix our family, so I took all our money from savings and bought that ridiculous yacht, a foolish decision. I could never compete financially with the man she'd fallen for. But I wanted to try and offer a glamorous life—whatever it took to keep us together. She'd ended things with him, but he wasn't the kind of man who would allow that. If he couldn't have your mother, then neither could I.

"After that day, after she drowned, he swore that he would take you from me because I took the woman he loved from him. The night that you found me shot, he had sent someone to the house looking for *you*. I tried to stop him. To take him down, but my lame arm . . ."

Oh, Dad. Autumn pulled up the man's image from her cell and showed it to her father. "Is this him?"

"That's his brother who works for him. With him."

"Why now? Why all of a sudden?"

"His brother, Mateo Santos, was released from prison a few

months ago and will be running the operation for Rafael, and it appears fulfilling his past threats to me is a top priority."

"Why didn't you tell me about this so I wouldn't be blind-sided? What about Nolan? Is he in danger too?"

Autumn hadn't known about her parents' issues. All of it weighed painfully on her heart, and she wanted to curl into a ball when she got home. But right now, she needed to see this through.

"As far as I know, he's only after you. You . . . You look just like her." Grief edged his words.

"If you intended to hide us when you left Topeka, why re-main a police chief? You'd be easy to find. You're not telling me everything, Dad."

"I wasn't hiding. Rafael and Mateo were finally captured and incarcerated, and I wasn't worried about him coming after you. Not until recently. Running and hiding was no kind of life for you. I brought you to your mother's childhood home, where you would know your grandparents, and for the last many years, I prayed this day would never come. That he would forget his threats and get over the past."

Autumn's heart jumped to her throat with her next question. "And what about Mom?"

He looked at her long and hard as if trying to learn if she already knew the truth, but he simply pursed his lips rather than tell her that her mother faked her own death to protect her family from the man she rejected.

But his response didn't satisfy Autumn.

"Where is she?"

"I honestly don't know, and I don't want to know."

Dad is lying to me, and to himself.

THIRTY

Grier walked out of the room, leaving Autumn with her father. He nodded at the officer at the door and made a beeline for the vending machine down the hallway, where he grabbed two black coffees.

He couldn't stand to hear more. He already knew a bad man was after her, but the reasons for that were heart-wrenching. Her mother was still alive? Man, how long had she known? What did learning that kind of hard truth do to a person?

He didn't have those kinds of family dynamics to deal with. He grew up in Indiana, but when he was nine, his parents died in a car accident, and he went to live with his aunt in Omaha. Then he headed off to college, and after his aunt died, he had no one else. So he got sucked into an obscure three-letter agency. He hadn't told Autumn the truth yet because he feared putting her in even more danger.

Right now he was playing the wait-and-see game.

But she was on a truth hunt, and his time would come. For now he would let her digest what her father had shared, including the criminal's name. That would go a long way in helping law enforcement take him down.

Again.

In the meantime, he handed off the extra coffee to the offi-cer standing outside the hospital room door. "You can let her know I'm in the waiting area." He gestured to the space at the end of the hall.

"Will do," the officer said. "Thanks for the coffee."

The agency had kept Grier's wanted status under wraps and in-house, but he looked for them to go public with it soon. If they couldn't bring him in quietly, then they would use other tactics. Now that the chief and Grier knew the name of the man after her and could share that with law enforcement, maybe he would be captured soon and Grier could disappear. Because if the chief was killed in all this mess—his *or* her mess—he couldn't live with himself.

Maybe he couldn't live with himself anyway because he was responsible for Krueger's death.

Krueger . . . his chest tightened. The man had sacrificed everything to help Grier. He never should have let Krueger try to secure the evidence to clear Grier's name. And he shouldn't allow the chief to help him either, but he wanted to protect her since she was entangled in someone else's mess through no fault of her own.

The sins of the father? Or the mother?

He headed for the waiting area, feeling the officer's eyes on his back. Anchorage—the Alaska mainland—was a long way from his hiding place in the Alaska Panhandle, and the skin on his back and neck prickled. He glanced at the time on his cell and took a seat.

While drinking the too-hot coffee, he thought about all the possible scenarios—good and bad—that could happen over the next hours and days. Working out all the possibilities would help him be prepared. And then when it was all over, would he still be alive? Would the chief be back in Shadow Gap safe and sound? Her father too?

Shoes squeaked up and down the hallway—nurses, doctors,

and medical staff coming and going. Monitors beeped and voices spoke in low tones.

"What are *you* doing here?" The familiar voice held accusation.

Grier tried not to bristle as he glanced up to face Nolan. Like sister, like brother. Where did he even start in answering that question? Grier stood and thrust his free hand out to shake Nolan's, surprised that his grip was met. "The chief asked me to come."

Nolan narrowed his gaze as he released Grier's hand. He hadn't realized the scope of Nolan's dislike of him, but maybe it was because the guy had the wrong idea about the two of them. Clearly, if something were going on between them—at least that they admitted to each other and the world—Grier wouldn't have Nolan's blessing when it came to his sister.

"Your father told the chief his story." Grier lifted his coffee cup. "You might have missed the best part, unless you already know, that is."

"Don't go anywhere." Nolan turned and headed to his father's room.

I wouldn't dream of it.

Nolan disappeared down the hall, and against his better judgment, Grier decided to follow—from a distance. He needed another cup of coffee. Yeah. That was it. He stood in front of the vending machine and heard voices.

Nolan and his sister had moved down the hall from her father's room and now stood against the wall behind him. He could see their reflections in the vending machine glass. They spoke in hushed tones, then she looked up and caught Grier watching in the reflection. Her ridiculously stunning eyes grew big as she stared unblinking at him. Those eyes, this woman, had captivated him from the first moment he'd seen her months ago when he'd entered the salmon fishing contest—Krueger's idea for situating him in the Shadow Gap community.

Nolan suddenly stared at him too. Grier focused on getting coffee and ignoring the siblings.

They obviously had issues to work through, and this wasn't his business. At least he now understood the kind of criminal that had set his sights on Chief Autumn Long.

But how did Grier keep her safe?

Was he arrogant to think she needed anyone's help or that he needed to be the one to do it? If she needed that from anyone, her brother was capable and had the connections. Another cup of coffee in his hands, Grier finally turned and stepped across the hall and into the middle of Nolan and the chief's heated discussion. He couldn't miss the stiff set of Nolan's jaw. The furrow in the chief's brow. The two stared as if waiting for him to inject his thoughts into their discussion.

He should keep his mouth shut. Wait and listen. He took a sip of the coffee that burned his tongue, but he downed it without complaint.

The chief huffed and gestured for him to follow her.

The three of them ended up sitting in Nolan's Chevy pickup. Like her father had been uncomfortable with Grier in his hospital room, Nolan appeared uncomfortable with Grier in his truck.

"Look, Nolan," the chief said. "Grier has proved himself to be invaluable, and I need him in this with me."

"Is he working with you in an official capacity? If he's not, that could be a problem when it comes to gathering evidence."

"Grier is working with me."

She hadn't added the "unofficially" part. But her words seemed to satisfy Nolan.

"Okay. Good enough. Now that that's settled, here's your gun." Nolan handed over her Staccato P that she'd given up after shooting the man who shot their father. "You're all cleared."

"And that's it?"

"That's it."

"Thanks. So what have you got?"

"The man who we believe abducted you is Mateo Santos. He works for his brother, Rafael, who runs a criminal organization out of Costa del Sol, a region in southern Spain practically overtaken by criminal organizations from across the world. They work together, specializing in different trafficking rings. Rafael remains in prison, and Mateo was recently released."

"I got some of the story from Dad, but I don't understand how our mother, a defense attorney in Kansas, could get mixed up with someone like this. It makes no sense."

"I've been digging, and I think she met him when her firm was representing one of Rafael's minions—someone starting a new distribution point in Kansas."

"Why would she represent someone like that?"

"To make sure he got a fair trial," Grier said. "That he wasn't framed or set up." Grier understood that perspective.

"Rafael was paying the firm through a shell company," Nolan offered. "I'm not sure that she was in love with him or planned to leave our family of her own accord."

"What are you saying?"

"I think Rafael was fascinated by her." Nolan turned to his sister. "You have her distinctive eyes. I'm sure you've experienced some unwanted attention from strangers."

Nolan worked his jaw—he'd intended the dig at Grier. But Nolan didn't understand that his sister *wanted* Grier's attention. He could almost smile inside at that.

The chief nodded. "So you think he threatened to hurt her family if she didn't go with him."

"I think it's possible," Nolan said. "When Rafael was extradited and then incarcerated, she thought she was free. I think that's when she agreed to try again with Dad. Mateo hadn't been captured yet and stepped in to end her," Nolan said. "So now you can understand why she—"

"Faked her own death. To protect us."

Grier sat back and listened, new questions forming in his mind. "What does this Rafael's organization traffic in?"

Nolan rubbed his forehead, then said, "I was only able to read a snippet of the file, which included the usual arms, drugs, people, but it seemed more like he majored in intellectual property and money laundering. His brother is still out there, and Dad was right, Autumn, you're in danger." Nolan's sigh was gruff and painful. "I think you should stay here with me. I'll get you twenty-four-hour protection until this is wrapped up."

Which was as it should be, so why did Grier bristle at the thought? This could be his real chance to walk away. He should encourage her. "He's right, Chief."

She glanced over her shoulder at him, and he didn't miss the hurt in her eyes before she blinked it away.

"I can't abandon my town and the two officers I have left. In the meantime, I'm working on an investigation that keeps me moving and not so easily targeted. That said, Grier and I have an appointment we need to keep. Thanks for the information, Nolan."

Without waiting for her brother's reaction, the chief opened the truck door and stepped out.

Nolan twisted to look at Grier. "Will you talk to her?"

"What makes you think she'll listen to me?"

Nolan scowled. "Then at the least, protect her."

"In case you hadn't noticed, your sister is an experienced police chief."

"Are you saying she can protect herself from the likes of Mateo? In cases like this, even the most skilled law enforcement officers out there need protection. Need someone to have their backs. And right now, it looks like you're all she'll allow. I hope you've got skills."

I hope I do too. Grier's turn to get out. He'd already tried to talk her into staying at a safe house, but this plan of remaining on the move was as good as going off-grid.

He followed Autumn to their rental vehicle. This time, she got into the passenger seat. He glanced at her before turning on the vehicle and cranking up the heat. He still hadn't grown accustomed to the high temperature being fifty-two degrees. He steered out of the parking lot and along Northern Lights Boulevard, hugging the perimeter fence of the airport, then followed the road south until he parked at Point Woronzof. They had time before their flight back.

He climbed out to give her space and walked around to lean against the front of the vehicle, though he hoped she would join him in looking across the waters of the Knick Arm at snow-capped Denali in the distance. Of all the areas he thought he'd end up, Alaska was the last place on earth he ever dreamed he would be, especially for the reasons he was here. And even more surprising, the woman he was with.

She got out and came around to stand next to him. "I might not know a lot about you, but I know you're not from Alaska. How'd you know about this place?"

"I skim tourist brochures here and there, when I'm waiting on you." He tossed her a grin. "Now we need to walk the trail to the beach. Are you up for it?"

Her features remained tight, and she hesitated.

"Come on, Chief. You could use the fresh air to clear your mind. We have a long flight home."

She nodded. "You're right."

She took off down the trail, and he strolled next to her. While he'd wanted a reprieve, and for the tension to drain out of them both, he couldn't let his guard down for even a moment. Others strolled the gray beach as well, so they weren't alone. They found a large chunk of driftwood—an old whitewashed tree trunk—to sit on.

If only for a few minutes.

He remained silent, listening to the lapping waves. Then finally, he said, "This is supposed to be a great place to see bald eagles."

When she didn't say anything, he was left to imagine what she was thinking. And her brother's words came back to him.

"Will you talk to her?"

Yeah. Sure. He would try.

Again.

He blew out a breath, then started in. "Listen, I don't think you can afford to alienate your brother. He's, well, your brother, for one. And he has resources. He's willing to bend a few rules to help the cause of justice. Maybe you should consider taking a few days off and staying in Anchorage. Nobody would fault you for it."

That earned him a glare, along with raised eyebrows. "Oh, but wouldn't they? We're having a crime spree in Shadow Gap and the police chief is a no-show?"

He shifted on the log, wanting to reach for her hand. To touch her cheek. He hated that the memory of their kiss flooded him now. "Look . . ." He'd never called her by her first name for his own reasons, but he desperately wanted to say it now, and the thought pinged around in his heart. "I get it. Your job is important. But it's not worth your life. That aside, I think you have bigger issues to talk about."

He let those words hang in the air, uncertain which issue she would bring up, but he thought he had an idea.

She stared straight ahead, and by the look in her eyes, he knew she was miles away. She blinked at unshed tears. "All these years, I believed it was my fault Mom died. She drowned swimming me to shore. Or so I'd thought."

And there it was—she had shared what had to be her deepest wound with him. He wasn't sure he deserved to hear it.

THIRTY-ONE

Once the proverbial gate had been opened, Autumn couldn't stop the flood of words. They'd been building up in her chest for far too long as it was, and she couldn't hold the emotions inside any longer. Grier was the man of the hour—the person who happened to be with her, so she hoped he was prepared to listen.

Tears surged, but she held them back. Police chiefs weren't supposed to cry.

"Hey," Grier said. "It's okay. I'm here."

Even in front of friends.

She gazed up at Grier and took in his dark-green eyes; strong, scruffy jaw; and thick hair. She couldn't think of anyone else she would rather share with. And maybe that was wrong of her.

"That day. Mom argued with the men who threatened her, threatened us. She rushed me off the boat, jumping with me. Then it exploded behind us. Debris rained down into the water. She tugged me out of the way and to safety, and then we began the long swim back. Mom mostly kept me going when I grew tired. At some point she was the one swimming for the both of us, holding me like I was an unconscious person. She never complained, and I never even thought about her growing tired."

"You were just a kid."

Autumn pressed her hands against her face. Gathered what she had left of her composure. Then looked out over the water. The blue sky was quickly filling with clouds, and she could no longer see Denali in the distance.

"I don't remember exactly what happened. I know that I crawled up the beach and laid on my back, exhausted and in shock. I might have passed out. I don't remember. I don't know how long I was there, but long enough that day turned to night, and eventually I was staring up at the stars. That night the sky was filled with a meteor shower. I finally had the energy to sit up and then realized . . . she was gone. She never made it to shore."

"And authorities assumed she drowned?"

"Yes. That she brought me far enough and released me, but a riptide must have taken her away. Basically, she was too tired by that point to fight back."

"That had to have been a traumatic experience for you."

She nodded. "I curled into myself after that. I know lots of conversation went on around me, with the authorities searching for her. The men were assumed dead with the boat, but clearly at least one of them survived. And according to Dad, so did Mom."

"When did your father know?"

"He didn't exactly say, but according to my grandfather, she contacted my grandparents about three years ago. That's when they learned their daughter was still alive. Nolan was with them when they heard from her, so he knew. Why did everyone keep this from me?"

"I don't have the answers, Chief"—his voice was gentle, compassionate—"but it sounds like she believed your lives were in danger as long as she remained alive. So she made the ultimate sacrifice by faking her death so that her presence in your life would no longer endanger you. I can't know the true reasons why this information was kept from you, but I can see how your family thought the news could bring tremendous pain. They wanted to spare you the hurt. It sounds like her goal is to remain dead to the rest of the world, so even now, you can't see her."

Grier stared out over the water, shaking his head. He appeared to be going through the pain of it with her even though he had his own serious problems.

Autumn nodded and drew in a harsh breath to shove back the gathering tears. "I made it my mission in life to be the best swimmer I could be. The best diver too. Every year I went back to the Caribbean—where it all started—to dive and chase away the fears. And now, to learn that she survived?"

Family secrets could shatter a person. Autumn stood and stepped closer to the water, but not so close that the waves soaked her shoes.

Grier sidled next to her, turned her to face him, and loosely gripped her arms. "You refused to let what happened in the past destroy you, and you won't let this news take you down either. You're the strongest person I know."

He offered a tenuous smile. And while she understood he struggled to know how to comfort her, the depth of emotion in his eyes told her how much he cared—and that smoothed away the pain wrinkling across her heart, her thoughts. She was glad he was here with her, because he was the only person who could truly comfort her at this moment.

Grier and, well, God.

For the life of her, Autumn wasn't sure God could fix this, if he even wanted to. She hung her head and listened to the rhythmic lap of the waves, a train running somewhere nearby, and the planes taking off. At this moment, she was glad she lived in Southeast Alaska in a veritable crook in the mountains, away from all the noise and chaos. And she understood Dad's choices a lot better now. He had wanted that quiet and solitude too.

Finally, she looked at Grier. "Thanks for your vote of confidence. I still have so many questions." At least one of her questions might have been answered—now she thought she understood what had driven Dad to drink, but there had to be a better way for him to work through his grief and find comfort. To find closure.

She didn't have time to waste on past regrets—not until they were no longer in danger. Autumn or Grier. She shrugged out of his grip and crossed her arms. "Now I want to hear *your* story, Grier Brenner. All of it."

He glanced at his cell. "You will, but right now we need to get to the airport so we don't miss our flight."

After the flight to Juneau, Carrie delivered Autumn and Grier to Skagway. She and Grier agreed that going back to Shadow Gap now was too dangerous. They booked two rooms at a hotel in downtown Skagway using cash and would be ready to meet Sarah in the morning, or rather, let Sarah find them.

Exhaustion weighed on her, but so did the questions. Autumn suggested dinner at the small hotel restaurant and then an early night. They were seated at the back of the room in the shadows where they could look out across the room. One small candle lit up the table.

Autumn yawned, then glanced across at Grier, who stared at the menu.

"I'm putting a lot of trust in you, Grier. I . . . I'd planned to run a background check on you when we got back, but we're already thick into this. Still, I want to know."

He glanced up from the menu. "I'm surprised you haven't done that already."

"I didn't have a legitimate reason, except now you've told me you're a fugitive. But I don't want to give Wally another tally on the scoresheet he's keeping on me. He could think I'm checking into you for . . . other reasons. The system is tracked, and I wouldn't put it past Craig to keep tabs." She could be criminally charged, in fact. Wally would use it if he could.

Grier set his menu on the table. "I know what I want, Chief. What about you?"

"And that's another thing. Haven't I already told you to call me Autumn?" She glanced at the menu, her appetite gone. But she needed to eat to keep up her strength. "I'm just having a burger."

"Same," Grier said. He sipped from the glass of water the waiter had already delivered.

The waiter returned and took their orders, then left them to stare at each other over the candle. The ambiance was romantic. Grier might be everything she wanted in a man . . . under different circumstances. She was attracted to him in every way, not just physically. And maybe, if she were honest with herself—brutally honest, that was—the fact that he remained a mystery intrigued her, drew her in and kept her there.

"I think it's time for you to come clean."

He grinned, and that alone charmed her. Disarmed her. Autumn had never been one to fall for good looks or charm, so maybe that's why she hadn't been guarding herself against the likes of him. Throw in all his heroics and the danger factor, and she'd walked onto the pages of a romantic thriller novel.

Thrills aside, this wasn't fiction. It was real, and their lives were on the line.

"What are you smiling for? This isn't funny."

"You want me to come clean. Your choice of words makes it sound like you believe I'm guilty."

"I'm counting on you being innocent." She leaned in and kept her voice low. "But the fact that you've successfully avoided telling me your story concerns me."

"I don't want to tell you because that would put you in more danger."

"Whatever is going on with you, the people after you, you can assume they believe I know everything."

"And that's on me." Grier stared at the flickering candle as if unwilling to look her in the eyes. "That's why I think your mother did the right thing. She protected you. Me? I was supposed to stay invisible in Shadow Gap. Not get close to anyone. Not draw attention. Not make friends. Or care."

Then he chose to look up, and the longing that stirred in his eyes seized her heart. She could barely breathe. "Grier, I . . ."

"I let myself care about you. Get involved in your life. And I wanted to protect you, but now with the trouble that followed me here, I see my mistake."

"Please don't talk to me like you're making a deathbed confession."

He hesitated, then huffed. "I don't know how I'm going to get out of this alive."

His words shocked her. She reached across the table and grabbed his hand. Willed him to feel how much she cared. Willed him to believe they were getting out of this alive. He would survive, and when the dust settled, he would be free. "You don't mean that. Of course you're going to live. And I'm going to help you."

The waiter brought their food and asked if they needed anything else. Autumn quickly dismissed him.

"You don't think I *can* help you, do you?"

"I don't want you in this. I should go meet Sarah myself, but there's the issue of this Mateo guy who's still at large. I would have preferred you stayed with your brother and he protected you. And then I could learn what I can from Sarah."

"And disappear again."

Lines appeared in his forehead. She'd never seen Grier this serious about anything. "First, I want to make sure you're safe. I hope they take down Mateo soon. This isn't how I thought things would turn out. I thought I had time. That Krueger would clear my name."

"Now that you brought him up, tell me everything. I want to be ready for our meeting with Sarah tomorrow."

He hung his head again and nodded. A few seconds ticked by, then he finally said, "I was a Navy SEAL."

Her heart lurched. "I knew it."

She waited a few more seconds, hoping he would tell her more.

"A cryptology technician, to be specific. But I went on to work with the NSA in their Scorpion Program—SCS, Special Collection Service. Officially, we don't exist."

"I've never heard of it. What would I find if I searched on the internet?"

"You would find sites that say it doesn't exist and others that say it does."

Realization dawned. "And that's why you're not on any official fugitive list."

"Exactly. SCS is a joint NSA-CIA program."

"Highly classified."

He nodded. "I shouldn't be telling you."

"But you think you're a dead man walking."

"Possibly."

"Well, you've told me this much. What happened to put you in the wanted fugitive category?"

"My job was to insert eavesdropping equipment in difficult-to-reach places. We went in under diplomatic cover to penetrate foreign communications networks. Does it sound like gibberish?"

"No. It's fascinating, actually." And her admiration for him exploded. Her instincts about him had been correct.

The waiter returned.

Of course. He planned to interrupt them every step of the way. "Is everything all right?"

She glanced at her burger. Grier's burger. Neither of them had touched their meal. Then she looked up at the waiter apologetically. "I'm sure the food is great, thank you. We need time to talk."

"Of course." He gave a nod, then stepped away. She stared at him until he got the message and went across the room to another table.

"I want to know what happened. Who was Martin Krueger?"

"Krueger was one of the CIA intelligence officers, operatives, I was working with, along with two others, including a technician. We intercepted and transmitted information, and often deciphered it. Unfortunately, we learned a foreign government official—"

"You're not going to tell me the names of the other agents or the official?"

"The names don't matter." He stared at the flame. "The official was funded by massive amounts of laundered money. Let's call the other agents Brown and Blue. Brown tried to steal the intercepted information and siphon money for himself, and when Blue learned of it, she was killed. Brown is framing me for the murder, going to his superiors with fake evidence about me, conveniently leaving out the stolen financial information. Brown intended to kill me so I couldn't counter his claim. Krueger sent me into hiding while he found solid evidence against Brown. In the meantime, Krueger went along with Brown and acted like he believed I was guilty."

"So he could keep working at finding the evidence to prove your innocence."

"Yes."

"Did Krueger witness any of it? If he did, then he could have cleared it all up. But I'm guessing he didn't, otherwise he wouldn't have needed to find the evidence. In which case, why did he believe you were innocent?"

His head bobbed. "Because like you, he knew me. Trusted me. He was already suspicious of Brown. Was already digging up evidence on him." He rubbed his mouth and chin. "I suspect that Krueger might have been put in place to watch Brown. But now he's gone." Grier frowned deeply. "Unfortunately, I believe I now understand why Krueger placed me in Shadow Gap."

She studied him. What was he getting at? "You mean other than it's in the middle of nowhere. Who would think to look for you there?"

Grier held her gaze as if willing her to make the connection on her own.

She'd had two Red Notice guys—international fugitives—in her backyard. A guy from an international criminal organization here in town to get revenge because of her mom. The guy who shot Dad, who was likely connected to said organization. And Grier's murdered Krueger—all tied together? The weight of it dropped in her stomach, and she groaned. She stilled her pounding heart, leaned in, and whispered.

"According to Nolan's information, Rafael's organization launders money. Are you saying he's the connection? That you were in Shadow Gap because of my connection to him? I don't get it."

"Krueger was an intelligence analyst before he became a field operative. We intercepted the transfer of information, but we still didn't know where it came from and were in the process of digging into that when Blue was killed and I had to make a run for it. Then Krueger told me he'd discovered that the criminal organization that had laundered the money and funded the official was out of Costa del Sol. He sent me to Shadow Gap to stay, well, in the shadows."

"Costa del Sol. According to Nolan, that's where Santos's organization is based. I still don't understand. What's the connection?"

"In unearthing everything about Rafael Santos, Krueger must have learned about the connection he had to a certain attorney who disappeared years ago. I suspect he heard chatter about something involving you, Chief Autumn Long—the daughter of the attorney. All I can figure is that Krueger wanted to monitor us and thought it would be easier to keep an eye on both of us in Shadow Gap. The only other thing I can think . . ." He trailed off, his frown deepening as he shook his head.

"He knew you would protect me if I was in danger—that you not only had the skills, but you would recognize the threat."

Grier nodded. "Except I didn't recognize the threat soon enough."

"And the Red Notice fugitives?"

"I can't know if they were here for you or for me. Brown could have sent them for me, or Mateo could have hired them to watch you or assist in taking you."

Autumn tried to wrap her mind around the fact that two separate entities bearing down on her and Grier were connected.

"I have a feeling we'll learn more once we talk to Sarah," he said.

"Agreed," she said. "I'm still not sure about why Kenny and Monica were shot back in May."

"Once we know who's behind Krueger's death, we'll have a better idea who shot them—or not. It's a start. I'm thinking that Monica and Kenny witnessed something and were taken out because of it."

"There's no evidence that Monica and Kenny even knew each other," Autumn said. "Her family was questioned about Kenny, and her parents told us she'd been heading to meet a girlfriend and never arrived. We never found her back in May when she went missing."

Grier leaned closer. "Hank didn't know Kenny was coming to see him, so let's assume Kenny was heading to meet his uncle to surprise him and never made it."

She nodded. "He bought the older snow machine off someone, which my officers confirmed. Maybe he witnessed someone shooting Monica? I don't know. I'm leaning toward she was at the wrong place at the wrong time and was abducted, taken up the mountain to dispose of. Kenny witnessed it, then was also shot and killed." Two people at the wrong place at the wrong time.

"And the avalanche buried their bodies."

"Perfect timing. Too bad it also didn't catch the murderer." She closed her eyes at the morbid images. The two had their whole lives ahead of them. Burning fury erupted inside.

She opened her eyes and searched Grier's gaze.

"Yeah, too bad." He hung his head.

"Something about Krueger's death and your story about Brown doesn't add up. If Brown learned where you were after torturing Krueger, why hasn't he killed you already? I think there's more to it. I think Krueger might have been tortured for another reason. You're not telling me everything. I think you must have information he wants."

With the deep respect that flickered in his gaze, she knew she'd hit the mark. "Grier? What does he want?"

He released a slow sigh. "The cold wallet."

Though she'd suspected something unexpected, hearing him say the words still surprised her. A wave of nausea ripped through her stomach. She hesitated a few breaths before she could ask. "A cold wallet? Where is it? *What* is it?"

"It's a USB drive that holds millions of bank account transfer codes, along with cryptocurrency private keys to convert to a hot wallet—or rather, give access to the funds or send them. It can't be compromised because it's not connected to the internet. In this case, the digital money is illicit. It's what he's after, along with making sure I can never tell another soul about any of it, of course. And if the money was taken from Santos's organization—intercepted before it was handed off to the official—then the Santos brothers want it back too, so they have more than one reason to be here." Grier lifted his head, his expression contemplative. "Part or all of it could be payment to the government official who could be the key to Rafael's release."

A knot lodged in her throat. "*Where* is it?"

"In a safe place."

"With you?" She studied him. "You have it."

"I put it in a safe place."

A cold chill crawled up her spine. Could she have trusted the wrong person, after all?

"Why did you take it?"

 # THIRTY-TWO

The accusation in her gaze gutted him. He never should have shared so much with her.

She slowly stood from the table and backed away. Given the look on her face, he wouldn't be surprised if she reached for her gun. But she turned and fled. Grier hurried after her. Instead of going to the elevator and up to her room, she rushed through the doors and into the cold night air and a still-busy downtown.

He hurried after her. "Chief!" He caught her arm and swung her around, bracing himself for any defensive moves she might use.

When she stared up at him, her face pale and her eyes pained, she shook her head. He hadn't expected to see so much hurt, and it filleted him.

"I'm innocent. Please let me finish."

I never should have told you.

Then again, this secret he'd held as he hid here in Alaska was what kept them apart—whether she knew the truth or not, it would always be there, standing between them. Better that she knew now before going any deeper with him.

236

An older couple walking by stared at them and quickened their pace. The man looked like he might reach out to the chief to ask if she needed help.

Grier ignored him and stepped closer. "Please . . ." *Autumn.* Now wasn't the time to use her name, because in a weird way, it would feel like he was taking advantage of this emotionally vulnerable moment.

Desperation flooded him. He didn't want to lose her.

I . . . love you.

Her eyes softened. "You have thirty seconds to explain."

He had one chance. One shot to make her understand. His palms slicked. "We can't let them have the money. I must keep it safe. Keep the evidence. Krueger couldn't have it on him. Please understand—I had to disappear with it."

"It makes you look guilty. It makes you look like Brown was telling the truth." Her eyes glistened.

She *cared* about him. He'd suspected. He'd hoped. But now he *saw* it in those eyes he adored, and it was what made this so much harder. But he also saw in her eyes more questions, and he braced himself.

"I need the truth. Are you really innocent? Did you murder Blue?"

If it weren't for the ache knifing through him that she'd asked him this question at all, he could almost smile at her use of his fictional names. "I promise that I'm innocent. You can arrest me yourself at any moment if you think I'm guilty." He thrust out his hands, wrists together, so she could cuff him. A few seconds of uncertainty passed, a few thumps of his heart, as he waited to learn his fate.

She stepped back. "What now, Grier? How do we prove you're innocent?"

With her question, relief blew through him. Though doubt still lingered, he recognized the hope surging in her eyes. She believed him, or just desperately *wanted* to believe him.

He needed to think through everything. "Let's head back in and see if our dinner hasn't been tossed. I'm still hungry."

Her eyes widened. "Seriously? I've completely lost my appetite."

Relief washed over him that they were back to normal—and normal was relative, of course.

"You're going to need your strength."

Back in the restaurant, they caught the waiter as he was clearing the table and took their seats again. He brought them fresh water. Their burgers were cold, but they ate anyway.

The chief leaned in. "We know Mateo is after me in Shadow Gap, but are we sure he knows you have the cold wallet?"

"I think he probably does, yes." Grier bit into his burger, which should have tasted fantastic but instead was flavorless. After he chewed and swallowed, he finished his thought. "He would have been trying to find out what happened to it and could have learned about our SIGINT—signals intelligence— operations. His organization has connections within the intelligence community."

They finished their meal in silence, both caught up in their thoughts. After dinner, he walked with her up to their connected hotel rooms and said good night. He figured she wouldn't sleep any better than he would, given everything that had been dumped in her lap today. Knowledge of her mother's survival trumped Grier's story, by far, but regardless, the danger factor had increased.

He rested in bed and stared out the second-floor window. The aurora borealis had taken up the night sky. Now that he knew Sarah was connected to Krueger, he believed she held the missing piece—the evidence that could clear him.

The next morning, Grier met Autumn downstairs, and they ate a quick breakfast.

"What now? Sarah didn't give us a meeting place."

"No, but we're here. She said she would find us."

The chief pushed her plate aside, after only eating half her eggs and toast. "That seems risky. For her to find us, we have to be out in the open. Others could find us too, if they're looking here."

"Nothing we can do about it." He finished his coffee, pulled out enough cash for breakfast and a tip, and set it on the table. "Let's walk around and see what happens."

"If you say so." Instead of her uniform, she was wearing a white blouse, blue jeans, and her Shadow Gap jacket, her badge still secured where it was visible. Her 9mm remained easily spotted in the holster at her waist.

He held the door for her to exit the restaurant. He waited a few seconds while they both took in their surroundings, then followed her when she started walking along the sidewalk.

"Let's hope she doesn't make us wait all day," she said. "I have things to do."

A woman peered out from the alley. Grier immediately recognized Sarah and stepped into the alley with her. The chief had seen her too and moved in close.

"We're here. Where do you want to talk?" Grier asked.

"What's she doing here? I told you to come alone." Sarah glanced down the alley as if she would flee.

Grier gently gripped her wrist. "Relax. She's with me. She's in this with me and in danger too. I trust her."

Sarah looked at the chief. "Does she . . ."

"I know everything."

The chief pressed her hands on her hips, and her gun was in full view. He hoped she wasn't intentionally intimidating Sarah.

Sarah frowned. "Maybe you don't know that someone followed me here. I was afraid to even look for you, but I easily found you. So maybe he did too." She stepped deeper into the shadows and rubbed her arms. "Meeting you was too risky."

"Who followed you?" Grier asked.

"I don't know who he is, but I've seen him in Shadow Gap. I know when I'm being followed. I almost didn't wait for you, but I have to tell you what I know before it's too late. So I bought us tickets for the train. We can talk there."

"The train?" the chief asked. "It goes nowhere."

"It's a two-hour excursion. Maybe he'll give up looking for me, but at least we can talk without fear. Let's go. We're going to miss our ride."

Grier wasn't so sure Sarah's idea was the best plan, and it almost sounded like a trap. But Sarah had answers he needed, and she was finally ready to talk. He looked at the chief to gauge her reaction.

She shrugged. "I guess we're going for a train ride."

———

The White Pass and Yukon Route railway was initially built during the Klondike Gold Rush to facilitate transporting passengers and equipment between the Yukon and the Port of Skagway. These days the narrow-gauge train transported tourists who wanted to see the breathtaking view along the Klondike Trail roundtrip from Skagway.

Grier sat with the women at the back of the vintage coach, waiting for the train to start moving. They were in the last car on the train, and the other cars looked almost full. Two older couples sat at the front of their car. A cast-iron heater kept the passengers warm. Each car was outfitted with platforms fortified with safety rails on both ends, as well as huge windows along the length of the cars that allowed for the scenic view. But he wasn't here for that.

A prerecorded female narrator resounded over the intercom, explaining that points of interest would be noted along the trip.

He didn't like how much time the ride would take or the reason behind their boarding a tourist train. Apprehension coursed through him, but he gritted his teeth. If this was what it took for Sarah to talk, then so be it. His patience was growing thin.

The train shifted slowly forward. At least they were moving.

The others at the front of the car were engrossed in their own conversations. He leaned in and kept his voice low. He couldn't wait any longer for answers. "What's your real name?"

"I'd prefer to simply keep it Sarah Frasier, the name I gave."

Understandable. "Why didn't you say anything when you were rescued? You could have told me then."

Sarah's brown eyes grew big in her pale face. "I couldn't exactly talk to you on the plane. Or in the hospital. You didn't show up. I had to get somewhere safe and figure out how to survive."

Made sense. At the time he rescued her, Grier had no idea she was connected with Krueger. "Did you happen to take a picture of the man you claim is following you here in Skagway?"

Sarah nodded. She pulled up the image on her cell and flipped it so he could see.

The chief got a glimpse too and lifted her gaze, held his.

Mateo was following Sarah? Did he believe that if he followed her, eventually he would find Grier and Autumn? If so, how had he learned about their meeting? Or was it that he'd learned she was connected to Krueger and Grier? And if that was the case, then it confirmed Mateo knew that Grier held the cold wallet.

"Maybe we shouldn't have gotten on the train," the chief said. "If we'd stayed in Skagway, we could've waited for him to show up."

"You want to face off with him?" Sarah said.

The chief lifted her chin. "Face off with Mateo Santos together, and we could take him down. I'm ready to be done with this game and get back to my life."

"What?" Sarah asked. "You two know who he is?"

"It's complicated," Autumn and Grier blurted at the same time.

The train lurched forward, traveling faster now—maybe twenty-five miles an hour, if that. The narrator droned on as the train slowly climbed its way to White Pass Summit—beyond that, British Columbia, but they weren't going into Canada.

"We don't have much time, Sarah," Grier said.

"It's only twenty miles to the summit," Sarah said, "but the train moves about twenty miles an hour so people can get pictures and stand on the platforms. Sometimes even slower on the steep grades around the tight curves. I hear it used to stop for photo ops but doesn't anymore. We have just over two hours."

"During which I need you to tell me everything that happened. How did Krueger end up in the shipwreck? How did you end up in the water?" Grier was especially eager to learn if Krueger had found out anything that could help. Otherwise, Krueger gave his life for nothing. "Sarah, who were you to Krueger?"

He had to have trusted her.

She closed her eyes. "We'd known each other for years. Dated in the past. I . . . I'd recently left a post with an agency, so he hired me to work for him—off the books. Martin needed someone he could trust, and apparently he had no one else. In the end, he was sorry that he'd involved me."

Tears slipped down her cheeks.

In the end, Grier wished he hadn't allowed Krueger to help him. "I'm sorry for what happened to him, and now to you. Help us end this." He would like to add that she would be safe if she helped, but he could promise nothing, and she no doubt already knew the risks.

Staring at her hands, she nodded. "I'll tell you what I know. Then, after today, you won't see me again."

"I understand." He wanted safety for Sarah and for the

chief. And for himself? He needed freedom from this prison and hoped she had the keys to open the prison doors.

She took a few breaths.

A pang stabbed through his chest. "It's okay. Just take your time."

"He'd set up a temporary office for us in Lisbon, Portugal. One day we were together, working. Men burst in and put bags over our heads. They must have drugged us. I woke up to see Martin had been beaten. Tortured for answers. He didn't tell them where you were. But then they focused their attention on me . . ." She stared at the ground. "He told them where he'd sent you, Grier. That you were hiding in Shadow Gap."

"Do you know who the men were connected to? Did Krueger know?"

"He told me they were connected to his counterpart who'd tried to frame you."

Sarah glanced at the chief, then back to Grier. "We were tied up and hidden away as we traveled on a private plane halfway around the world. I lost track of time and where we were exactly. At some point we were put on a boat, and we traveled up the Alaska Marine Highway to the waters near Shadow Gap." She angled her head to look at him, grief filling her eyes. "He hid you well, Grier, but it would have been better if he didn't know where you were." She shrugged. "I guess they planned to use us against you in some way after they located you. They needed to confirm that Martin wasn't lying about your location."

"Didn't you try to escape? Krueger had skills."

"Several times. That only earned more beatings. More torture. If he hadn't hired me, if I hadn't been working for him, maybe things would have turned out differently. I don't know."

Or they would have found some other way to compel Krueger to give away Grier's location. His gut seized. Brown was going to pay for the murders, one way or another.

Sarah wiped her nose. "That day . . . that day you found me.

We were on the boat when one of them returned from visiting Shadow Gap and had found you near the water overlooking the inlet. Said you'd been diving. And because they'd found you, they no longer needed Martin." Sarah covered her face then, and her shoulders bobbed up and down.

"And that's when they shot him?" *In the head*.

Hands still covering her face, she nodded.

Grier wasn't sure how to comfort her. Krueger should never have been put in this position.

"Why was he put in the shipwreck?"

"I listened and only caught some of their comments. They spoke Spanish. Unlike Krueger, I'm not fluent in several languages. They didn't want his body to wash ashore. One of the guys had been diving earlier and found the shipwreck. I think he thought it was a joke of some kind to put Martin down there. Some kind of weird irony, maybe, since you were a Navy SEAL before."

"They didn't put him there as a warning to me?" With Brown's twisted personality, Grier could see that happening.

She shuddered out a breath. "I don't know what they were thinking. Maybe that was the plan. All I know is that I was next. Maybe after they used me to get to you. I don't know. They were waiting on you that day. Waiting to make their move. Had planned to turn the boat and steer over to where you'd been spotted. A whale caught their attention, and I took advantage of the distraction and slipped off the boat, preferring to take my chances in the cold water. It was better than dying at their hands. And I thought if you were near, there was a chance you could help me from the water. A long shot, really, but one I was willing to take.

"I stayed underwater until I saw the boat take off. I think the seaplane scared them away. Maybe they thought I had gone belowdecks and didn't discover I was gone until it was too late. Once I came up out of the water, I saw the plane in the distance. I started swimming for shore, but I wouldn't have made it without your help. And then . . . I was terrified. I had to get away. I'm sorry about that. I should have warned you as soon as I was able, but I was scared. I fled the first chance I got. I'm ashamed of my actions."

Grier fisted his hands. Opened. Closed. Opened. Closed. As the train entered a tunnel through the mountain, he stared into the darkness.

He'd love to get his hands on the men responsible for Krueger's death. "I'm so sorry about everything, Sarah. I don't want his death to be for nothing. We have to take the killers down. If Martin Krueger found the evidence he was looking for, did he tell you what it was?"

In the darkness, he barely heard her whisper.

 # THIRTY-THREE

s they passed through the tunnel, laughter erupted from the people standing on the platforms at each end of the cars and echoed off the carved rock walls. A chill crept over Autumn, and it had nothing to do with the cooler air in the higher altitude. She squeezed the grip of her Staccato P, expecting danger at any moment.

The train finally exited the tunnel, and she released a slow, easy breath, but tension remained in her shoulders. The familiar sensation of being watched tickled her back.

But how could they be watched here? The two couples in the front were retirees and paid them no attention, so they certainly were not involved with Mateo or Brown.

Sarah stood and pressed a hand on the seat to steady herself. "I . . . I'm going to splash water on my face." Then she headed for the restrooms at the very back of the car.

Autumn studied Grier. He must be grieving over his colleague, but angry as well about what happened. The injustice of it all. Sometimes it felt like the bad guys always won. But she would fight to the end and help to prove Grier was innocent. And she'd really like to know what Sarah said in answer to his question.

She leaned forward and kept her voice low. "I couldn't hear what she said, Grier. What did Martin Krueger find as evidence?"

He watched out the windows of the car as they entered another cloud that reduced visibility. According to the tour narrator, they approached a bridge.

"She only told me that she knew, but she didn't tell me *what* she knew." He leaned back and scraped his hand over his jaw, then covered his mouth.

"Well, is she going to tell you or not?" Seemed to Autumn that Sarah still held on to the most important information they needed, and really, the whole purpose for meeting with her.

Wind whipped through the train car, alerting them that a door had been opened. Autumn glanced to the back of the train. Grier stood, then slowly made his way to the door.

Palming her gun, she pulled it from the holster and followed Grier. Fortunately, the two older couples were caught up in the scenery and hadn't yet noticed the police officer wielding a gun. She knocked on the restroom door. "Sarah?"

"She's outside." Grier stepped out onto the platform, protected by rails to prevent riders from falling, and held the door for Autumn to join him.

"What are you doing out here?" Grier asked Sarah.

Wind whipped her brown hair across her face as she turned to him, shivering. "He's here."

The words stabbed through Autumn. She tensed. "Who?"

"The man you called Mateo. I came out of the restroom, and I saw him standing at the window in the door on the front of the car, and then he was gone. I should have said something, but I didn't want to make a scene or scare the other passengers. I knew you'd follow me. What are we going to do?"

"Get back into the car." Grier ushered her back inside. "Get down and stay hidden. The chief and I will handle this. We'll protect you."

Sarah opened her bag and revealed a gun. "I'm not defense-less."

Maybe not, but she was letting the fear get to her.

Once they were inside the car again, Autumn held her gun ready, unsure what Mateo had in mind. Meeting on this train with tourists aboard had been a flawed plan. And this time, the two couples sharing the car with them noticed.

A silver-haired man wearing a blue baseball cap slowly stood. "Excuse me, what's going on?"

"Sir, please remain seated." They needed off this train. Engaging Mateo in this setting was a disaster waiting to happen.

She marched to the front of the train car where Grier stood, holding his gun next to his leg. Sarah followed and sat nearby. Would Mateo face off with the three of them? Autumn thought through their options, then whispered, "Everyone on this train is in danger. He could use anyone as a hostage."

"Women. Children." Sarah's voice shook. She'd apparently been a desk jockey and was not accustomed to fieldwork.

Autumn peered through the window in the door, trying to see into the next car. "What's he planning?"

"He's here to keep tabs on us," Sarah said.

"But he could make his move at the right moment," Autumn said.

"What move?" Grier huffed a growl. "Maybe he has no real plan."

"But he has a goal." Autumn was tempted to cross over into the other car. At the moment, she saw no one on the platforms between these two cars.

She peered at the distance between them, then looked down. "The railway coupling!" Mateo could try to detach the last car.

Autumn shared a look with Grier. Images flashed in her mind of their car slipping backward and rolling downhill, picking up speed, then plunging off into Dead Horse Gulch.

"No," Grier said. "He's not going to separate our car. I don't think he could so easily do that if he wanted to. Besides, he wants us alive. He wants you for whatever purpose Rafael might use you for."

"But if he knows about the cold wallet, Grier, then he could want you and Sarah for that reason." She pulled out her cell and found the images of the men associated with the cabin the day Ross was shot and showed them to Sarah.

"Recognize these guys?"

She slowly nodded and held Autumn's gaze. "They were on the boat. That one"—she pointed at Alberto Acosta—"killed Martin Krueger."

Grier growled and huffed. He rubbed his eyes, then finally looked up, locking his gaze on Autumn. "By placing me in Shadow Gap to wait and hide, Krueger put your whole town in danger."

Autumn heard the concern in his tone. He sounded almost defeated, but she knew he wouldn't quit. And neither would she. "It doesn't matter how Brown found you or how Mateo found me. What matters is that we're the good guys, and we're going to win the day. Remember, Grier, Alaska is my home turf, not Mateo's or Rafael's or the rogue CIA operative's. We have the advantage."

Though, now that the words were out, *we* wasn't exactly appropriate since Grier hadn't lived in Alaska long. But he had the advantage because she was on his team.

His expression hardened, resolve stoking his gaze. "Okay. Let's use that advantage then. Try to get a signal and call for backup to meet us at White Pass Summit. We can try to force Mateo off the train and get him away from the passengers. Trap him."

Autumn nodded and held her cell to start the call, but she watched Grier and recognized that look on his face—he was concocting a plan. That was fine by her, as long as he shared it with her. But she wasn't so sure he planned to.

Sarah stood. "We're approaching the last tunnel before the summit."

Grier glanced at Autumn. "Stay here and guard Sarah."

He opened the door and stepped out before she could react. Then he shut it in her face.

"Grier . . . wait!"

 # THIRTY-FOUR

T he wind hit Grier with greater force than he'd expected as he stepped outside while the train rushed through the tunnel. The locomotive clanked and vibrated, the sounds echoing against the chiseled rock walls.

Darkness surrounded him, but the light at the end of the tunnel created the silhouette of the man standing on the platform of the car in front of him. Mateo Santos. The man who abducted Autumn.

Grier held his gun at his side, pointed downward to avoid bringing a gunfight into this volatile situation. "What do you want, Santos?" He ground out the words loud enough the man wouldn't mistake his question.

"I've been sent to retrieve only two things. The police chief with the strange eyes and the money you stole, neither of which belong to you."

Mateo's choice of words surprised Grier and sent anger slicing through him. "I don't have the money, and you're not taking her. She belongs to no one. Either way, you'll have to go through me."

In a flash, Mateo hopped over the rail and jumped between the cars as if he were a much younger man practiced in parkour.

He landed next to Grier on the platform and immediately thrust a knife at him.

Grier dodged and parried. The train exited the tunnel, and brightness momentarily blinded him.

He had to get out of this space. Overpowering this maniac wouldn't be so easy, and the longer it took, the greater the risk to those inside the car, especially Sarah and the chief. He had a feeling the chief was about to burst through the door to help him. And the only way to keep her safe, to keep everyone safe, was to get Mateo off this train.

Grier was too close to use his gun effectively without risk. Instead . . .

Aiming for Mateo's midsection, Grier rushed forward, knocking the knife from his hand at the same time he lifted the surprised man off his feet. They both toppled over the rails and onto the rise near the tracks. Pain ignited in Grier's shoulder and back as he rolled down the incline. He tried to stop his momentum before he tumbled into the woods, digging his hands into the meadow grass, dirt, and rock. Finally, he stopped. Caught his breath. Ignoring the pain, he scrambled to his feet, then up the hill, and grabbed the gun he'd dropped when he slammed into the ground.

Grier quickly glanced around and spotted Mateo at the tree line about ten yards from the tracks, getting to his feet. The man scowled at Grier then took off.

"Grier!"

The chief called from the back of the last car as it continued rolling toward White Pass Summit. *God, please let her stay on that train.*

Grier might never recover from the fact Krueger had given his life for him, but he wouldn't fail the chief . . . Autumn . . . the woman he loved. He *must* take this guy down.

He started for Mateo, racing through the woods and cutting between the trees. The thick clouds at this altitude reduced visibility, and he quickly lost sight of the man. He paused to listen.

Hearing footfalls, Grier hunkered behind thick foliage and waited. Was Mateo getting closer or farther away? Hard to tell. The chief stepped out of the fog, then made her way to him.

"What happened to *we* stick together?" She glared at him.

That was fair. But . . . "I saw a chance to take him out, get him off the train, and I took it."

She nodded, respect in her eyes. "I would have done the same thing if given the chance."

"All we have to do is find him," he said. "Secure him and take him for transport."

"Oh, is that all?"

"I think he's going to find his way back to the train for a ride back down. If we don't get up there, he'll slip through our fingers again."

"You're probably right. He could jump on the passenger train and ride back down since it's round trip or go into Canada and disappear or take the bus back at Mount Frasier. But it's risky. They'll definitely be looking for him, so he won't be entering across the official border."

"I don't think he planned to be thrown from the train. No one is out there waiting to pick him up."

They shared a look.

"Sarah!"

She was alone on the train. If Mateo made his way back to the train, he could get to her. They started for the tracks.

"She has her gun, and she knows to stay alert. I'll try her on her cell. I got her new number before I left the train."

They climbed back up the incline to the train tracks.

"Anything?"

"I couldn't get a signal, so I sent a text. Maybe it will go through at some point."

Together they followed the tracks.

"Hear that?" Autumn gasped out. "A chopper. Could be our backup."

"We hope." He picked up his speed. If only he could have gotten his hands on Mateo. "You don't think it's a ride for Mateo, do you?"

Adrenaline surged, and he pushed forward, navigating the rails and the ties. This was easier than traveling the stones along the grade. Finally, they approached the train, which had stopped to switch out the engine and go back down the track.

The chief breathed hard next to him, and he joined her, gasping for breath. The engine was already in the process of switching. They could hop on here and find Sarah. Grier jogged up and climbed onto the last car, then assisted the chief up and over the protective rails.

Sarah wasn't on the last car, and the two couples who'd been on the car must have moved to the next car while the train was stopped, and perhaps complained to the conductor about what had happened.

"I hope she's still on the train," the chief said. "Maybe she moved up to another car too."

"Only one way to find out."

Grier and the chief hopped between cars—against the rules, of course—and made their way through all the train cars, even as the train was getting ready to head back down to Skagway. Grier spotted both couples from their car seated in the most crowded car. Smart people.

Sarah wasn't anywhere. "You think she got off the train?"

The chief pulled out her cell and tried calling Sarah again, then shook her head. "She isn't responding. Let's find the conductor or engineer or whoever is in charge."

He followed her around to the back of the train, which was now the front of the train since the engine had been switched. While the chief flashed her badge and spoke with someone, requesting the train be held up for a few more moments, Grier stood by and watched the helicopter search for a place to land. He looked for Mateo in case the chopper was his ride instead of their backup.

She stepped off the engine and walked toward Grier. "I told him we want to make sure a dangerous criminal isn't on the train. He told me that he'd already been informed to hold the train." She gestured to the helicopter. "Let's go talk to these guys."

Two men had hopped off the helicopter and were headed toward them. The chief again flashed her credentials as they approached.

"I'm Shadow Gap Police Chief Autumn Long. We called for backup. A dangerous international criminal, Mateo Santos, was on the train, but he escaped. He can't get far in this rough terrain." The chief glanced around. "But we'll need more resources to search for him than just you two."

The tall, broad-shouldered agent with dark hair spoke first as he flashed his credentials. "I'm Deputy US Marshal Flanders, and this is DS Special Agent Knap."

Agent Knap flashed his credentials as well.

Identifications aside, wariness crept over Grier. This wasn't the kind of backup they had expected. To show up at this summit so quickly, these guys must have been already closing in on Mateo. All good, except he had a bad feeling about this and almost wanted to take a step back and away. But he stood his ground.

"Have we met before, Agent Knap?" the chief asked. "You seem familiar."

He half smiled, though his eyes remained cold. "I would have remembered."

"Well, I'm glad you were close. Santos can't go far in this wilderness. We suspected he would try to escape on the train. Or find his way onto a bus on the return trip or try to disappear into Canada."

"Ma'am, we're not here for Santos. We're here for Grier

Brenner, a.k.a. Troy Fox." The marshal looked over Autumn's shoulder at Grier and stepped forward, holding out handcuffs. The other agent held his gun as if he thought Grier would flee.

"On what charges is he being arrested?" The chief stepped forward as if she would defend Grier against these two federal agents.

And at that moment, he knew his heart was forever hers.

But what a tragic ending for them both.

"Mr. Fox is wanted for questioning in a murder case, but today we're charging him with passport fraud."

Of course. He'd had an undercover identity on his assignment, all sanctioned by his agency. But Krueger had secured him a new cover and identity while he hid in Alaska, necessary when exfiltrated or removed from immediate danger and put into a safe zone. Alaska was no longer that for him. Now that new identity was being used against him, since the Diplomatic Security Service majored in counterfeit documents. Grier swallowed the impossibly large knot in his throat. So . . . they had finally caught up to him. He eyed the two agents. If he'd thought he could trust anyone, he would have already turned himself in and allowed justice to run its course. With the chief standing next to him, he wouldn't put up a battle. She would be caught in the crossfire.

Marshal Flanders stepped forward, pressing his hand on his gun. "Please step aside."

"Now hold on a minute!" The chief blocked the marshal's path. "Mateo Santos is a *dangerous* international criminal. That's the man you want. The reason I called for backup."

"Chief Long, we aren't aware of your call for backup. We received word that a wanted international fugitive was on the train, and now we're taking him into custody."

Who had called to inform these agents? The only other person who knew was Sarah. Or Mateo or Brown? Which meant Grier should remain wary. Maybe he shouldn't trust these guys.

But he would leave with them, to protect the chief.

"Fine. Take me in," he said.

Marshal Flanders cuffed Grier and led him to the helicopter.

Grier tensed, tried to hold it together, but he tossed the chief an apologetic look, because really, regret that he'd involved her carved a deep, gaping hole in his chest.

 # THIRTY-FIVE

They escorted Grier toward the helicopter.

"No!" Autumn wanted to rush after the federal agents. "You have it all wrong. This man is innocent."

Agent Knap blocked her path this time, while the marshal loaded Grier onto the helicopter. "Chief Long, we'll have questions for you regarding your time spent working with this fugitive."

His cold eyes held a threat, as if he would try to charge her as well.

"He's not a fugitive. He isn't on any wanted list available to me."

The man gave her a smug look. "We'll be in touch."

Autumn looked over her shoulder. "The train is leaving, and with Mateo out there, it's not safe. Give me a lift back to Shadow Gap."

The agent conferred with the deputy marshal and then returned to her and nodded. "We'll drop you in Skagway, and you can make your way home from there."

Shadow Gap was not even a fifteen-minute flight from Skagway, but she wouldn't complain or else he might deny her. She didn't care where they dropped her. She wanted a few more minutes with Grier. She had so much to say.

This was wrong. Maybe she and Grier could spend their remaining time together convincing these two of his innocence. But she doubted they would listen, and she seemed to be digging her own proverbial grave with every attempt to defend Grier. No. She needed that proof Sarah had mentioned, only Sarah didn't tell them what it was or where to find it.

Without solid evidence, Grier wasn't getting out of this.

Even *with* that proof, Autumn wasn't sure where to take the information to produce results. After all, Martin Krueger had hidden the evidence, or rather, he hadn't shared it with his superiors. Autumn climbed into the chopper and sat across from the DS agent, donning headphones and a mic. To her right was the deputy marshal, and in handcuffs, Grier sat in the seat across from the marshal. The sight twisted her heart a hundred different ways, but she kept her features flat and expressionless to match the federal agents' expressions. More outbursts would win her no points with them. To keep her emotions under control, she had to stare out the window. If she looked at Grier, the two men arresting him would read in her expression what she was trying so hard to hide from herself.

I love him.

She blinked back tears. Autumn needed to remain professional or she would lose credibility. She wanted to glance at Grier—offer him just a glimpse of her heart—but how could she with two law enforcement professionals watching her? She got the feeling they considered she might make a move to free Grier.

If she could free him, would she make that move?

The idea that yes, yes she would, ripped through her, sending a jolt across her chest that scared her. She pushed down the rising breaths, the fast heartbeats, the raw panic.

Enough of this. She blinked back the tears, pulled in a long breath, then shifted to face the men—full-on, no-nonsense police chief.

"Marshal Flanders. As I understand it, your job is to bring in fugitives. So what are you going to do about Santos? He's still out there running around. Are you going to call in reinforcements to find and take him down? He's been hanging around Shadow Gap, and I want him out of my town. My state. Mateo Santos is a dangerous man. I understand he was recently released from prison, but he is back to his criminal activity. He brought violence and murder to Shadow Gap, and he also abducted me."

Agent Knap was the one to answer. "We'll send reinforcements for Santos. We were already on Fox's trail after we learned he'd boarded the White Pass excursion."

Maybe Autumn should have stayed behind and focused on getting the Alaska State Troopers to the area for a manhunt, but that meant she would have been on her own until they arrived, and she wasn't taking Mateo down without backup.

Then again, she knew she was in the right place. She needed a few more minutes with Grier, and she'd like to talk to him too, if given the chance.

The helicopter landed in Skagway—her stop.

"Can I have a minute?" she asked the marshal. He shook his head.

"Fine." She looked at Grier. She didn't think his eyes had ever left her. "You're innocent. I'll find the evidence to free you."

He shook his head so subtly, she thought she might have imagined it. She recalled he'd told her he would be killed, murdered, while in custody.

She held his gaze while she asked the other two men, "Where will you take him from here?"

"Not your concern."

"Your cards, gentlemen?" Autumn wasn't moving until she got their contact information.

They each handed her an agency card, and she glanced at them to make sure they reflected the credentials the men had shown her. "I'll be contacting your superiors. In the meantime, treat this innocent man with respect and dignity."

Agent Knap got off the helicopter and offered his hand as if to both urge her out and assist her down. The helicopter hadn't powered down, and the rotor wash overwhelmed her.

She gave Grier a look filled with all the hope, determination, and yes, love, she could muster, then turned and walked away.

An hour later as Autumn walked into the Shadow Gap Police Department, Tanya rushed forward, blocking her from entering her office.

"Are you okay?" Tanya's big brown eyes were filled with concern and compassion.

Unable to fully answer, Autumn stared at her. Tanya stepped forward and hugged her—good, long, and hard. Autumn returned the hug. She hadn't realized how much she needed one. Her friend stepped back and gripped her arms. Her actions seemed natural, considering how long the woman had known Autumn, but something else was going on.

"Spill it." Autumn shrugged out of her grip and beelined for her office.

Tanya followed and sat at the desk across from her. "I don't know the details, but I got the news that you were working with an international fugitive and the city council has called an emergency meeting, which doesn't include you."

Autumn sank into her seat. "Thanks for giving me a heads-up."

That meant her time was limited, so she needed to use her resources efficiently.

"Chief, what's going on? What can I do to help? I've got your back. I don't believe what I heard. But even if it's true, I know you had your reasons, and I've still got your back."

Autumn booted up her computer, then stared across at Tanya. "Grier Brenner, a.k.a. Troy Fox, was arrested at White Pass Summit. Mateo Santos is the criminal who should be caught and arrested." She gestured at the image she'd put on the board on the wall. "He's dangerous, and he's still out there. Grier is innocent."

"Did you know he was a wanted fugitive?"

"Not until recently, but it's complicated, Tanya. It's all connected, and Grier is being framed."

Tanya pursed her lips and gave her a searching look. "And you *know* this how?"

"I trust him. I know enough that, yes, I know. I just need to help him prove it."

"Are you sure your judgment isn't compromised? Because, well . . . I've seen the way you look at him."

Her words surprised Autumn.

"Relax. You don't have to be concerned that others noticed. They're all too self-absorbed, and it wasn't obvious. But I've known you for so long, and known you well. There's a lot of . . . let's say, electricity in the air when you two are in the room together." Tanya offered a small smile.

Autumn hung her head and smiled to herself, even in this worst-case scenario. Then she lifted her head. "I'm glad I have a friend. You might want to distance yourself from me because I have a feeling that things are about to get weird around here."

Tanya laughed. "They were already weird. Hello, this is Shadow Gap."

"Poor choice of words. How about, things are about to get messy around here." Because Craig was about to be chief. He made a good officer, though she questioned his attitude toward her sometimes. But she had issues too.

Tanya stood. "And if they do, I'll be your inside man."

"I don't want you to risk your job for me."

Walking over to the side wall, Tanya stood next to the Scripture plaque and read it. "'To act justly and to love mercy and to walk humbly with your God. Micah 6:8.' I was here when your grandparents presented this plaque to your father. That's all you're doing, all any of us are doing. You've been unjustly targeted by a council member or two who have connections. Hang in there, Chief. It'll work out."

Tanya slightly bowed her head, then stepped out, only to peek back in. "Get ready. The gavel is here."

Oh . . . the mayor.

Autumn stared at Mateo's picture.

A slight knock came at the door, and Mayor White walked in. Per her usual compassionate self, she offered a smile—this time, a sympathetic one.

"Mayor White. Cindy. What a surprise to see you." Autumn felt an inward eye roll coming on but kept her composure. Autumn gestured at the one chair across from her desk. "Please have a seat. I only have a few minutes. I'm in the middle of an investigation and closing in on the person behind the recent crime wave." She could hold on to hope that Cindy wasn't here to fire her, or if she was, maybe Autumn's news would stay her hand.

"Look . . ." Cindy huffed, her discomfort apparent.

Autumn felt a punch to her gut, which she'd expected. She *hadn't* expected the strength to flood out of her, her palms to sweat, and her heart to pound.

"Please, let me finish this investigation," Autumn said.

"Then you know why I'm here."

"I'm hoping my suspicions are wrong."

Cindy stared at her hands in her lap, then back up at Autumn. "I was the one who let the news leak so that Tanya would know and prepare you."

Her way of acting like a friend?

"Thank you. I think."

Cindy's eyes shimmered. "This is the part of my job that I

hate, and it's not something I have to do often, but I can't ignore the latest news that you've been gallivanting around the Panhandle with a wanted fugitive. Chief . . . Autumn, how could you let yourself get sucked in to working with him?"

Autumn stood and stared down at the mayor. "We're talking about the town hero, Cindy. Grier Brenner—"

"You mean Troy Fox. I hear that's his real name."

Autumn should have at least learned the truth about that from him, because she didn't know which was his true name. "Whatever a person's name is, it's their character that shows us who they really are. You know him and who he really is and what he's done for the people of this town. Go over to the Lively Moose right now and take a show of hands to learn who believes he's innocent."

"None of that matters. The city council has voted you out."

Autumn wanted to slink into her chair, the fight slipping out of her. Not really the fight as much as she needed to choose her battles, and she wanted to help Grier. She had the energy and determination left to help him. To do justice.

"And who will be acting police chief?" *Let me guess . . .*

"You know who's in line. Craig Atkins."

"He and Wally have been out to get me ever since I was elected."

"Be that as it may, it's out of my hands, Autumn. Now, I suggest you take some time to rest—you look a wreck—and go home and spend time with your father. I hear he's coming home today. Nolan is accompanying him."

What? Autumn hadn't heard the news.

"I called the hospital to find out where things stood with him. Nolan mentioned not wanting to distract you and preferring to surprise you, so now I've blown that surprise, but I figured you needed some good news. Believe it or not, I care about you and your family."

Cindy stood and clasped her hands in front of her. No cookies this time. "Between you and me, you've been a great police chief. I hope the future has wonderful doors open for you, even if that means being right back here in the office. I've said enough, and probably too much." Cindy opened the door, then turned back. "Oh, the council expects you to gather your personal items and be out of the office by the end of the day."

"Thank you for keeping me informed." Autumn stared at the door after it was shut.

The breath whooshed out of her.

I do not have time for this.

She turned back to the computer, but her fingers trembled and she couldn't effectively type. She removed her Staccato P and the holster and set it on the desk. Then placed her credentials next to it. Bile rose in her throat as she stared at her gun and badge.

I can't let this crush me.

She stood and grabbed all her stuff, which amounted to very little, and put it into a cardboard box she had sitting in her office. She reached for the plaque but hesitated. It had been gifted to her father, and she stood by the Scripture—a motto of sorts. She pulled her hand back. Whether she agreed with the city council's decision didn't matter in terms of fighting for justice. She hoped, believed, that Craig would meet the same standards, and he might need this reminder from Scripture.

She dropped her hand and turned to head for the door. Tanya stood there, the door cracked. "I didn't mean to spy. I was just coming to tell you that Craig is headed over." She gestured to the plaque. "You did the right thing in leaving it." Tanya's lips spread into a sad smile.

Autumn tore her gaze from her friend, held her head high, and carried her box of personal items out the front door. She headed for her Ford Interceptor, then stopped.

Oh.

That vehicle no longer belonged to her either. Maybe . . .

maybe she could at least be a police officer. Nah. At this point, she couldn't stomach working for Craig. As she headed across the street to the Lively Moose, she thought she caught a few people staring at her through the windows, but they quickly averted their gazes. She pushed through the door and headed through the restaurant, to the back stairs, and climbed up to the guest room. After dropping the box onto the floor, she plopped onto the bed.

Could this day get any worse? She pressed fingers against her closed eyes and groaned. She was tougher than this, or at least she thought she was.

Oh yeah. Dad was coming home tonight. She needed to go home instead and maybe bake a cake, hang a "Welcome Home" sign, and make lasagna. She was glad he was alive and coming home—but he was still in danger. She didn't know if law enforcement had heeded her request to search for Mateo near White Pass Summit or on the train.

And what had happened to Sarah? Worst of all—Grier? What could she do to help him now that she wasn't police chief? She didn't have access to information like she had before. She wanted in to those fugitive databases—something gnawed at the back of her mind.

A slight knock came at the door. Autumn didn't answer and hoped that whoever was there—Birdy or Grandpa Ike—would think she was taking a nap and leave. The door opened and she could tell it was Birdy who slipped inside, closing it behind her. Her grandmother sat on the bed next to her, then she grabbed her hand and squeezed it.

She didn't say anything. No words of encouragement. Then, finally, she asked, "What now?"

"I don't know, Birdy. I was working with a notorious fugitive, remember? Not like I can go out and get another job in law enforcement." At least not yet.

Birdy huffed and stood. Autumn opened her eyes and saw

her grandmother had crossed her arms. "Now you listen to me. That young man is innocent, and you know it."

The burden of it weighed on her. "You don't know what you're talking about."

"Maybe I don't, but I'm absolutely sure you wouldn't have been working with him if he were guilty. You're not an idiot, Autumn Emma Long."

"What do you suggest I do? I just got fired!"

"All the better to help him. There's nothing, no one, holding you back. You don't have to answer to anyone now. You're still the same determined woman with or without your badge."

With those words, Birdy turned and walked out. Autumn sat up.

Stood.

Birdy's words had the wanted effect, and actually, that came as no surprise to Autumn. She didn't have time to feel sorry for herself. She would ask Grandpa Ike to drive her home, then she could use Dad's old truck until she got her own vehicle. She lifted the box she'd brought from her office, opened the door, and glanced down at the contents. Mateo's wanted fugitive picture stared back at her.

The image jogged her memory. Why hadn't she realized this sooner?

God, please don't let it be too late.

# THIRTY-SIX

Still cuffed, Grier stared straight ahead in the small gray room. Gray walls. Gray floor. Gray table.

Cameras in the upper corners. And one mirrored window. He'd been left alone for two hours or more. Nothing to eat or drink. No use of the facilities.

He'd lost track of time, or maybe it was that he hadn't been keeping track. Maybe he should start. Once they dropped the chief off in Skagway, they hadn't traveled far, so he knew they hadn't gone to Anchorage. But that was all he knew. Their strategy of leaving him alone with his thoughts provided the perfect psychological torture.

He was his own worst enemy—he had failed those closest to him.

His safe haven had been discovered and violated. Krueger had been murdered, and the woman he loved was out there, still in danger. While being left alone with his thoughts was an opportunity to figure out a plan, instead he was left with self-recriminations and concern for Autumn.

She was in real danger. He hoped Nolan had made protecting her a priority, especially once he learned that Grier had been arrested. He could do nothing for her now.

Or could he? Was he giving up after such a long, hard struggle? And he still hadn't obtained the vital information from Sarah that Krueger had collected to clear his name.

Heaviness pressed in on him from all sides.

The two men who arrested him walked the walk and talked the talk, but so did trained assassins and operatives. If the two were, in fact, feds, that meant his name was on a fugitive list. How could that be? Because putting him officially on any list would bring to light a covert operation. He doubted capturing him was worth the aftermath of that disclosure.

He could be sure of nothing.

Grier calmed his pounding heart and sent up multiple prayers that Chief Autumn Long would be safe and her predator would be taken down. But ultimately, she was in God's hands. Had always been in God's hands.

And Grier, too, was in his hands.

For the first time—maybe ever—he was grateful his aunt had sent him to Sunday school and drilled Bible verses into him, because when he got quiet and still before God, and had hit rock bottom, the needed Scripture floated from his heart to his mind as if he'd just read it yesterday.

"Fear not, for I am with you; be not dismayed . . ."

"Okay, God, I'm trying not to be afraid, but I don't know what to do anymore." He'd been all about doing the right thing. Doing good in this world. But it had all come back to bite him, or at least it seemed that way when someone else's wrongdoings were pinned on him. "I guess I'm not in control of this. I've never been in control, so . . . what do I do now?"

Sit here and wait. Do nothing? Be still?

Otis's words—had it been only a few days since he said them?—drifted back to him.

"I knew the first time we met that God brought you here for a purpose greater than your own."

Greater purpose. What greater purpose, God? I'm all ears.
But in response, he got nothing but silence. He shouldn't be surprised. And yet, an uncanny peace settled in his heart.
Your purpose, God, not mine.
The door suddenly banged opened, startling him after all the hours of quiet. Grier instantly knew something was off when Agent Knap walked in, and behind him, Cyrus Brown, the CIA operative who killed their team member Charlotte O'Dare, whom Grier had called Blue when sharing the story with Autumn. The thing was, Brown was still Brown.
He crossed his arms and glared down at Grier.
Knap half sneered at Grier. "I'm sure you remember your associate, Brown."
Grier angled his head and held Brown's gaze. A thousand retorts came to mind, but he remained silent. Well, maybe not. "Agent Knap, your life is in danger. This man is a murderer, and since he's CIA, he cannot legally operate inside the United States or gather intelligence on American citizens. So I'm not sure why he's here. Unless, of course, you're in this highly illegal operation with him."
Grier shifted his gaze to Knap's arctic-cold eyes, and then he knew. This guy wasn't an agent, or else he'd gone rogue like Brown.
"I'll ask you exactly one time," Brown said. "Where is it?"
"I don't know what you're talking about."
"You're not going to waste my time." The door opened and in walked a couple more bullies. One carried a bucket of water and the other a towel. Great . . . waterboarding.
Knap's expression flinched. "What's going on? You said he would talk to you."
"Are you really going to allow him to use this inhumane form of torture on me?"
"What's the matter, *Agent Knap*?" Brown emphasized his name. "Are you squeamish?"

The way Brown emphasized Knap's name—as if mocking it—confirmed to Grier it wasn't the man's name, after all.

"No. I . . . almost drowned once. I'm not staying here to watch."

Knap took a step toward Brown, who pulled out his gun and shot the man, point-blank, in the chest. Knap's cold eyes widened as he glanced down at the red bloom spreading across his shirt, then he collapsed.

Anguish twisting inside, Grier focused on one point on the wall.

"Even if I tell you what you want to know, you're just going to kill me like you shot your partners. Knap wouldn't be the first, would he? You've sold your soul, Brown." Grier, Charlotte, and Krueger had learned the hard way that Cyrus Brown was out for himself and could not be trusted.

As the men prepped to waterboard him, Grier wasn't at all certain why he was holding out, but he'd better find his why—his reason—and fast. He would need it to survive this.

Did doing good mean keeping the illicit money from the bad guys, no matter the cost? The two men tilted his chair back. Then placed a towel over his face and poured water over his mouth, creating the sensation that he was drowning. The pain, the torture, engulfed him.

Would crush him. Then it suddenly stopped—before he drowned due to lack of oxygen—only to be started again.

Grier was subjected to the water in his airways. Over and over.

Until he wished he would just die.

A purpose greater than your own.

A purpose greater than your own.

A purpose greater than your own.

God, just let me die . . .

He would never give them what they wanted.

The men pushed the chair so all four legs were flat against

the floor again, and Grier leaned forward, coughing up water. He would have collapsed onto the floor, but they'd tied him to the chair.

Brown crouched to eye level. "I know someone who will make you talk. I heard you have a soft spot for a certain police chief."

Grier squeezed his eyes shut. *God, please, no.*

 # THIRTY-SEVEN

Grandpa Ike had delivered her home, and she stood in the living room spilling the news to Nolan and her father, who was in his recliner.

"At least one of the so-called men who arrested Grier is impersonating a federal agent."

Both stared at her with wide eyes. Nolan shook his head, and Dad's expression paled.

"When I saw Mateo's image in that box, it jogged my memory that I'd seen Agent Knap's picture before—he's a wanted fugitive and not a federal agent at all. But I can't get access to the system. They changed my login. Craig locked me out—must have been the first thing he did when he took over." She fisted her hands. "Of all the low-down things to do."

Actually, she was surprised Craig hadn't arrested her for partnering with a fugitive. That might be in her near future.

"Autumn." Nolan ground out the words. "This isn't the time or place. Dad's recovering."

"Yes. I know." Maybe she shouldn't dump it on him, at least not so quickly. "I'm sorry, Dad. I'm glad you're home." Autumn rushed forward and kissed him on the cheek. "Nolan's right. You need to rest, and I'm not helping you with that. Can . . . can

I make your favorite dinner?" Lame. She was so lame. Autumn should have made Dad's homecoming special, but someone she cared deeply about was in danger.

"I don't need coddling," Dad growled. "And Nolan, enough of this. Both of you—Grier Brenner is in trouble. That man has saved lives in this town, mine included. He saved your sister. Now"—Dad began hacking—"it's time to save *him*."

Autumn watched Nolan, willing him to finally look her way. When he did, he subtly nodded. "Dad, are you sure?"

"I'll be fine as long as I know you two are working to help someone in need. He's one of our own, a resident of Shadow Gap."

Autumn found herself smiling at that slight untruth, because surely, over the past few short months, it had become the truth. Even though he was an outsider, Grier had made a place for himself in her small town. Although she suspected that even if she cleared his name, he would go back to his world when this nightmare was all over.

Nolan and Autumn moved the table into the living room near Dad's recliner and set up their laptops.

"I can log in to databases remotely," Nolan said. "So what am I looking for?"

She shook her head. "I spent hours scouring the fugitive lists on Interpol, and I would need to be the one to look. Pull them up, and I'll scan through them as I work. In the meantime, do me a favor." She pulled out the two business cards the federal agents had given to her. "Call and see if he's legitimate. Call his boss. Whatever. Explain the situation. It could be that the real Agent Knap is in trouble or dead, killed by the man impersonating him."

Nolan snatched the cards. "Got it."

After he logged in to his database access, he twisted the laptop to face her. "You look, I'll call."

Before she started searching, Autumn sent a text to the last number she had for Sarah. She hated that she truly had no idea if Sarah was safe now—if she'd gotten away from Mateo or if the man had her. But Sarah had told them they would not see her again.

The only problem was that Sarah had not shared the most vital information—the evidence needed to clear Grier. Autumn called the number and sent a text but got no answer.

Anguish grew in her heart, squeezed her chest until she couldn't breathe. She couldn't let Dad or Nolan see how this situation affected her. She'd been fired, after all. She'd failed the people of Shadow Gap.

She'd failed Grier.

Nolan pressed his hand over hers and squeezed. She glanced at him.

"Breathe. You're doing the right thing, Autumn."

She had to smile at that. "I thought you were going to give me a hard time and tell me that you'd been right all along about Grier and that he was trouble. I shouldn't trust him. Blah, blah, blah."

A half grin hitched his dimpled cheek. "I was right about some of it—you do have a thing for him."

Pain burned behind her eyes. "I . . . do. Yes."

"No pressure or anything, but you're the right person to do this."

And the only person, it would seem. "Grandpa Ike said something to that effect."

"Well, there you go, then. I'm here to help if I can."

Grandpa Ike's words came back to her.

"You're here now, in this place and in this position, because God put you here. You need to believe that and know you're the exact person needed for this hour."

Nolan dialed a number and pressed the cell against his ear. "Hold on. Someone is answering." He stood and paced the room, deep in conversation. Autumn could only make out some of the words.

If only Autumn knew where Grier was taken, but she had no clue. Still, if she could somehow find the evidence Krueger had died for—

A text from an unknown number came through on her cell.

Postcard from Miami.

What did that mean?

Nolan ended the call. "I had to call several numbers and was finally put through to a supervisor, who had to call regarding my badge number. Normally he wouldn't share the information, but I had information to trade. Basically, the real Agent Knap is recovering in the hospital after a hit-and-run, and considering he has an imposter, they're now going to look into the incident as being deliberate."

"And help? Are they going to help us?"

"I've given them what information I know. But Autumn, there's more."

"Well?"

"Knap had no ongoing operations with the marshals."

"Are you saying neither of the men who took Grier are legit?"

"I have a call in to the regional US Marshals' offices, but it looks like that's a strong possibility. In the meantime, did you find the guy impersonating Knap?"

"Not yet, but I got a text from an unknown number. Could be Sarah. It simply says, 'Postcard from Miami.'"

"What could that mean?"

Dad coughed again. Cleared his throat. "It means you go to Grier's cabin and look through his mail. If I didn't learn enough after decades in law enforcement, then I've read enough spy novels in my retirement to know a clue when I see one. In this case, hear one."

Autumn grabbed her jacket and rushed to her father. Kissed him on the cheek. "Thanks, Dad."

"Where are you going?" Nolan asked.

"To Grier's cabin, where else?" She headed for the door.

"Not alone, you're not." Nolan stood halfway between her and Dad, hands on his hips.

"It's fine, Nolan. I'm still packing my Sig, so I can protect myself. Plus, someone should probably check on his dog, Cap." Maybe Grier had already arranged for the dog to be cared for. She couldn't believe she was just now thinking about that.

"Autumn, I don't feel comfortable with you taking off alone. Not with Santos still out there. But we need to stay here and care for Dad. Protect him too."

"Don't treat me like an invalid," Dad said. "Hand me my shotgun. Nobody will get the best of me ever again."

Nolan glanced between Autumn and Dad, then nodded. "I'm coming with you, Autumn."

"Stay with Dad."

"Will you two stop it?" Dad stared at his cell and punched a few buttons. "See? I'm calling the cavalry. Actually, Tanya texted almost an hour ago that she's bringing a casserole. And I'm calling Ike. I won't be alone. You two kids go save the day."

Autumn shared a look with Nolan. Were they making a mistake? Nolan handed Dad his shotgun, and the doorbell rang. Nolan and Autumn both reached for their guns, and Nolan peered out the window. "It's Tanya."

Autumn opened the door and held it wide. "Just in time."

Tanya held up a casserole and a few bags hanging off her wrists. "I thought you could use some help with the party." She winked.

"Let me get that." Autumn relieved her of the casserole and set it on the counter in the kitchen. "This is perfect timing, as I mentioned. Can you stay with Dad for a bit until Grandpa Ike gets here? Nolan and I have some errands to run."

"Of course. I'm not the only one heading out this way. Some of your dad's friends will be stopping by. Everyone's coming to welcome him home."

Sounded like more than a simple welcome. "I should have done more—"

"Nonsense. I knew you were busy. Oh"—Tanya reached into her back pocket and pulled out a folded slip of paper—"I thought you might want this."

Autumn opened the paper, which contained an image of the international fugitive who had been impersonating Agent Knap. Her jaw opened, but no words came out. Then finally, she said, "How did you—"

"My cousin was flying the helicopter that landed at White Pass Summit. The transport service was shorthanded, and he got called in. He always has his GoPro going. Since this involved you, he sent the footage to me. Said he had a bad feeling about the men. I was stunned when I recognized one of them from the list of wanted fugitives you'd been scouring, so I got busy searching."

Autumn shook her head, trying to comprehend Tanya's resourcefulness. She shouldn't have been surprised. "I can't thank you enough. I owe you, Tanya. But where did your cousin take them?"

She shrugged. "He landed in Juneau. They disappeared inside the airport terminal."

"Grier's in danger." Closing her eyes, she sucked in a breath. He could already be dead.

He'd told her this could happen. *Please, Lord, let him be alive.*

Tanya touched her arm. "Chief, are you okay?"

Autumn opened her eyes. "You know I'm not the chief anymore."

"Autumn. You're still the same person you were. Now, please tell me more about what's going on."

"Grier once told me that if he was captured, incarcerated, he would be murdered while being held."

Nolan stepped into the kitchen. "All the more reason we need to get on top of this. You ready?"

"Go." Tanya pushed Autumn toward the door. "I won't let the party get out of hand."

Autumn rushed out the door and climbed into Dad's old Ford. Nolan got in too. "Party? What party?"

"A few friends from town are showing up. Tanya brought food."

She floored it out of the driveway and down the road and was heading to Grier's cabin when she remembered the image Tanya had printed. Holding the steering wheel, she stretched her legs and reached into her pocket to pull out the paper. She tossed it to Nolan. "That's the fugitive who was impersonating Agent Knap."

"I'll take a picture of it and send it to the contact I just spoke with and let them know."

"What about the Alaska State Troopers? Can you update them on what's happening? Tanya said her cousin flew the helicopter that delivered me to Skagway, then stopped at Juneau. They could still be there. Let's not let them escape by boat or air or road. They're not going to leave this state with Grier."

"I've been keeping my superior informed, and the information is being passed up the line. Troopers are looking for the fugitive impersonating Agent Knap. It's probable the deputy US marshal has also been impersonated. I'm sending the images now, or at least when you stop. I can't take a picture with all this bouncing around."

Autumn accelerated through town. Flashing lights and a siren behind her drew her attention to the mirror. "Oh, for crying out loud. Is that Craig? He's going to pull me over?"

"Let me handle it," Nolan said.

"I'm not stopping until I get to the cabin."

Nolan touched her arm. "Autumn, just stop the truck. This will go a lot easier and faster if you do."

She pulled over to the side of the road.

"Stay here." Before she could argue, Nolan hopped out and rushed around the truck to Craig.

Their voices rose, and she reached for the handle and barely opened the door. *Should I?* Nah.

His face red, the new Shadow Gap police chief, Craig Atkins, threw his hands up and went back to the Ford Interceptor she used to drive. Man, she loved that vehicle.

Nolan jogged back around and got in.

"Let's go."

"What? Just like that?"

"You're wasting time. Let's get to the cabin."

She steered back onto the road. "Am I okay to speed?"

"Yes."

"What did you tell him?"

"I told him I was given a tip that I need to investigate. Official Alaska State Troopers business."

"Oh, is that all?"

Nolan laughed. "And I told him to back off. I know things about bribes and the review board."

"Wait. What?" Autumn almost steered right off the road and had to correct the truck. "What are you talking about?"

"You didn't hear it from me. I shouldn't tell you. It's under internal investigation."

"So you mean . . . I shouldn't have lost my certification."

"I don't know anything, Autumn, but Craig reacted very strongly to my threat, so there must be something to that story. But right now, let's help your friend, Grier Brenner, get his life back."

Troy Fox or Grier Brenner. She didn't know.

"Okay." She took a hard right onto muddy tracks that led up to the one-room cabin. The truck bounced along the drive as tree limbs scraped the sides.

At Grier's cabin, she put the truck in park and hopped out,

almost forgetting to turn it off. Nolan followed. With their guns out, they cleared the area in case they weren't the only ones with the same knowledge, the same idea. At the door, Autumn found it locked. Nolan kicked it in, and they cleared the cabin too.

"Someone's been here," she said. "Grier boxed up his stuff and his laptop, but as you can see, the computer is gone. His things have been dumped out."

"What are we looking for?"

"And Cap's food and water bowl are gone. I hope the right people took the dog."

"Cap?"

"You know, it's short for Captain America."

"Right. Okay." Nolan riffled through the few clothes.

Autumn felt seriously ill. Nausea rippled through her. Grier wouldn't give them the cold wallet, so they came here looking for it. The fear for him crushing her, she bent over her thighs.

"Breathe, Autumn." Nolan spoke from across the room.

He knew her too well. She couldn't lose it now. She had to help—Grier could need her help. He could still be alive.

"Hey. What's this?" Nolan asked.

She crossed the cold, small space to the kitchen. A postcard was stuck to the fridge with a magnet. Palm trees and . . . "Miami." She took the card, flipped it over, and read the words. "See you soon, Steve Rogers."

"Who's that?" Nolan asked.

"I don't know. He has a dog named Captain America, and now a friend in Miami named Steve Rogers."

"I don't see how this can help us find him."

"I'm just going to keep this, while we think on it." She thrust the postcard into her back pocket.

The door burst open. Nolan and Autumn aimed their guns at the new threat.

In walked Grier.

Behind him, a man held a gun to his head.

THIRTY-EIGHT

G rier's insides wound into a painful knot.

"Lower your weapons now, or I'll kill him." Kresky, one of the two men who'd assisted Brown in waterboarding Grier, pressed the muzzle of his Ruger 9mm pistol against Grier's temple.

Why were Nolan and the chief in his cabin anyway?

Autumn immediately dropped her gun, but Nolan hesitated.

"Nolan, drop it," she said.

He lowered his gun, easing it onto the floor.

"Kick both guns over." Kresky increased the pressure against Grier's head, igniting pain. "The weapons at your ankles too."

Nguyen, Kresky's waterboarding partner, entered behind them, his weapon drawn.

Autumn and Nolan shared a look, and she shook her head, warning him off. Good. *Do as these guys tell you, Chief, or you're going to die.*

Autumn and her brother did as they were asked. Grier looked between the two, hoping they could read the regret in his eyes, but in theirs, he saw only determination.

Kresky shoved him all the way into the small space in which he'd spent four of, yes, the best months of his life, falling in love with this woman whom he'd now endangered. Then pushed him to sit on the old sofa.

Nguyen yanked Autumn forward, but she elbowed his nose and he cried out in pain. Grabbing her by the hair, he pushed her head down so she was bent at the waist and pressed a gun into the back of her head. Nolan reacted, and Brown rushed in from outside and slammed his head with the butt of his gun, knocking him out cold.

Or was he? Grier held on to hope that between the three of them, they could outsmart and overpower these criminals who had chased him all the way to this hidden fjord in Alaska.

Brown stared at Grier.

"Now, give me what I want or he'll blow her head off."

She gasped and struggled, angling her head up slightly so that he could see the sweat beading on her temple. She looked up at Grier from beneath her brows—those stunning, amazing, one-of-a-kind eyes. An ache he'd never felt before surged behind his own. Tears. He held them back.

"I . . . I can lead you to where I've hidden it. You'll never find it on your own."

Brown smirked. "I knew I could make you talk. That's why you should never fall in love." He gestured at Nguyen, who released Autumn.

She stood tall, lifted her chin. He wanted to smile at her bravery, her determination, but what was he thinking? None of them were going to make it out of this alive.

But Grier had to try.

He had a purpose greater than himself. Right?

He stood from the sofa, and one of the jerks started to push him back down, but Brown spoke up. "Leave him."

"I'll take you to it, but you won't get your hands on it until Autumn and her brother are free."

"We'll see if I like what you give me. Now, how do we get there. Boat? Airplane? Any travel involved will require planning.

You're not going to best me, thinking you can lead me on a fat goose chase and escape."

The expression is "wild goose chase," you idiot. "We have to hike into these woods."

The man's eyes widened. "You're going to try to escape in the wilderness."

"No. I'm going to take you to the place where I hid the cold wallet that you stole after murdering an operative. More than one, I should say."

"No. You committed the murders." Brown glanced at Autumn, as if hoping she would believe his lie. "I'm only retrieving what you stole."

"Let's go." Grier headed for the door.

"Hold up there. She's going with a gun to her spine. If she flinches, if she trips, if she makes me nervous, I'll kill her. If *you* flinch or trip or make me nervous, I'll kill her."

Grier didn't glance at Nolan for fear Brown would simply shoot him where he lay. As if reading his mind, Brown pointed his gun at Nolan.

"You shoot him, and you get nothing." Grier had to win this.

"But she lives, right?"

"She would never forgive me if I let you shoot her brother." His wrists cuffed in front, he stepped forward and ground out the words. "You shoot him, hurt him more than what you've already done, and you get nothing. I won't tell you. The same goes for Autumn. Hurt her. I won't tell you."

Brown searched Grier's eyes, and what he saw must have convinced him that it wasn't worth the risk. Grier thought he detected a subtle sigh of relief from Autumn.

"You." Brown addressed Nguyen. "You stay with him. If he tries to escape, shoot him." Then he looked at Grier and shrugged. "It's all I can offer."

"Can we get this over with?" He continued to hold Brown's gaze.

"Lead on. You'd better give me something before it gets dark. I don't want to hike these woods at night."

Afraid of Bigfoot? "Then we'd better hurry." Grier pushed through the door that now hung on one hinge. If he survived this, he'd have to pay for those repairs. He almost laughed at the simplistic thought—wouldn't he love to return to everyday life?

Brown marched behind Grier, holding a gun at his back. Autumn was behind him, and Kresky held a gun on her as they hiked.

God, what am I doing? Where am I going?

He had no plan, really, except to try to escape and save Autumn. No matter what he did, she was there in the middle. He'd tried to buy them time. He wanted to lead them to where he'd hidden the USB drive, but other lives would then be in the line of fire. He hiked in the opposite direction of where he should be taking them.

God, forgive me.

Autumn, forgive me.

He heard a scuffle and a grunt behind him and expected a shot to the head per Brown's warnings. He whirled around.

Autumn had knocked Kresky out and taken his gun, which she now aimed at Brown, who pointed his gun at her. Since Grier's hands remained cuffed, he had few options. He rushed Brown, slamming him into a tree, and the impact knocked the gun from Brown's hand. The rogue agent elbowed Grier in the face, sending blinding pain through his skull.

Grier had imagined this moment for far too long.

Pain would not stop him.

Brown scrambled away from him, and Grier knocked into him from the back, sending them down an incline. They rolled apart but kept sliding.

Grier dug his hands, his fingertips, into the wet ground, stopping his fall before he hit a tree.

He sucked in a breath, but his heart still pounded.

Brown.

He glanced up. Around. There.

Brown lay unmoving against a large boulder, his neck at an awkward angle. His lifeless eyes were open.

Grier started forward, stunned at the fact that Brown was gone for good. He dug around in the man's pockets until he found the keys to the cuffs. Then after a few failed attempts, Grier released the cuffs from his wrists.

"Grier!" Autumn shouted.

Something in her scream sent a chill racing through him. He slowly turned and looked up the hill.

Another man held her now, a gun to her head.

Deputy US Marshal Flanders, or was it? Grier hadn't seen him since the helicopter ride.

"Give me the money, or I kill her. You have three minutes to tell me where it is."

"I have to show you! I can't tell you. You'll never find it."

"Then I guess she dies."

"No! Wait . . . wait!" Grier scrambled up the hill. Something about this guy . . . he'd bided his time, waiting until the others were all out of the picture. Brown and his men, as well as Knap. Had Brown been clueless that Flanders was waiting for the right moment to act? As Grier's aunt used to say, "There's no honor among thieves." Did Flanders know that his competition, Mateo, was in town?

God, I'm not in control. I was never in control. Please, help me to do good. Help justice win today.

A bark resounded in the woods. Two dogs barked, getting closer.

No. No, no, no, no.

"Put the gun down, or I'll blow a hole into you." Hank's voice rang out, echoing through the woods.

A standoff.

"You're surrounded!" Sandford?

"On all sides!" And Otis too?

Flanders gripped Autumn even tighter, pulling her impossibly close. No one would risk the shot or they could hit Autumn—and Flanders knew it.

Autumn elbowed Flanders, then dove forward. Gunfire rang out. His heart in his throat, Grier climbed up the hill. Who had taken the shot?

As he topped the hill, he saw Autumn on her knees and Flanders lying motionless on the ground from a gunshot wound to the middle of his chest. Grier raced forward and helped her to her feet, then pulled her to him and wrapped his arms around her. She held on to him just as tight. He had so much to say, and yet no words could adequately convey the emotions flooding through him. His heart pounded against his ribs. He felt her deep breaths as he tangled his hands in her hair, wanting more—so much more.

"You know this isn't over yet," he whispered. "Mateo is still out there, and he wants the wallet, plus he wants you."

Cap dashed forward and jumped on him, and he released Autumn, though he didn't want to. He knelt and hugged Cap. "I missed you, boy."

Cap licked his face. Hank, Sandford, and Otis approached, and the three of them looked at Flanders's lifeless body.

"Well, who took the shot?" Grier asked.

Otis cleared his throat. "Hank got him."

"Hank," Autumn said. "Thank you for your help. Thank all of you for your help. But how did you know?"

"I didn't. Sandford and Otis were at the house." Hank frowned and peered at Grier. "All this news about our boy Grier here upset us. I guess you could say we were commiserating. Then something stirred the dogs up. You know I pay attention. I let them out, and we all followed them. I was hoping to find Bigfoot, but instead, I found this guy holding you hostage. Can't have that, now, can we?"

"No, I guess not." The chief smiled. Thinking of her as anything but the police chief would be hard.

"So we spread out and planned to take the two hiking you up the hill out. But things got dicey when this guy showed up. He hadn't seen us, but we hadn't seen him either. Sorry we let him get to you."

"I can't thank you men enough," Grier said.

Autumn looked at Grier. "Where is the cold wallet? Where were you taking us?"

Grier crouched again, and while Cap licked his face, he took off the dog's collar. He opened it up and removed the USB drive from inside a protective covering, then held it out for Hank, Sandford, Otis, and Autumn to see. "This is it. This is what they all want. This is why Brown killed so many people."

"And you kept it on your dog's collar?" Incredulity edged her tone.

He gave her an indignant look. "Not just any dog, this is *Captain America*."

She burst out laughing, and he'd never heard anything so beautiful. He longed to hold her, to kiss her thoroughly, but this wasn't the time. He wasn't sure it would ever come.

"Besides, it's in protective plastic and has a tracking device, so I won't lose it."

"You've thought of everything." Autumn's eyes widened. "But there's still a bad guy at the cabin. We need to rescue my brother. Hank? Sandford? Otis? You ready to surround the cabin in case we need your help?"

"Always," the three answered.

"I'm here!" Nolan hiked up the trail with a bloodied temple. Autumn rushed to him.

"Are you okay?"

He touched his head, then brought his fingers back to look at the blood. "I'll live."

She reached up as if to touch his head but resisted the urge. "You look terrible."

He chuckled. "You know the old joke—you should see the other guy."

She gasped. "Is he—"

"Tied up. I had to get the advantage to come and save your hide, but it looks like you took care of yourself. Or at least had some help."

Nolan, Hank, Sandford, and Otis started talking at the same time, asking questions and sharing as if they were on the adventure of a lifetime.

Grier watched Autumn, who suddenly glanced at her cell. She stared down at the screen.

"What is it?" he asked.

"A text from the same unknown—" She gasped and covered her mouth.

"Autumn, what is it?" He peered at the cell in her hands.

Mateo and another man are holding your
mother and me, Sarah, hostage. Bring the USB
drive—fifteen minutes.

Grier cursed the day they intercepted that money-laundering scheme.

THIRTY-NINE

F ifteen minutes?" Autumn stared at the cell. "And my *mother?*"

Her outburst caught Nolan's attention. "What's going on?"

She showed him the text. "Mom—if this can be believed—she's here and being held for that stupid cold wallet. I mean, it's a USB drive, let's just call it that."

"And we don't have any time to think or talk about it," Grier said.

"Hank, you and the guys go back to your cabin." Autumn talked to them like she was still chief. What was she doing?

"We can help."

"I'll contact you if we need you," Nolan said.

Hank nodded and waved for Sandford and Otis to follow him. The dogs trailed them.

Autumn was glad they didn't have to spend time convincing them to go home. Now for the other two . . .

"Grier, you're with me. Nolan, stay here and call your fellow troopers. Contact the local PD and get these bodies taken care of, your tied-up guy arrested."

"For someone who isn't officially the police chief, you sure are bossy. I'll make the calls on the way. I'm going with you."

"Where are we supposed to meet them?" Grier asked.

"The airstrip. I'm not sure we can even make it, so let's move it!"

Autumn snatched the USB drive out of Grier's hand and started down the hill, half sliding, half running.

"Wait. We need to think about this. Plan something," Grier called after her.

He and Nolan followed.

"No time to plan." No time to argue.

She slid down the last incline, falling on her backside, then scrambled back to her feet and dashed to the truck. Nolan and Grier emerged from the woods. Another vehicle sat there waiting for someone who would never arrive to drive it away.

"Wait up! You can't just go barging in there." Grier rushed forward and yanked the USB drive from her. "I need to be the one to deliver it. Me and me alone. They're not getting you."

"They have Sarah and my mother."

"You don't know that." Nolan closed in.

"What? Now you're taking *his* side?"

"Look, they're at the airstrip. That means they're looking to make a fast getaway. They didn't give us time to call in the cavalry. They know we're on our own. I'll send a text to my superior and request assistance, but any help we're getting is hours away."

Yep. They were on their own. Even the local PD—just one police chief, Craig, and one officer, Angie, couldn't make it in time or change the outcome.

She opened the truck door and got in. Grier and Nolan scrambled round to the other side and climbed onto the bench seat, Grier squeezing in next to her and Nolan up against the passenger-side door and on his cell. Any other time, and Autumn would have smiled to herself.

She sped out of the drive. "I see Hank in the rearview. He's calling the dogs back. They decided to come after us."

"I'm not so sure the gang shouldn't have come too. You know, for backup," Grier said. "They saved us."

"We're taking the advantage back, Grier. These cheechakos, outsiders"—she glanced his way, then back to the road as she swerved—"let me clarify. You have skills, Grier, so I'm not referring to you. But these international criminal intruders think they can come into my state and create chaos without repercussions. Well, I think it's time we gave them a proper Alaskan welcome."

"And what exactly would that be?" Grier shifted next to her. "I don't think I got one."

"The kind of welcome she's referring to isn't one you want," Nolan said.

"What? You pull a grizzly out of your back pocket? I need to know the plan."

"Grier, get the cell out of my pocket, will you? I can't reach it." She twisted, and he pressed impossibly close but snagged the cell.

"Now what?"

"Send a reply that we're five minutes out."

"The map says that we'll be there in three."

She steered across the bridge and turned off the road into the forest and slammed on the brakes. "Okay. We've got two minutes. Everybody out."

"What's going on?" Grier asked.

Autumn hopped out and opened the decked toolbox in the truck bed. "There are only two vests in here. One of them fits only me."

She tossed the Kevlar to the side. "You guys decide who is wearing the other vest. Nolan, you get the rifles." She glanced at Grier. "This is Dad's truck. He packs everything."

Grier stared at her. "And what are you going to do?"

"Mateo is after me. I heard him on the train tell you he was after me and the money. I was on the other side of that door when you were shouting at each other. So we'll *try* to exchange the USB for my mother and Sarah, and if that doesn't work, I'll trade myself *and* the USB for them."

He shook his head violently. "That's not going to work. You're not letting them take you."

"I'm not a fan either," Nolan said.

"If it comes to that. I figure once they're safe—because Mom and Sarah are the priority here, right?—then you two can take out the bad guys. I'll use whatever advantage I can get."

"And what if they get you into the helicopter or airplane or whatever they've got at the airstrip and fly off?" Grier clearly wasn't going to let her do this.

"No." And neither was Nolan.

But she had news for them. "You know that if that's what they want, we don't have a choice if we want Mom and Sarah back. Now, get ready. We're running out of time."

Autumn donned her vest, then stepped to the driver's-side door. Grier stood in her way. "You do this, Chief, I'm going with you. I'm not playing sniper in the woods."

"I'm not the chief anymore, so when are you going to call me by my name?"

His gaze roamed her face, lingered on her lips, sending heat rushing through her, then settled on her eyes. Half his cheek hitched in that grin. "When this is over—"

The sound of rotors jarred Autumn into action. A helicopter was firing up. They were out of time. "Let's do this!"

She climbed into the driver's seat, and Grier got in on the passenger side. Nolan took off into the woods toward the airstrip to get into place. "Nolan's an expert marksman. He'll take care of us."

"I still wish there was another way. I'm sorry that I got you into this. Everyone into this—"

"Nothing to apologize for. You ready?" She floored it, racing the old truck over the bumpy road through the woods and around a steep ridge, then emerged from the forest near the opposite end of the airstrip—a 1,200-foot-long down-sloping gravel runway. Carrie James's hangar sat at the other end of the airstrip next to the Goldrock River for use with floatplanes.

In the middle of the strip—the helicopter waited, rotors powered up.

Autumn continued forward. She needed to get close but not too close. Heart pounding, she pressed hard on the brakes and the truck skidded to a stop about fifty feet from the helicopter that supposedly held her mother and Sarah.

This feels too close.

But they needed to negotiate.

"Let's do this," she said.

Grier dangled the USB drive out the window, signaling that he had what they wanted. He started to open the door.

"No, let me do the talking—at least for now." Autumn slid out of the truck but remained near the door.

Dressed in tactical gear like a soldier, Mateo hopped from what appeared to be a stolen, doors-off, tour-company helicopter. Her heart rate kicked up.

"I want to see them right now," she shouted. "You're not getting anything until they're free. Right here. Right now."

Another man stepped out—Rafael? He was out of prison?—and assisted two women out of the helicopter. They were bound and gagged. At the sight of the two sets of fear-filled eyes, Autumn thought her knees might buckle.

Mom . . .

She didn't have time to unpack the flood of emotions at seeing the woman she thought was dead all these years. The blame she'd held on to.

Grier got out and held up the USB drive.

Autumn sidled up next to him. "Give it to me," she whispered.

He walked forward. "Send the women over, and I'll walk to you. Get close enough to toss it to you."

"Grier, what are you doing?" Autumn whispered behind him. "They want me, not you."

"Precisely why you're not making the exchange." He started forward again and glanced over his shoulder. "You stay here and wait for Sarah and your mom. Be prepared for anything."

Rafael remained at the helicopter while Mateo ushered the two women forward, holding each of them with an iron grip. With their hands bound, they could run but couldn't fight.

 # FORTY

Grier walked forward and stopped in front of Mateo, though not too close. Just out of the man's reach.

He looked at Sarah and then at the chief's mother—who had very similar blue-and-amber eyes. Rafael had been fascinated by her, unwilling to let her go. But he apparently was willing to let her go for money. If appearances could be trusted.

Grier dipped his chin. "Did they hurt you?"

The waterboarding memories raced across his mind.

The women shook their heads, but Sarah's eyes held a message. She was going to try something? He pretended not to notice and telegraph that she wanted to communicate. He didn't hold her gaze, just remained aware of their surroundings.

He lifted the USB drive. "It's yours. Take it. They can walk back with me."

Mateo smirked in a weird, tough-guy way. "You come with the drive. Once we verify it contains the information we need, then you're free to go."

You're not a very good liar. "Not happening."

His only goal was to get the women to safety, and maybe he was playing the tough guy as well.

Mateo thrust the muzzle of his gun into the base of the woman's head. Autumn's mother. Jessie. "You come with the drive, or I take her or the police chief with me."

Okay. He was going with them. He threw his hands out in surrender. "Whoa, whoa. Easy there. Let them go, and I'll come with you."

At least he could be relieved that the brothers were not demanding to take the chief or keep her mother now. Their tactics had shifted, for some unknown reason. He didn't care what it was.

He nodded at both women and took a step forward, expecting them to do the same. Mateo shoved Jessie forward, and she slightly stumbled but righted herself. Mateo kept his weapon trained on her. Grier's insides tensed. What was going on?

Sarah headbutted Mateo. Gunfire blasted around them.

"Get down!" Grier shouted.

He dropped to the ground, along with Sarah and Jessie and even Mateo. Grier jammed the drive into his pocket for now.

More gunfire ensued, but it echoed off the mountain. Their secret-weapon sniper.

"Get out of here, Sarah. Get Jessie to safety. I'll take care of this guy."

Grier got back up and started for Mateo, but he rolled out of the way and scrambled to his feet. He shoved Grier to the ground and pointed his pistol at him.

The guy stood over Grier, making himself a big, fat target.

Take the shot, Nolan!

Either Nolan would take Mateo out, or Grier was going to die. *Come on, Nolan, what's taking so long?*

"Mateo!" someone shouted from behind them.

Grier focused on Mateo, whose eyes suddenly grew wide. He kept his gun pointed at Grier.

"If you don't come with me now, your women"—Mateo gestured toward the old Ford truck where they were hiding—"will never be safe."

Grier understood that reality. More than anything, he wanted to take these two men down today. The chief and her mother would never be safe, and he would have to continue to look over his shoulder too. Rifle fire echoed. Mateo instinctively ducked and scrambled toward the helicopter. Grier took in the situation. Rafael held his gut—a gunshot wound.

Nolan's work?

Grier scratched his head. Mateo didn't even take the USB drive. Grier glanced behind him, and his heart rate kicked into overdrive.

A two-hundred-foot-long wall of mud, boulders, sand, and trees crept down the hill toward the airstrip. It moved at a slower speed than some he'd heard about that had left a trail of bodies and missing persons. But it was almost to the truck. Nolan emerged from the woods and raced forward.

Grier could run to them, but he wasn't going to make it. He glanced at the helicopter. He didn't want to lose these criminals, though he was not law enforcement and had no arrest authority. He'd learned from Autumn that, in Alaska, you made do with what you had available.

Everyone piled into the truck, and Autumn sped away from the slide and shouted out the window.

"Grier! Come on, get in!"

"Don't try to save me. You'll be buried." He had no idea if she'd heard him—probably not—but she could see he had different plans, and she wouldn't risk the lives of the others.

Grier sprinted toward the helicopter, which was now lifting off the ground. Then he jumped and grabbed the skids, hanging on. Weirdly, Mateo thrust his hand out and assisted Grier onto the chopper. He had no idea what that would look like to the others—it could very well make it appear that he was guilty, after all. He climbed into a seat, and Mateo pointed his gun at him.

Rafael could only look on—sweating and bleeding as he

was. He would die if he didn't get immediate medical attention. Mateo didn't seem worried, and maybe Rafael's death would work out better for Mateo, who had lived his life in his brother's shadow.

Maybe Grier was crazy to go looking for trouble. To chase it. But he was done hiding. Done playing games. He was taking his life back now, or he would die trying.

Either way, neither Mateo nor Rafael would come for Autumn or her mother again.

"The drive for your woman's life."

Mateo could just shoot him and take it, but maybe he wasn't completely sure Grier still had it. Now it was Grier's turn to smirk. "You're never getting your hands on it." He glanced at the mudslide. "I tossed it."

Or he would . . . right into the river. Next chance he got. He wasn't here to hand over the money to them. He was here to take them out.

Mateo's face reddened.

The hairs on the back of Grier's arms tingled, and he instinctively rolled out of the seat as three bullets hit the leather. He thrust his fist into Mateo's face but received three punches to his gut in return.

He and Mateo fought, wrestling in the helicopter as both gripped the weapon. Grier ground out his words. "You need to get your brother to the hospital or he's . . . going . . . to die."

"Hay una temporada para todo. My mamá made sure I attended the best Catholic schools. It means, there is a season for everything."

Mateo freed his weapon from Grier's grip and then aimed at Rafael and fired at the exact moment the helicopter shifted, and Rafael's body with it, so he missed. But then he turned the gun back on Grier.

"He was too focused on the women, the both of them. I had to come all the way here to set my eyes on her to make sure

299

she was in this forsaken hole! It was cold and snowing, and I hated it."

Could it be that Mateo had been here in May, scouting the place out? "You. You're the one who killed Kenny and Monica."

"I don't know who you're talking about."

"On the mountain back in May."

Mateo's dark eyes flashed. "I didn't need witnesses. As for Rafael's obsession over the Long women, our organization is suffering because of it. Now it's time for me to have my moment at the top."

"And that's all it's going to be—a moment!"

The helicopter suddenly took a dive and then whirled. The pilot shifted forward against the dash, bleeding from a bullet hole in his head. Mateo had missed his brother but shot the pilot! As the helicopter spun again, Mateo slipped through the open door, letting go of his gun to grab on to the skid with both hands, his feet and body dangling over the Goldrock River below.

"Help me!"

"Here, take my hand!" Grier reached for him, but the helicopter's incessant spin caused Mateo to lose his grip.

He screamed on the way down and hit the water.

That's exactly where the helicopter was going too, and Grier could not free himself from the building inertia of the spinning bird.

FORTY-ONE

ang on!" Autumn floored the truck, heading perpendicular to the mudslide to get out of the way.

Mom and Sarah were crowded in the truck cab with her, and Nolan held on in the truck bed. He hit the top of the cab and shouted, "We're not going to make it!"

She pressed the accelerator all the way to the floor. The engine roared, and the truck's tires spun out in the saturated ground, then got traction. Still, the truck wasn't fast enough. If she could get them as far as she could . . . preferably to higher ground.

Nolan signaled, and she suspected he was tracking with her.

"Get out," she said. "Nolan is signaling for you to climb out the window."

"What?" Sarah asked. "I can't do that. It's too dangerous."

"He's going to help you to get up on top of the truck. Trust me."

"What's the point? We can't make it."

Nolan reached into the window on the far side and practically pulled their mother through the window. Mom was in the bed of the truck with him now.

"Okay, Sarah. Your turn. You can do this. Go."

"What about you?"

Out the passenger window, the rush of mud and boulders and tree trunks moved toward them, increasing in speed as if competing with Autumn, trying to prevent their escape.

"Go. Now!"

Sarah scooted toward the passenger-side window and slid out so she was sitting on the edge. Autumn's gut remained clenched as she willed this plan to work. Nolan assisted Sarah the rest of the way out of the window as the truck bounced over uneven ground. Finally, Sarah joined Mom and Nolan in the bed.

If Autumn left the truck, it would stop, and she needed to get them out of the path of debris, but she was losing the battle. The mud edged forward and caught the truck's front wheels.

They were so close. Almost there.

God . . . help us. Just. Get. There.

Feet. Just a few feet.

The woods angled up an incline away from the trail of destruction.

Autumn floored the accelerator, hoping the back tires could give them enough push to get to safety, but the truck shifted toward the river, pushed by the debris.

Time to leave.

She started to climb through the driver's-side window, and Nolan pulled her out as if she was a bag of potatoes. Either that or adrenaline was driving his every move.

"Hurry! Go now, Mom!" he shouted. "Climb across the top and jump. We can make it!"

She leapt over the cab, then pivoted off the hood, landing out of the mudslide's path. Then she crawled up the incline and turned around to watch. The slide pushed the truck toward the water, bending and crumpling the metal. Sarah screamed, and Nolan caught her before she fell. Autumn clung to the truck bed. This vehicle was about to crush under the weight of tons of earth.

"Come on!" Nolan shouted. "We have to do this together or we're not going to make it."

"I'm right behind you!" Autumn shouted. "Go!"

Nolan hung back, waiting for Autumn to make her move.

"Go!" She urged him again.

Frowning, he grabbed Sarah. "We'll jump together. Let's go!"

The two crawled over the cab and leaped across the hood as the truck twisted again, and Autumn held on. She crawled onto the cab.

Heart hammering, she stepped onto the hood and started to jump. The truck suddenly shivered and tilted, the metal frame twisting and crunching. Autumn's feet slipped out from under her and she slid across the hood and onto the ground between the truck and the river. She bolted to her feet, fear gripping her. Paralyzing her.

The truck and the mud would crush her. She had to get out of the path.

Voices shouted. Nolan, Mom, and Sarah watched from safety, their voices amping up Autumn's terror.

She raced toward them, but it was too late.

She couldn't make it.

Instead, she turned and ran away from the mudslide toward the water.

The slide, crunching and creeping behind her, along with the grind of trees and boulders stuck in its path, nipped at her heels and caught her as she reached the water. Pushed her forward and out as it slowly ate her.

She pulled in a breath as a tree trunk forced her down deep into the cold water. But the water worked to break up the mud, and the log floated to the surface, releasing her.

She dove deeper as she swam away, heading toward the middle of the river. She'd never been more grateful for her diving and swimming training. She pushed forward, able to hold her breath for long periods—it was almost as if she'd been preparing for this moment her entire life. And she didn't stop as the mudslide pushed debris farther into the river, threatening to take her under and drown her.

Autumn swam for her life.

More.

Harder.

Deeper.

Longer.

Until . . . finally, her lungs screamed. The cold had zapped her energy. She had no choice but to swim to the surface and pray she'd made it far enough out of the mudslide's path and into the river that she was out of danger.

Breaching the water, she took in a breath. Shouts from the shore drew her attention, and she lifted her hand. The current was slower where she'd emerged, or else she'd be fighting the river now. Still, she could feel the slow, gentle tug.

"I'm here. I made it!"

Nolan waved. She spotted Hank over by Carrie's unharmed hangar on the other side of the mudslide from where the rest had found safety. He'd come to help, after all. He pointed and gestured and shouted, but she couldn't make out his words. Then he aimed his rifle . . . at her?

Oh. He was signaling about something *behind* her? Treading water, she whirled around.

Mateo?

He reached for her.

Autumn growled. "I've had enough of you!"

Her adrenaline surged. With all the power she could muster, she swung her fist straight into his nose, then delivered a blow to his most vulnerable parts, though the water slowed her momentum. Mateo grabbed his nose and groaned in pain. Would he be able to stay above the water or swim to safety in his condition?

Behind him, the helicopter was tipped into the water and sinking fast.

Grier . . .

He floated on his back. With the last of her energy, she swam toward him, leaving Mateo behind.

At least Grier was of the mind to float, but he must be injured. "Grier, are you okay? Where are you hurt?"

"Chief." His voice sounded entirely too weak. She lifted her hands from the water and saw the blood.

Too much blood.

FORTY-TWO

G rier!"

She searched for the wound and found a chunk of metal sticking out of his midsection. A massive fist crushed her heart. *No, no, no, no.* Autumn pressed her cold, slippery hands against the wound and around the metal to staunch the blood flow. Fear squeezed her insides.

God, I can't lose him! Help!

"Just hang on." She tried to keep her voice steady but failed. "You're going to be just fine. Everyone made it out. We're all alive, thanks to you."

He was losing too much blood, and the chill in the water wasn't helping either of them.

In her peripheral vision, she saw Dad's boat—the *Long Gone*—speeding toward them. "Help!" She waved her hands in the air.

Craig slowed the boat and steered closer. Tanya, Sandford, and Otis rushed to the side and leaned over.

"Help me! Grier needs immediate medical attention."

He's not going to die. He's not going to die. He can't die.

Grier was quickly lifted into the boat, and Autumn climbed the ladder. She rushed below deck, where they'd taken Grier.

Tanya threw a blanket around Autumn as she dropped to her knees next to Grier on the floor. "We need to get him to the hospital now."

Or he's not going to make it.

"Move out of the way." Craig forced her aside, dropping the medical kit next to him. "Sandford, take us back. Call an ambulance to meet us. Tanya, get another boat out here to retrieve the others."

"I can help," Autumn said.

"You're shivering and in no condition to help. Now let me save him."

She shifted so Craig could get at the wound. He paused as if he might have already given up, then suddenly started working as though his own life depended on it.

"Don't worry, he's going to make it." Craig glanced at Autumn, more compassion in his eyes than she'd ever seen or known he possessed.

She peered at Grier's pale face, leaned closer, and pressed her forehead against his. Squeezing her eyes shut, she couldn't prevent the tears from falling. She didn't care if she cried now. Why had she *ever* cared? Autumn let go of the control she always held over her emotions, the control she thought she had over her life.

"Autumn . . ."

Grier whispered her name so faintly—but he'd said it, finally. The sound of it on his lips sent tingles of warmth through her, but it was bittersweet. She moved back slightly as she opened her eyes and smiled, her tears dripping over Grier's lips and chin. "Yes. I'm here. You called me by my name, finally."

"Told you. Would."

"Yes. After this was over. And it's over, thanks to you."

"Never. Seen. You. Cry." He closed his eyes, and she feared he would never open them again.

"I love you, Grier."

Why hadn't she told him sooner, so much sooner—while

they still had a chance? She pressed her forehead against his again, wanting the contact and willing him to live. And she prayed harder than she'd ever prayed. Voices sounded around her. Shouts. Bodies. Arms grabbed her and pulled her away.

"No!" She reached for him, then realized EMTs had come to transport him off the boat and take him to the hospital. Their small, limited trauma hospital.

He needed much more care, but how could he live long enough for that trip? Autumn followed them up the stairs and onto the deck, then off the boat, walking behind them all the way to the ambulance, sticking close to this man she adored.

"Don't worry, Chief," Dooley said. "We'll stabilize him. A helicopter is already waiting to transport him."

She watched as he and another EMT loaded Grier into the ambulance and it sped away—but not nearly fast enough for Autumn.

Tanya approached and wrapped the blanket that Autumn had dropped around her. "You know, you have cuts and bruises and might be going into shock. You need to see a doctor too."

"He called me Chief."

"What? Who?"

"Dooley. I'm not the chief anymore."

Nolan appeared at her side. She should have registered his presence, but she felt numb all over. "Where'd you come from?" she asked.

"Tex got us in his boat. Mom and Sarah. We're all okay. We pulled Mateo from the water too. Craig will keep him in the local jail until AST can transport him."

Autumn turned and spotted Craig ushering a handcuffed Mateo forward toward his Ford Interceptor.

"What about the others?" Autumn asked.

He shook his head. "Pilot's dead. Rafael too."

"Where'd he come from anyway?"

"He escaped according to his plan, and Mateo was supposed

to have recovered the USB drive by then and gotten you too. They were to rendezvous and go underground before Rafael was recaptured."

But their plans were thwarted. "He told you this?"

Nolan lifted a shoulder. "More or less."

"We'll need to recover the bodies." Oh. What was she thinking? Someone else would need to recover the bodies.

Not her.

And not Grier.

"Where *are* Mom and Sarah?"

Autumn had no idea how to approach her mother—the woman she had thought dead for so long. And she also needed to talk to Sarah about the information that could clear Grier.

He would live.

He had to live.

She wouldn't dwell on any other outcome. And somehow, she had to muster both the emotional and physical strength to finish this.

"Heading to the hospital, just to get checked out." He gestured to the right.

She hadn't seen the other ambulance.

"You should go too," he said. "Tanya can take us. I'll go with you."

Ignoring his words, she angled her head and looked at Nolan. "Did you get a chance to talk to her?"

He held her gaze. "To our mother? Not really." He looked away, and by his expression, she could tell he was as confused as she was, though he'd known longer than her that Mom had survived.

"Does Dad know she's here? In town? Birdy and Grandpa Ike?"

"They will soon enough."

Autumn sat in Tanya's vehicle. She didn't remember the walk over. Nolan sat in the back, and Tanya drove them to the hospital.

Autumn's thoughts swirled in chaos. The mother she thought dead was very much alive and had chosen to stay away. The man she loved . . . was dying.

A bone-deep exhaustion gripped her body and soul.

If Grier somehow survived, his fate still hung in the balance until he could prove his innocence. Grier had saved their lives by sacrificing his own.

Autumn would clear his name—if it was the last thing she did.

———

At the hospital, after one of the physician assistants checked out Autumn's superficial wounds, she found her way to Sarah and Nolan, who spoke in hushed tones.

"What is it? What's happening? Where's Mom? And Grier? Where is he? I couldn't get anyone to tell me anything."

Nolan gently touched her arm. "Just breathe, Autumn. Grier's been transported to Juneau, and then possibly to Seattle or Anchorage. And Mom is getting stitches. She had a gash in her leg."

Okay. She needed to talk to her mother. "Dad?"

"He's in there with her."

Wow. "Did you talk to her, Nolan? What did you say after all these years?"

"I should go and let you two talk." Sarah started to walk away.

Autumn grabbed her arm. "No. Wait. I need your help to clear Grier. I still don't know what Martin Krueger found."

Dad slowly approached. "Autumn, I'm glad you're here. Your mother wants to talk to you. The doctor said it would be okay if you see her."

She glanced between Sarah and Dad. "Okay, but—"

"Go. I'll wait here." Sarah smiled. "Don't worry. I won't leave until I've helped you prove his innocence. After all, what has this been for, if we don't accomplish this one thing? I don't want Martin's death to be for nothing."

Autumn nodded. "Agreed." She looked at Dad. "Are you coming?"

"No, you and Nolan go. I'll let you talk alone." He shuffled toward the waiting area.

She walked with Nolan down the hallway. "I thought she was only getting a few stitches."

"Maybe she's still getting them." He pushed the door open, and Autumn went in.

Her heart seized. Again. Seeing her mother—although she was older, yes, definitely older—overwhelmed her. She couldn't control the tears, the joy and resentment that tangled up in her heart, and she rushed forward to hug her mother in a tight grip. She would never let her go. They sobbed together, tears of joy.

Autumn could sort out her chaotic thoughts later.

Nolan cleared his throat. "Can I get a hug in there somewhere?"

Autumn chuckled and stepped back. She wiped her eyes and let Nolan hug their mom. She might have been making up for all the years she'd refused to shed a tear. She'd had to be a tough cop and then a tough police chief, after all.

Nolan finally released Mom.

Mom smiled and wiped the tears from her cheeks. When Autumn was a child, she'd thought her mother was the most beautiful woman. But seeing her now again in person, even after years, she realized how truly stunning Mom was. For her, that had been a curse, because Rafael Santos had obsessed over her and destroyed her life. Their lives.

"I'm so sorry," Mom said. "I've missed you so much."

She opened her mouth to say more but hesitated. Finally, she said, "I stayed away to protect you. I hope you can somehow understand and find it in your hearts to forgive me. I knew he would never stop."

"But he went to prison, Mom."

"That didn't matter. He was the head of a huge international organized crime syndicate with a global reach. If I was dead, then you were no longer in danger. I never stopped keeping tabs on you. Watching your lives, only from a distance."

"Just where were you all this time?" Autumn asked.

"Alaska. Where else can a person so easily disappear and start a brand-new life?" Mom's smile was tenuous but hopeful.

Autumn wondered if Dad had known all along—and that's the real reason he'd relocated to Alaska, but she doubted she would ever learn that truth. And honestly? Knowing that truth might be too painful. She was fine with not knowing.

"Except, Rafael found you again this time, didn't he?"

"No. I found him."

Ah. "Birdy told you what was happening."

"Yes, and I intercepted Rafael to stop this madness. I contacted someone from his organization who I knew could get a message to him. But my plan didn't work, because some sort of USB drive containing billions of dollars of syndicate money was at stake."

Dr. Combs entered the room. "Georgiana will bring you the discharge papers and instructions for caring for your wound. I'd elevate your leg for the next twelve hours, at least. You're good to go." He stared at her as if expecting questions. Maybe he was just taking in her exotic beauty.

"Thanks." Mom smiled.

The doctor nodded, then exited the room.

Dad lumbered in and smiled—he only had eyes for Mom. "Are you ready to go home?"

"I'll help get her and Dad to the house," Nolan said to Autumn. "I believe you have some unfinished business with Sarah. Let me know whatever help you need."

"I will." Autumn turned to rush out, but Nolan grabbed her arm, leaned in, and whispered, "Clearing his name clears yours. Remember that."

Actually, she'd forgotten, because it was imperative that she clear Grier. Her job had seemed important to her before, but it was the least of her concerns now. She exited the room and went in search of Sarah. Now it was Autumn's turn to stop the madness.

Should she just tell him the truth, or wait for the doctor? She'd seen patients respond well to being told, but some lost what clarity they had when assaulted with too much information. Autumn felt she was walking a tightrope.

FORTY-THREE

The low murmur of voices echoed from the hall.

Grier didn't want to open his eyes. He wasn't sure how long he'd been in the hospital. The only things he knew for sure were that he had an aching skull, a throbbing midsection, and his wrist was handcuffed to the bed rail.

Like he could go anywhere, even if he wanted to.

He couldn't believe he'd survived that ordeal. The doctor had come in at some point after he'd woken up and explained his injury. For the life of him, he couldn't recall what he'd been told. A bullet to the gut made sense, but he didn't think that's what happened.

Nor could he remember.

He recalled one thing, though, and for that he was so grateful. *Thank you, God.*

But maybe he shouldn't be happy that he'd remembered. Maybe forgetting was the best thing for everyone involved.

What did it matter that Autumn had told him she loved him, since he would soon be carted off to prison or killed on the way? He hadn't been told if the Santos brothers had fared any better than he had. If they'd survived or been captured and incarcerated. Or maybe he had been told but didn't remember

314

that either. He was still in agony and on pain medication too. Thinking about it too much made his head hurt that much more and zapped his mental energy.

Sensing someone had entered the room, he frowned. He didn't want to talk to anyone. Then a finger touched his hand, followed by a palm and a squeeze.

"Grier." A whisper.

The familiar voice sent warmth through him that curled around his heart.

For this moment, he would open his eyes. Grier squinted against the harsh lights, turned his head—more pounding ensued—but he kept his expression as pain-free as he could manage while he looked at the feisty chief.

He had thought he was dying at the time, but those memories of what he assumed were his last moments on earth hadn't left him.

Autumn's tears as she leaned over him.

Her confession of love.

"Chief." He tried to grin, but his lips felt funny.

He was rewarded with a pain-filled smile from her. Sitting in a nearby chair, she leaned close and squeezed his hand again. "You called me Autumn. I want to hear that from you now instead of Chief. Besides, I'm no longer in charge."

He tried to reach up and cup her cheek, but the handcuff on his wrist prevented him. The jangling cuffs startled him and broke the magic. He turned away from her and closed his eyes.

"You shouldn't be here."

What are you doing, man?

She released his hand. Just as well. Then she rushed around to the other side of the bed.

He opened his eyes and peered into those stunning mismatched irises.

"What are you saying, Grier? Why wouldn't you want me here?"

"My being in your town, in your life, has already caused too many problems. Just . . . let me go, Autumn."

Tears shimmered in her eyes. "I can open those cuffs for you. You can disappear again."

He pursed his lips, and even that small movement caused him pain. "If I could disappear again, I wouldn't leave." He closed his eyes. What was he saying? He just tried to push her away, and now, well . . . "I wouldn't leave because of you." He shouldn't say it. He shouldn't tell her that he loved her too. That he'd heard her. She needed to let go and move on.

She gripped his hand as if she would never let go. "Listen, I found the evidence to clear you. Sarah and I figured it out. It was on the postcard from Miami. You'd put it on your refrigerator. Do you remember that?"

He opened his eyes again. "From Steve Rogers. Martin Krueger's alias. I didn't see anything in the message. I'd thought to go to Miami and look, but there wasn't time."

"Martin found Brown's communication with a third party, possibly the government official's enemy who knew the man was being financed with illicit funds and wanted those funds, agreeing to pay Brown a huge percentage if he intercepted them. But that's all still under investigation. We know he hired mercenaries Alberto Acosta and Oscar Evans, the guy who shot Ross, to torture Krueger and find you. But the most important news is that the information proved Brown was behind the other agent's murder, not you. He was playing both sides, or rather all sides. Sounds like he answered to the highest bidder and had no real loyalties."

"And look where that got him." Grier felt the tightness in his chest ease for the first time in months.

"That proof was in a microdot on the postcard."

Really? What an idiot he'd been. Krueger had sent him what he needed the week before this all started.

"Microdots are old-school, really. Concealed messages—

steganography—are as old as WW2. In modern technology, we just take it further with new encryption techniques."

Like she wanted to know any of that. An ache shot through his head, and he shut his eyes to let the pain pass.

"You need to rest, and my being here is taxing you."

"You could have put yourself into more danger."

"Grier, it's okay. I've given the information to the proper authorities."

Oh no. "We . . . were trying to learn who we could trust."

"Nolan and Sarah worked together to gather several figures from the NSA, CIA, and FBI."

How long had he been here? "And yet I'm still in handcuffs."

"You should be cleared by now. But maybe they're hoping to regain the cold wallet. What did you do with it?"

"I dropped it into the river. I was floating. Thought I was dying. But I was able to pull it out of my pocket and just let it go. Since it includes a tracker beacon, we can retrieve it."

"You did it, Grier. You saved us all."

"I couldn't let you have all the glory, could I?" He felt his love for her all the way to his marrow.

Autumn came closer, then leaned in until her face was mere centimeters away. She pressed her lips gently against his, and for a few seconds he forgot all the pain in his body and let go of the fear of what came next.

Medical staff entered the room, and Autumn ended the kiss. "I'll be back to check on you."

Grier turned to look at her as she walked out of the room, groaning with the effort, but he had to catch a glimpse . . . remember this—the last time he would ever see her.

 # FORTY-FOUR

Autumn exited her office and stopped at Tanya's desk.

"Hey, Chief. How does it feel to be back?"

"Like the last few weeks were just a blur and I never left."

Tanya laughed. "It's good to be back to normal around here." She returned her attention to her computer, and Autumn stepped out into a welcoming, sunshiny day. She would walk a few blocks and enjoy the day and the quiet—no one had been shot or murdered or gone missing in almost a month. Gray skies and snow would descend on them soon enough, with winter around the corner.

Craig wasn't such a bad guy, after all. The way he'd worked to save Grier wiped away any animosity she'd ever had toward him. But as it turned out, he decided to move to Hawaii and marry a woman he met online. They'd been dating for three years. At least that was the story he gave everyone. But, honestly, she suspected he wanted to get out from under his uncle's thumb, especially before the internal investigation into bribes came knocking on Wally's door.

Wally apologized profusely to her since it turned out that

Grier had, in fact, been framed and wasn't an international fugitive. Wally had chosen to listen to the wrong information. Mayor Cindy White had reinstated Autumn as police chief—though Autumn had taken a day to think about whether she truly wanted to hold that position again.

The day after she was reinstated, Wally announced he was moving to Arizona, where it was warm. In a matter of a few weeks, Shadow Gap had shifted and changed, but at the same time, had stayed the same. As she walked across the street, she spotted Sandford and Otis sitting at their usual booth at the Lively Moose—without Grier. Otis's old truck with the Jesus symbols sat out front.

And Ross would return next week. But until he did, with Craig gone, it was just Angie and Autumn. And she hoped to hire another officer soon—in case they had to endure another crime spree. Because now and then, she spotted outsiders hanging around, some who even stayed.

But no Grier.

Her heart heavy, she headed to the Lively Moose.

Soon Mom and Dad would be leaving Alaska on a trip to the Outside, what the locals called any place outside the great state. She understood they needed to forge a new future and get to know each other again, though it was clear they both remained in love.

As for Autumn's love life?

Grier had disappeared, after all. But he was taken against his will. She'd gone back to the hospital, but he'd been taken into custody. Federal agents transferred him to a secure location after they retrieved the USB drive, the cold wallet. At least that was the story she was given. She tried to contact him and find out more, but her calls went unanswered. Nolan reassured her that they had done all they could do to prove Grier's innocence.

At least Mateo had confessed to killing the two on the

mountain back in May. Mateo hadn't known their names—Kenneth Duncan and Monica Nobel—only that he hadn't wanted witnesses to his presence in Shadow Gap.

Because Autumn was the police chief, Mateo and Rafael had taken their time in planning how to abduct her. But after Mateo committed the murders, he decided to stay away for a few months. Folks tended to look closely at strangers when someone went missing.

Then their organization was hit hard when the cold wallet was stolen, and their focus had shifted to tracking it down all the way back to Shadow Gap, where Autumn ended up killing Mateo's right-hand man the night Dad was shot.

What a tangled mess, and she hoped never to be caught in such a web again.

All she wanted was to talk to Grier. Just . . . to hear from him and know he was all right.

Sarah was the one to inform Autumn that Grier had been released from federal custody. But he hadn't come back to Shadow Gap. And with that, Autumn had to accept that she would never see him again. That's what she got for letting an outsider get under her skin. But the thought didn't do anything to take away the ache in her heart.

That evening, she went home and sat on the porch steps near the water alone, watching the sunset. Soon the stars would come out. Maybe, finally, she could look at the star-filled sky without remembering that horrible night so long ago when she thought she'd lost her mother.

A dog barked in the distance, then something stirred close to her. She turned just in time to see Cap before he dove in and licked her face. Autumn laughed. Hank had kept the dog in Grier's absence.

"What are you doing here?" she asked.

She finally righted herself as someone marched down the steps and sat next to her. "It's Chief Long, again, I hear."

Her heart might have stopped.

She sucked in a breath. "Grier?"

Autumn was stunned to see him. Relieved and hopeful. Joy surged inside, but she had to remain cautious.

"Yes, it's me. Grier Young."

"Young, as in . . ."

"That's my real name."

"You used Grier even as a cover name?"

"Troy Fox was my undercover name while working with Krueger, and then Grier Brenner was the name he gave me while I was staying in Shadow Gap. I wanted to answer to my real first name, at least while hiding, and Brown wouldn't look for me under Grier anyway." He stared at her long and hard as if gauging whether she was glad to see him or not. If he'd made a mistake in coming back.

Fox. Brenner. Young. She didn't care. "I thought I would never see you again. You just . . . disappeared."

"Thank you for everything you did to clear my name. I had to spend a lot of time debriefing, and then I shut down that chapter of my life. It took longer than I expected."

"Meaning?"

"I'm not going back."

"Does that mean you're staying? I need to know, Grier. I mean, this was never your home. We can't offer you the world or the exciting life that you're accustomed to as a cryptologist or operative or—"

"Will you stop, already?" He grabbed her up in a kiss. Tender and inviting, and then he pulled her harder, tighter, against him and kissed her thoroughly. He eased away from her, but not too far. "Does that answer your questions?"

Dazed, she could only say, "I think so."

"You're all I want. I love you. Nothing else matters to me. And for the record, I adore Shadow Gap. I found my place, my home, my friends, and you here in this isolated corner of

Alaska. I'm not going anywhere ever again. Unless you leave. I'm with you, Autumn Long. That is, if you still want me."

She leaned in and kissed him. "You know I do." She smiled and leaned back, taking his hand. "I could really use another officer around here. It's down to just me and Angie for at least another week, and Craig moved to Hawaii."

"And you still can't afford me."

She laughed. "You seem to work for free anyway."

His smile was all she needed.

Grier was all she needed. She gazed up at the stars and thought, maybe, just maybe, she was ready to make new memories. Because for her . . . memories made under the stars lasted forever.

ACKNOWLEDGMENTS

As always, I thank God for giving me this writing dream, guiding me along the journey, and then making the dream come true. Along the way I've met so many writers who've encouraged and inspired me, and some who've become more than simply writing buddies—they've been the dearest of friends.

To Lisa, Shannon, Sharon, Susan, Chawna, Michele, Lynette, Lynn, Patricia—thank you for being there to answer questions, brainstorm, pray, hold my hand, and listen to my vents. And thanks for just being the best of friends.

To Wesley Harris—thank you for answering my police procedural questions and for your guidance and encouragement to so many Christian writers.

To my Alaska friends—you know who you are, and I so appreciate all your input.

To my precious children, Rachel, Christopher, Jonathan, and Andrew—thank you for inspiring me, encouraging me, and keeping me laughing at myself, or rather, reminding me not to take myself so seriously.

And Gabriel—what a wondrous gift from God you are! You fill my nonwriting days with joy!

To Dan—you are the sunshine of my life. We're good together, aren't we?

To my Revell team—you guys are the absolute best publishing team on the planet. I appreciate all you do, and I'm so glad I landed with you.

To Steve Laube—I'm grateful you're in my corner, and you've been there from the beginning, well, at least from those very early writing years when you signed me! Thanks for all you do!

Return to Alaska for the
next thrilling case in the

MISSING
IN ALASKA
SERIES

"Before opening this book, brace yourself.
Elizabeth Goddard has a knack for leaving you breathless
while stealing your heart at the same time."

The Suspense Zone

The old cargo plane vibrated as the pilot descended into the air-drop zone, the turbulence shuddering through Carrie James. She braced herself on a bench a few feet from the secured freight—emergency supplies that could mean the difference between life and death in a food-starved, war-torn country.

Battle-scarred was exactly how her heart felt, especially with Darius Aster sitting so close. She struggled to comprehend his betrayal.

My heart is splitting in two.

Good thing Bongani and his brother, Tariq, piloted today.

Darius released the safety harness and stood over her, his dark eyes flashing as he steadied himself against the fuselage. Plowing his free hand through black hair, he worked his stubbled jaw.

How would he explain himself?

"Choose me." Desperation flooded his voice. "Choose *us*."

Carrie didn't miss the warning that surfaced behind the anguish in his eyes.

"You're the one who's throwing everything away!" Her voice shook. How had he snuck the contraband worth millions on the plane without her noticing? "You're a good man. I don't believe . . . I can't believe you would do this."

"Believe it." His expression shifted. She'd never seen that look in his eyes before.

Who are you?

Unshed tears burned her eyes. She stared at this man who had been her world.

Her everything.

"This isn't what we do. What we're about." She loved this job. Loved flying in the much-needed supplies to isolated African villages. Aiding people in a way she never could in her military career. Reminding them they were important too and weren't forgotten. "We're supposed to help people, not *steal* from them."

"Don't you see?" Darius huffed. "This is our ticket to freedom."

Nausea churned in her stomach. She stood too so that he couldn't hover over and intimidate her. And Darius moved to manually open the door specifically designed to eject supplies.

God, help me to make him understand, please. She had to shout her next words to be heard over the wind. "Stealing precious resources won't give you freedom. It means living a lie, always looking over your shoulder."

He took an unsteady step closer. "Nobody knows. Nobody cares about this God-forsaken continent."

The tears surged forward now and no manner of trying to close herself off to this outrage could hold them back.

I wish I had a way off.

A way out.

Had Darius assumed she would go along with his theft? He'd already committed the crime, only admitting his actions after she'd spotted the uncut gems nestled inside the crate and questioned him.

God, help me. What do I do? What do I do?

Her breaths came too hard. Too fast.

His gaze softened, and he took a step back. "Just relax, will you? I'll handle everything."

He might hope he could persuade her, but he would be wrong. "Why didn't you ask me before you made this decision for us? You should've known I would never agree."

"That's exactly why I didn't ask. I figured I'd tell you, eventually. You shouldn't have been nosing around."

"Well, I did. So, now what?" She glared, trying to challenge him, threaten him, and *will* him to choose the path of love all in one look.

Raw pain flickered in his eyes and pinged through her heart. *There—he's still there. Please come back to me.*

Pulling her against his chest, he crushed her lips with a desperate kiss that bruised body and soul. Did he think this was love? She shoved him off, freeing herself.

"Get away from me." She loved him, but he'd ripped her heart from her chest. "I can't be part of this. Please, choose us. Choose me."

"I've already been paid. Now I must deliver. And for the record, I *am* choosing us. I'm choosing to save us."

How could she have been so wrong about him? Such a fool?

"Count me out. I can't be part of it."

He stared at her, long and hard, then his gaze turned dark.

Cold.

Empty.

A chill shivered through her. Before she could dart out of his reach, he seized her arm and dragged her to the open door of the cargo plane.

Wind rushed at her from behind. Roared in her ears. Fear paralyzed her.

He wouldn't. He couldn't.

Heart in her throat, she took in the man before her, now a stranger. "Please! Don't do this. You don't have to do this."

But his eyes held a cruelty she'd never seen before. She couldn't have dreamed or imagined he could harbor so much darkness.

Evil.

"I'm sorry. We could have been good together. But I can't . . . I can't trust you now!"

The man she loved shoved her chest, punching the breath from her, knocking her out of the airplane.

Elizabeth Goddard is the *USA Today* bestselling and award-winning author of more than fifty novels, including *Present Danger*, *Deadly Target*, and the Uncommon Justice series. Her books have sold over one million copies. She is a Carol Award winner and a Daphne du Maurier Award finalist. When she's not writing, she loves spending time with her family, traveling to find inspiration for her next book, and serving with her husband in ministry. For more information about her books, visit her website at www.elizabethgoddard.com.

Discover more from
Elizabeth Goddard with the
Rocky Mountain Courage series

"Goddard increases the stakes and highlights
the power of hope, faith, and trusting God
in the darkest times in this rush of a series."

Publishers Weekly

Revell
a division of Baker Publishing Group
www.RevellBooks.com

Available wherever books and ebooks are sold.

CONNECT WITH
ELIZABETH GODDARD

Get news, sign up for her mailing list, and more
at **ElizabethGoddard.com**

FIND HER ON